of cats and men

THE DIAL PRESS

# of cats and men

stories

Nina de Gramont

The Dial Press

Published by
The Dial Press
Random House, Inc.
1540 Broadway
New York, New York 10036

The Dial Press® is a registered trademark of
Random House, Inc., and the colophon is a trademark
of Random House, Inc.

Library of Congress Cataloging-in-Publication Data
Gramont, Nina de.
Of cats and men : stories / Nina de Gramont.
        p.   cm.
ISBN 0-385-33508-3
I. Title.
PS3557.R24 O38 2001
813'.6—dc21   00-052353

Book design by Laurie Jewell

Manufactured in the United States of America
Published simultaneously in Canada

May 2001

10 9 8 7 6 5 4 3 2 1
BVG

For David

contents

of cats and men

the nature of the beast

I found the magazines one weekend when Jack was winter camping. I'd been looking for the letter he'd just received from Stella, his ex-girlfriend, which we'd both agreed I shouldn't read. Prior to me, Stella had been the undisputed love of Jack's life, the topic of pages and pages of his most passionate prose. Though married now and living back east, Stella had no compunction about writing long and lovelorn letters to my fiancé. The fact that she'd been equally faithless when she was Jack's girlfriend did give me a little comfort. I soothed myself by recalling tales of her many blatant infidelities, and contrasting them to my own example of unwavering devotion. Still, I'd hoped that our engagement—several months old by now— might curb Stella's correspondence. I liked to think of myself as tolerant, confident, and progressive. Stella's boundary-crossing made me feel just the opposite: narrow-minded, jealous, and insecure.

A month earlier, Stella had called Jack in tears. His first collection of short stories had just hit the bookstores, and she was dismayed that her name did not appear in the acknowledgments. Sitting just a few feet away from Jack as he reasoned with Stella—within earshot of her inappropriately tearful voice—I decided to ignore the issue altogether. This was an important time in Jack's life: his first book, the beginning of his career after years of hard work. I did not want to dampen his happiness. And I could even, to some degree, understand how Stella felt—watching Jack achieve his goals long after her exit from his life. Jack's romantic dedication ("to Eve, my only Muse") clearly marked me as the winner. While she whined about the acknowledgments, I reminded myself that I, not Stella, sat beside Jack now—sharing his good fortune, his home, his two cats. His future.

Still. It was hard not to be curious. "Why bother?" Jack said, when I asked if I could read Stella's latest letter. "It doesn't mean anything to me, and it's just going to make you angry." I agreed, recognizing Jack's words as rational and mature. When his friend Tony arrived Friday morning to pick Jack up, I bid him good-bye with the purest intentions. I watched them drive away, then headed to work—Stella's letter the furthest thing from my mind.

That day turned out to be particularly grueling. At my desk in the district attorney's office, I spent the afternoon trying to convince a well-dressed, well-spoken woman, who asked to be called Mrs. Lloyd, not to return home with Mr. Lloyd— who'd just been released on bail after blackening both her eyes. If I had ever suspected that spousal abuse was limited to the lower income brackets, its victims uneducated, this job had taught me otherwise. Four years before I'd taken the position as a victim's advocate, considering it a possible segue to law school. At the time I hadn't imagined any crimes were actually committed in our picturesque university town. Every window in the Pearl DA's office framed a view of the Rocky Mountains, making the utilitarian building seem more like a resort hotel.

But while Pearl lacked its share of murders and back-alley stabbings, it had no dearth of domestic violence, and thanks to the college, there were plenty of acquaintance rapes. My job provided ample stimulation and frustration—as much if not more than a career in law, without the accompanying debt and pressure.

Now, in response to my gentle but persistent prodding, Mrs. Lloyd took the safe house address, her silk blouse rustling as she reached, but said no thank you to a ride. "My car's right outside," she explained, smiling through swollen lips. She promised to drive directly to the shelter. With Amy, the other victim's advocate, I watched through the window as Mrs. Lloyd met her husband in the parking lot. Standing against a backdrop of blue skies and mountains, the couple embraced. Then she handed him the keys to her BMW.

"Eve," Amy said. "I think we need a martini."

That night, when I crawled into bed, my brain slightly fuzzy with gin, I remembered Stella's letter. But the sheets smelled comfortingly of Jack: that good mix of sandalwood soap, cotton bond paper, and worn flannel. And finding me alone in bed, the cats had curled up companionably. More than a year after I'd moved in they had barely accepted me as their own, but were always very affectionate in Jack's absence. Beatrix slept politely at my feet, while the more brazen Pip took Jack's place, cuddled against my chest with his head on Jack's pillow. I smiled. Who cares about Stella, I thought. I fell asleep slowly, able to enjoy the vague loneliness, knowing that Jack would be home soon.

•   •   •

Saturday unfolded more gently. In the morning I met a friend at the autumn farmer's market and went for a long run by Pearl Creek in the afternoon. Weaving around the cheerful crowds on the bike path—college students, strollers, everyone looking healthy and happy—renewed my faith in the town's wholesomeness. At home, I refused to be upset by the message from Stella on our answering machine—her second call in just over a week.

At dinnertime I picked up videos and take-out Chinese, and never entertained a thought of disturbing Jack's study. I'd already erased Stella's message, deciding not to mention it. That, I thought, should be duplicity enough. I concentrated on remembering my place in Jack's heart, my permanence in his life. Long-gone Stella, I reminded myself, was not a threat.

But by Sunday morning the temptation and opportunity became too much to bear. I knew Jack would keep the letter—he kept everything of an emotional nature, not necessarily out of sentimentality, but for possible use in his writing. I got out of bed, brushed my teeth, and still wearing pajamas, let myself into Jack's study.

The first thing I found, as I crawled under Jack's desk on my hands and knees, was an enormous dead magpie—its wings spread and its neck broken. The bird undoubtedly had been murdered by Pip. Jack's cats each had a hunting style as signature as a serial killer's. Fat, long-haired Beatrix was meticulous and persnickety. Spare, rangy Pip was savage and hedonistic. I could always tell when Beatrix had killed a cricket because its left leg would be missing, while Pip's crickets turned up half-eaten with their little heads crushed. Unlike Beatrix, who preyed almost exclusively on insects and small rodents, Pip's trophies ran the gamut, including other unfortunates as startlingly large as this magpie—ravens, pigeons, even an occasional rabbit. If Pip meant to make a gift for Jack, the animal would be left—pristine as a stuffed teddy bear—on the floor at the end of our bed. Usually he presented Jack with his larger kills, and we often awoke to corvid or rabbit corpses proudly laid at our feet. Beatrix, on the other hand, would provide for Jack by leaving mice on the back doorstep. If she wanted the animal for herself, she would either eat the entire body, down to its tail, or roll her victim on its back and eviscerate it. To our later horror, we'd stumble upon the gleaming mouse guts on our lawn or living room rug, the tiny torso gaping as if a miniature cardiologist had wandered off in the middle of open-heart surgery. Pip never left mice for Jack, but always treated himself by eating their heads and immediately vomiting—leaving a doubly revolting mess.

I crawled backward, away from the dead bird, without considering cleaning it up. Though I usually rejected gender roles, disposing of corpses struck me as a man's job. Besides: Jack's cat, Jack's study. Clearly, the onus of the dead bird belonged to him.

I stood up and slid back the closet door. Though Jack claimed to be hyper-organized, the haphazard placement of boxes, shoes, sporting equipment, and piles of manuscripts suggested otherwise. The first half-open cardboard box I peered into contained his tuxedo, dusty and ringed with tufts of cat fur—a favorite napping spot for Beatrix. Underneath it lay a more solid, heavier box which—below a few bank statements and university catalogues—contained a naked woman.

I sat back, vaguely surprised. At a glance, the woman in the photograph looked comical and unreal: gazing up at me with smug triumph, apparently disdainful of my baggy flannel sleepwear.

The letter from Stella still my foremost mission, I pushed the magazine aside. Beneath it lay another, and another, and another—an impressive and lovingly frayed collection. I couldn't help but smile, the way I might at stumbling across a little boy's stash of Snickers bars. Jack's penchant for pornography did not exactly come as a shock. One of the stories in his book, an anecdotal piece that had also appeared in *Granta,* hilariously detailed an attachment to commercial smut.

But while I knew he'd enjoyed this literature in the past, he'd led me to believe this indulgence was behind him. In fact, Jack often complimented me by claiming he hadn't "perused" a magazine in the two years we'd been together. What's more, Jack had promised that his collection had been tossed into the Dumpster just before I moved into this very house.

I sat back and let the cardboard flap drop shut, feeling suddenly dirty and ashamed of myself. Not only for breaking Jack's trust and rooting through his belongings, but for asking him to throw out the magazines in the first place. Who was I to police his primal inclinations? Couldn't a demand like the one I had made (subverting a relatively harmless fetish) be likened to a kind of psychic castration? Why be so controlling? So *shrewish?*

Poor Jack, I thought. I returned the bank statements and university catalogues to their pathetic attempt at camouflage, then carefully balanced the tuxedo box in its original position. The only magazine I'd seen—the one on top—had some vaguely exonerating data printed to the right of the sneering bimbo: February 1989. Obviously, the magazines in Jack's closet were long-ago favorites, no longer needed but still too precious to discard. What if I left him? What if I died? Surely, Jack was entitled to some sort of sexual security blanket.

I closed the door to his study tightly, resolved to develop a more generous heart, and a more open mind.

I've always hated to be alone on Sunday. The long, languid daylight, luxurious with company, felt stultifying without. To make matters worse, the rain clouds that had only gathered in early morning burst themselves before noon. It would be snowing in the mountains, and I surprised myself by feeling a vindictive jolt of pleasure at the thought of Jack and Tony making their slow and dangerous drive down icy, barely visible roads.

I got dressed, had coffee, and threw myself on the bed with a Sunday crossword. Pip picked his way carefully across the bedside table, as if he knew the Cape Cod lamp from Jack's mother—our only engagement present—was precious. He did not show the same consideration to me, but pounced on top of the weekly magazine, obscuring both clues and puzzle. His immediate purr, which usually delighted me, roused inexplicable rancor. Remembering the dead magpie in Jack's study, I rolled onto my back and pushed Pip off the bed. "Get away from me, you murderer," I said. Pip bristled, then jumped back on top of me—settling precisely on my chest, forcing me to hold the crossword above my head, making it almost impossible to put pressure on the pen and fill in the squares.

I had not lost my liberal resolve. I really did forgive Jack the magazines in his closet. Still. While I struggled with seven-letter words, voices from Jack's study called to me: like sirens from stormy seas.

Apparently, *Playboy* was too tame for Jack. His collection consisted almost exclusively of *Penthouse*. I leafed through several magazines, scanning captions: "Our 38-24-36-inch Pet admits that sex is her favorite pastime." And cartoons: "I'm really in for rape," a convict tells his cell mate. "The murder part was accidental." Digging down deeper, I found myself relieved to discover a swimsuit edition of *Sports Illustrated*.

This I could understand. The familiar faces of supermodels comforted me with their unreachable yet readable beauty. I was used to feeling inferior to these women, accustomed to aspiring hopelessly toward their voluptuous and lanky splendor. They might not be my friends, but I knew them. They had given me tips to enhance my own freckled prettiness. We had shared clothes, hairstyles, makeup. I could watch a man ogle any one of them and find myself in tune with his aesthetic. While these models might surpass my beauty in leaps and bounds, at least they hailed from the same home planet.

Shana, Eloise, Samantha, and Desiree were a different breed entirely, holding the lips of their vaginas open with vermilion fingernails. As I took in these photographs, I searched for their subjects' beauty and felt a rising panic at finding none. To me they looked beyond caricature, one step away from plastic blow-up dolls with gaping holes for mouths. They all seemed to share the same body: plasticine skin, pale trimmed pubic hair, and bulbous breasts pointing skyward, as if someone working a bicycle pump had stopped just short of explosion. Their hair spiraled out in uniform waves. Their lips curled and sneered, baring teeth and tongues. They seemed so devoid of humanity, I honestly couldn't imagine them experiencing sexual pleasure.

"Our surprisingly practical Pet is enrolled in secretarial school." Nicolette posed above this biographical snippet with her vulva gaping. "Takes shorthand at 80, types a wild 65, and her sultry phone manner leaves heavy breathers gasping for air."

When the subject of pornography and its appeal came up in conversation, as it sometimes did since the publication of his *Granta* piece, Jack liked to cite a study he'd read where chimpanzees had masturbated to *Playboy*. He always relayed this information with a gleeful air of finality, as if it proved the ultimate truth of Playmates' sexual allure.

"The most interesting thing about that study," I told Jack the last time he mentioned it, "is that you consider it such a triumph. Are primates your point of reference for sexual conduct? I wonder if David Berkowitz justifies himself with Jane Goodall's essays about psychopathic chimpanzees."

Now, surrounded by the objects of Jack's most private lust, I found myself incapable of pithy comebacks. In fact, I felt lost and lonesome, flooded by my own erotic idiocy. Jack knew my carnal nature in all its detail—which suddenly seemed tame and uninteresting. Worse, I understood—because I could find nothing in me that wanted to emulate any aspect of these women—that I knew nothing of his.

Beatrix appeared, curving her back against mine—not so much in greeting but to inform me that I blocked entry to the tuxedo box. I gathered up the magazines and stacked them in their original order. Standing to return them to their hiding place, I made my last discovery. At the bottom of the box lay a far less yellowed edition than these relics from Jack's past. Its cover promised a "Summer Spectacular of Peerless Beauties" and a "Parade of Chinese Dolls." The date hung over the satirically sultry, platinum cover girl. June, this past. The very month Jack had presented me with his grandmother's engagement ring.

"You're pathetic," Amy said, when I called her that afternoon. "They're just magazines. Welcome to the world. Men love those things."

"But he *lied* to me," I objected.

"And you rifled through his things the minute he left town," Amy said. "Nobody's perfect."

"Not the minute."

"Look," Amy said. "You should be glad. You got off easy. You could have found evidence of an actual other woman. You could have found skin magazines starring prepubescent boys. But all you found was a *Penthouse* or two. God. Think of the women who come into our office. The men they live with. You should be celebrating, if that's the worst thing Jack's got in his closet."

"But I just keep thinking . . . if that's what he finds attractive, what does he see in me?"

"Do you think Jack would be seen in public with any of those women?" Amy asked. "Do you think he'd introduce them to his mother? Grow up, Eve. It's called fantasy."

"Hey, sweetie." Sunday evening Jack entered the house on the scent of campfire and freezing air. His cheek when he pressed it to mine felt flushed and icy. "I missed you," he said, crunching the bones of my back with his hug.

He hauled his gear though the door. Tony came in behind him, carrying Jack's tent, and I greeted him with insincere warmth. I knew that Tony's serene charm belied a treacherous nature: the kind of man who cheated on his wife without ever leaving a trace. Devoid of a telltale heart, he would continue guiltlessly after every liaison. Very much in contrast, I had always believed, to Jack—who had a candid heart, beating unapologetically on his sleeve.

"How was it?" I asked. I was determined to emulate Tony, thinking that she who snoops gets what she deserves. I did not plan to confront Jack with what I'd found—which would, after all, require my own confession.

"Cold," Jack said. "Very cold. I could use a bath." Baths were one of Jack's concessions to his feminine side. He spent hours soaking in hot water. Most men were difficult to buy gifts for, but not Jack: give him a jar of Epsom salts and he'd be in heaven.

Tony said his good-byes and left. Jack went into the bathroom and turned on the faucet, then came into the living room while the tub filled. As he sat down on the couch, Beatrix hurried to him on mincing steps and leapt into his lap, abandoning me as usual upon Jack's return. Jack let loose a string of endearments with the baby talk he only used with Beatrix, and on rare occasions me.

"Why are you sitting all the way over there?" he asked, as I lowered myself into the armchair. Beatrix looked like the epitome of female satisfaction: her eyes closed, her back arched, her throat pulsing with loud purrs. I remembered the first time I saw Jack hold Beatrix. He'd struck me as rugged and Hemingwayesque, until he started cooing to that fat, fluffy cat. How could I not have fallen in love with him?

"Come sit with me," Jack said now. "I missed you."

"Liar." I kept my tone flat, as if not joking.

Jack pushed Beatrix aside and held out his arms. I cuddled up obediently, pressing my face into his neck. Filled as I was with the aching and humiliated love of the cuckold, the strength of his embrace almost made me cry. I felt stripped of desirability, relegated to the unglamorous role of everyday partner. Half against my will, I let out a shuddering sigh.

"Hey," Jack said. "What's wrong?"

"Do you think I'm pretty?" I asked him.

"I think you're beautiful," he said. "You know that."

It was no use. Jack had lied about the magazines in his closet. Now anything he ever said would be suspect.

On Monday morning Jack woke up early and went into his study. "God damn it," he yelled. Still in bed, I froze—sure he'd detected my espionage. "Fucking Pip," he said, and I remembered the dead magpie.

"You could have cleaned this up, you know," Jack called. Pip was stretched out on his back just above my pillow—

companionship left over from the weekend. With his paws in the air, he pressed against my head, purring ecstatically.

"I didn't see it," I called back. Then added, "Cleaned up what?"

Jack laughed. He appeared in the doorway, dangling the magpie sideways. Stretched out to its full, impressive wingspan, the bird nearly reached the ground. A trail of blue and black feathers fanned out behind Jack.

"Look at you," Jack said. "You're cozied up with a vile assassin."

"I know," I said. I pulled Pip, pliable as a rag doll, over my head, bending him into a rock-a-bye curl. His purr rose to crescendo. When I squeezed him too tightly he let out a squeak and then went back to purring, eyes closed above an inarguable smile.

"I can't help it," I told Jack. "I love him."

Pip stretched in sensuous agreement, pressing one paw against my cheek—gentle as an infant.

Before lunch on Monday, I met with a sorority girl named Missy—one of several who'd been victims in a series of Rohypnol rapes. Because all the girls had experienced memory loss, the police were slow to arrest the two predatory male students. I'd last met with Missy more than six months earlier, just after the assault. She'd been devastated, looking childlike and stricken in a hooded sweatshirt, her hair skinned back into a ponytail, her face scrubbed.

Now Missy seemed to have recovered with the alacrity of youth. I barely recognized her. She wore her long hair in a flood of overtended curls. Her breasts strained impressively against a tight pink sweater. Her face—which I remembered as sweet and snub-nosed—wore an armorlike layer of makeup, applied thickly and expertly. A few days before, my attitude toward her would have been purely solicitous. I certainly would have no reason to consider Missy (a *rape* victim, I reminded myself) in conjunction with Jack. Now, my voice a study in compassion and experience, I coached Missy on her testimony. But I couldn't help thinking: this is just the kind of girl Jack likes.

Usually when I dressed for work, I concentrated on respectability over attractiveness. Today I wore a loose, boxy jacket and had my hair rolled into a bun. Sitting beside this poised and luscious victim, I felt like a sexless lump. A girl next door, minus the allure.

I had always been the kind of woman men dated. The kind of woman men fell in love with, and brought home to their mothers, and now wanted to marry. But I had never, I suddenly realized, been the kind of woman men wanted to *fuck*. At least not at first glance. I had barely bothered to cultivate sexuality into my appearance. I had hardly noticed women who did.

Poor Jack, I thought. No wonder he had to resort to magazines.

"How's she doing?" Amy asked, as Missy left the office.

"A lot better," I said. Inwardly I chastised myself again.

"Did you tell her she can't dress like that for court?"

"I forgot," I said. "I'll call her at home."

I picked up the phone and dialed Jack. "Hey," I said when he picked up. "What's wrong? You sound kind of breathless."

"I had to run to get the phone," Jack said. "I was writing."

"Oh. Sorry about that."

"It's okay." Pause. "Did you want something, sweetie?"

"No. Just to say hi."

"Hi," Jack said. I tried to concentrate on the sound of his voice, which was gentle and generous. But I could only think of a parade of pink sweaters, and pages and pages of glossy photographs.

. . .

Tuesday afternoon I surprised Jack by coming home for lunch. I rapped loudly on his study door. "Jack? What are you doing in there?"

He opened the door fully clothed, no disarray.

"Writing," he said. "What do you think?"

Over the next week, every time he left the house, I broke into his study to check the order of the magazines. Every time I saw Nicolette—on top of the pile where she belonged—I'd sit back with a sigh of relief.

In bed with Jack that weekend, I wriggled half-naked into one corner. While my bra rode up above my breasts, I spread my legs diagonally. I threw my head back, sneered, and fingered my clitoris.

"What are you doing?" Jack asked.

"Nothing," I said. My legs shut quickly, my head snapped up. "I thought this was what you liked."

"Why would you think that?"

"No reason."

"Come here," Jack said. He pulled me back to him and recommenced normal lovemaking. I responded with guilty and desperate enthusiasm.

"Hey," Jack said. "Wait." He kissed my cheek, then pulled a pillow from the disrupted stack and placed it carefully under my head. The gesture was so tender—so thoughtful and typical of Jack—I burst into tears.

"Jesus," Jack said. He rolled back, stroking the hair from my forehead. "What's wrong, Eve?"

"Nothing," I said. "Nothing's wrong. Sometimes I just feel like everything is a lie. Like a person grows up with all these expectations about life, and love, only to have them smashed into tiny little pieces."

"Is this about something at work?" Jack said. When I didn't respond, he continued stroking my head without further questions. If he suspected the real catalyst for my outburst, he didn't breathe a word. I sniffled into his chest.

"This is weltschmerz," I told him, "not PMS."

"Maybe you should think about law school again," Jack said.

"Why?" I said, my voice suddenly sharp. "Don't you think what I do is important?"

"Of course I do," Jack said. He kissed me. "Don't worry," he said. "Don't worry about anything."

"I'll try," I promised, settling down, and vowing to erase the magazines from my mind. "I'll try."

The following Tuesday Jack phoned the DA's office at three-fifteen. I was in a foul mood. I'd forgotten to call Missy about her wardrobe. That morning in trial, the girl's moving, intelligent, and practiced testimony had been completely undermined by her short skirt and scarlet lipstick.

"Eve," Jack said. "Guess what?" I reminded myself that Missy's improper attire was not Jack's fault but my own. I knew from the time—just after mail delivery—that Jack was about to relay a piece of writing news. I braced myself to respond with pride and excitement.

"I got a story in *Playboy*," Jack said. "Three thousand bucks."

"Great." I stamped my stapler on a pile of papers, accidentally including an index finger. "Shit," I said.

"What's wrong?"

"Nothing. I stapled myself." I put the finger in my mouth and sucked a few drops of tinny blood.

"Ouch," Jack said sympathetically. "But hey. Isn't that great news?"

Life made it hard to abandon unhealthy fixations. I wanted to congratulate Jack. I wanted to be happy for him. But at that precise moment, I couldn't quite muster it.

"That's pretty good news," I said. "If you like *Playboy*."

"Forget *Playboy*," he said. "Three thousand bucks. And it's prestigious. Isaac Bashevis Singer has had work in *Playboy*. John Updike."

"No offense," I said. "I'm sure it's very literary. It's just a little tame for me."

"What are you talking about?"

"You know. It's kind of mainstream. It doesn't give me that extra, illicit jolt. It's not so exciting as getting a story published in, let's say, for instance, *Penthouse*."

Silence on the other end.

"Don't you agree?" I asked.

"I'm hanging up now," Jack said. "But thanks for your support."

"Don't mention it," I said, then frowned at the sudden dial tone—probably the closest to hanging up on someone that Jack had ever come.

Amy, passing by my desk, must have noticed my expression. "Don't worry," she soothed. "We've got five more victims testifying. We'll get those boys locked up."

I nodded, profoundly guilty. I decided to pick up groceries and champagne on the way home, to make amends and celebrate Jack's victory properly.

"Jack!" I called his name for no logical reason—his car wasn't in the driveway, so I knew he wouldn't answer. I put down my bags and threw the shrimp into the refrigerator—out of Pip's reach. I wondered where he could be: it wasn't like him to go out and not leave a note.

"Jack?" I poked my head into his study. Not finding him, I started to leave—very innocently. But I couldn't help noticing, out of the corner of my eye. His closet door was open just a tad wider than Beatrix would need.

Sure enough: Shana had made her way to the top of the pile.

So, I thought. That's what Jack's in the mood for this week. Tall, blond Shana, whose firefighter boyfriend was thrilled to see the apple of his eye in *Penthouse*—though he did worry some other man might try to "put out her fire."

I heard a crash from the bedroom and jumped. I tossed Shana back into her box, pulled the closet door shut, and hurried into the hall.

Beatrix had destroyed the Cape Cod lamp from Jack's mother. It lay shattered on the bedroom floor. Making its half-blind way around the blue and white shards was a terrified mole. The cat pounced in graceful recapture, picking the rodent up in her mouth and squeezing it to momentary lifelessness. Then she dropped it to the ground. Frustrated by its stillness, Beatrix poked it with retracted claws. When it came to, she sat back—allowing its fleet-footed retreat under the bed. "Beatrix," I said sharply. The cat turned and stared, her eyes dopey as if stirred from a trance. Then, with murderous expertise, she recommenced her stalking.

The back door slammed. "Jack," I screamed. "Jack, come quick. Beatrix is killing a mole."

Valiantly, Jack attempted an impossible rescue—the mole of course regarding him as another predator. With a broom, he tried to guide it into a paper bag. Beatrix stormed around the bedroom, scandalized by this dilettante's interference.

"It's no use," Jack finally said. "We should just let Beatrix finish the job."

We closed the door, limiting the slaughter to that one room, and went together into the kitchen.

Jack had done the same thing as me: on the kitchen table sat his bag of groceries and another bottle of champagne. But Jack hadn't had time for my caution, and Pip perched on the table, methodically removing sirloin tips from their wrapper with curved Pooh-bear paws.

"Goddamn cats," Jack said, pushing Pip off the table.

"Don't worry," I said. "I bought shrimp."

Jack lit a fire, I lit candles. We ate shrimp and drank champagne, not saying a word about that morning's altercation.

Jack, after all, was the best man I knew. He stood miles above his friends, miles above the male attorneys at my office, and thousands of miles above the parade of subhumans they prosecuted. A pile of dirty magazines, I decided, was the absolute most minor of offenses. I loved Jack. Jack loved me. What else mattered? Not even the occasional rumble from our bedroom—the tussle of Beatrix and her sadistic undertaking—could interfere with our reconciliation.

Until the phone rang.

"Stella," Jack said, glancing at me ruefully. "What's up?"

Jack stood, pacing, with the cordless receiver to his ear. I waited, listening to his "uh-huhs" and "yeahs." Finally he paced himself into his study and out of listening range.

I sat by the fire, sipping champagne, my right foot beating out an increasingly angry rhythm—measuring the length of Jack's absence.

"Sorry about that," Jack said, when he came back too many minutes later.

"No problem," I said, still tapping my foot and not looking at Jack as he sat down beside me. "How's Stella?"

"Fine," he said. "Crazy, as usual."

"Really?" I said. "How so?"

"Oh, you know. Just the same old stuff. You don't want to hear it."

"Really?" I said again. "Well, Jack, maybe I do. Maybe I do want to hear it."

"I'll tell you another time," Jack said. "You don't seem very receptive at the moment."

"Don't I?"

Jack kissed my cheek. "Come on, Eve," he said. "Don't let her ruin this evening. Let's talk about something else."

"Fine," I said. "Would you like to discuss your great literary triumph? Your new brotherhood with Isaac Singer, John Updike, and Kilgore Trout? You know. All the great icons of wide-open-beaver lit?"

"Why don't you just come out with it," Jack said. "You've been like Raskolnikov for two weeks. You're so obviously wallowing in guilt and fury."

"Why don't *you* come out with it," I said, "if your conscience is so clear."

Jack tossed the rest of his champagne on the fire. "This is bullshit," he said. "I don't have to take this." He stalked out, and in a minute I heard the sound of running bathwater. I downed the rest of my champagne and poured another. Then I stomped to the bedroom for refuge—where I was greeted by the freshly killed mole. The animals left by Pip and Beatrix never looked peaceful in their deaths, but pained and tortured, eyes closed tightly in a clear line of misery. It always seemed their little souls hovered just above, crying outrage at premature demise. I fled to the bathroom, where Jack reclined in the tub.

"Jack," I said. "You didn't get the mole. It's dead in the bedroom."

"I'm taking a bath," he said, his voice still measured and angry.

"Look," I said. "It's not my fault Stella called in the middle of our celebration."

"It's not my fault either," Jack said.

"You could have called her back."

"Like you wouldn't have gotten pissed when I did."

"You could just do what you normally do, and call her the second I leave the house."

"Listen to you. You're so full of venom."

"Listen to you," I countered. "You're so self-righteous and smug."

"At least I'm not a prude."

"Who? Me? You're calling me a prude?"

Jack leaned back in the hot water, closing his eyes. "Leave me alone," he said. "Let me bathe in peace."

"No," I said. "You think I'm a prude?"

"You may not be a prude," Jack said. "But you're extremely irrational. I wish you could hear yourself."

"You think I'm being irrational?"

"Anyone would think you're being irrational."

"Really. Let's see. Let's just investigate that." I left the bathroom and went into Jack's study. Loudly and with great dramatic flair, I rolled back his closet door.

"We'll ask your girlfriends," I yelled. I collected the magazines and carried the naked armload back to the bathroom—pressed to my chest like schoolbooks.

Jack stared up at me from the tub, resolved to quietly take his punishment, however inequitable. I plucked Shana off the top of the stack.

"What do you think, Shana?" I shook the magazine open and asked the centerfold, who glared provocatively from beneath her fireman's cap. "Do you think I'm being irrational?

"What do you know?" I said to Jack. "Shana's not talking." I tossed the magazine into the tub.

Reflexively, Jack pitched forward to rescue Shana from her watery grave, but in sudden deference to me he pulled back. It was a touching and athletic gesture—the instant recoiling, snapping his hands back, allowing Shana and her firefighting paraphernalia to sink heavily to the bottom of the tub, newsprint smearing her face like runny mascara. Sacrificing her to spare my feelings.

I was not so moved that I didn't query Desiree, Samantha, and Nicolette. Each silent, vacant-eyed response was rewarded by a scuba diving trip into our bathtub. Finally I dumped the entire stack, which fell with a flutter and a glug—while Jack sat with his knees drawn in to his chest, trapped in the ink-muddied water.

I stepped back and Jack stood, holding his breath, dripping, nude: suddenly very vulnerable and unjustly exposed. I ran from the bathroom, hopped over the dead mole, and dove into bed.

I heard Jack dry himself off and put on his robe. I saw him pass the bedroom door once, then again—this time with a large garbage bag. I heard splashing as he plunged in his arm to retrieve the magazines, then the deep-throated gulp of the drain when he pulled the plug.

Jack came into the bedroom, dragging the dripping garbage bag behind him. He picked up the mole by its tail and swung it in, on top of the magazines. The pictures were visible through the pale green bag—leering faces and blown-up boobs pressing against the translucent plastic as if trying to escape. Jack heaved the load over his shoulder and left the room, looking like a pornographic Santa. I watched him through the bedroom window as he walked across the backyard and over to the Dumpster—still in his bare feet and bathrobe.

He returned to the house and crawled into bed, his wet hair crunchy with frost and his feet ice-cold. He pulled the covers tight around us and shivered.

"You need another bath," I told him, rubbing his hands between mine.

"No thank you," Jack said, and we laughed. The moisture soaked through Jack's bathrobe, through my shirt, and to my skin.

Jack and I lay that way, quietly, huddled into the changing dampness, finding a kind of diplomacy in our respective culpability. When the chilled condensation had turned warm again, Beatrix decided to join us, balancing her weight between our two bodies. Soon Pip was sacked out above our heads, stretching across the pillows.

We clung together, not so much cavalier toward our own and each other's evils, but simply bearing with them awhile. As Pip and Beatrix, amused by such innocence, kindly calmed our embrace with their own knowing and lenient purr.

the closest place

One thing nobody tells you about the mentally ill is how infuriating they are. This, what Tessa thinks as she scrubs the top of her washing machine where her twenty-eight-year-old brother-in-law, recently diagnosed as schizoaffective, has written "Tessa and Ben are sex fiends" in red ink. Tessa has just begun her second month of pregnancy, her waves of nausea are unpredictable, and she finds this extraneous task particularly galling. She used to feel sympathy toward the insane, romanticizing them, identifying with them—as catalysts, protagonists. Vincent van Gogh. Zelda Fitzgerald. Tortured. Beautiful. The madness that necessarily accompanies creativity, the breaking of societal norms, the evolution of genius.

A week with Andy has cured her of these notions. Tessa sees no genius in him, no charm or rebel spark. After traveling west from the Florida Panhandle—disappearing from his mother's house without warning or explanation—he arrived sullenly on their doorstep, his eyes bruised, like a consumptive craving dry heat. About why he left, Andy will tell Ben only that their step-father has an air of the State Department. "That entire part of Florida," Andy says, as if he had not grown up there. "It's like a third world country."

Ben listens to his younger brother with saintly concern. It seems to Tessa that he regards Andy through the film of memory: granting him humor and intelligence which may have existed once, but now are undistinguishable through so much misfired thought. To Tessa, Andy is a man her own age and twice her size, with a distinctly ominous bearing.

He sleeps in what will be the baby's room, keeping his residence with Tessa and Ben under two conditions: that he take his medication (antipsychotics and antidepressants) and that he look for a job. Tessa has not yet seen evidence of either. What she has seen is lots of muttering, heavy sighs, slamming doors, thousands of cigarette butts. When she steps out onto their deck, Tessa almost chokes on the stale odor—so profuse, it's taken over the very air (formerly clean, crisp) of their mountain home.

Their mountain home sits in an idyllic suburb, two-acre lots in the foothills outside a Colorado university town. A few years after moving in, Tessa still feels a newcomer's delight. The house itself is nothing special: beige siding tacked on flimsy construction, every noise audible behind paper-thin walls. But she loves the outside, the expanse of weeds and pine, the pebbles and dust flying up from her tires when she shifts her car into first to climb the last hill before their driveway. She loves the herd of deer that roam the neighborhood, hud-dling under their deck when it rains. There are coyotes, foxes, owls, and a cougar is rumored to claim the surrounding territory as its own. At dusk each evening Tessa brings her cat, Sancho, inside: summoning him from his crouch in the long grass, his wake of tiny corpses. Twilight the hour when predator might metamorphose into prey.

Scrubbing the graffiti from her washing machine, Tessa sees the sun begin its orange-melted dip behind Long's Peak. She throws down her sponge, walks out front, and calls Sancho, who always (to her vague surprise) comes cantering in, obediently. He is not an affectionate animal. "Purely decorative," Ben likes to say. Tessa bought Sancho on a whim from a mall pet store, despite her intrinsic disapproval of peddling live animals. That day he'd been hard to resist: behind the glass window, a kittenish ball of marmalade. China blue eyes. She and Ben had just moved into their mountain house. They needed a pet.

Now Sancho, fitting at least the visual bill, carries his full-grown self through the living room. "Outside's closed," Tessa tells him in a singsong voice that echoes her pre-brother-in-law cheer. Tessa loves the cat—never mind his aloofness, his aversion to anything like cuddling. Sancho has his own way of staying close, shadowing Tessa throughout the day. Whenever he's indoors, he follows her from room to room, never in her lap or wanting to be petted. But always there, purring when she gives him the milk remains of her morning cereal, surreptitiously alighting on her side of the bed (never Ben's) after the lights have been turned out.

Sancho and Tessa walk into the kitchen, where Andy is sliding open the glass door to the deck. "Be careful," Tessa says to him. "Don't let the cat out." Twice since Andy's arrival, Sancho has escaped after dark, through doors Andy neglected to close.

Andy glares at her, insulted by the order, letting the door gape as he lights his cigarette. Smoke wafts inside as Sancho tiptoes across linoleum toward the deck. Tessa reaches out and pushes the door closed herself, a snapping, frustrated movement.

Andy is an adult, a graduate of an Ivy League college, but he conducts himself with the indolent rancor of an adolescent.

Tessa cups her hand to her not-yet-burgeoning belly like an apology and forcibly coughs, as if she can expel the smoke from her lungs before it reaches her resting fetus. She averts her eyes from Andy and the brooding, pathetic figure he cuts: shoulders slumped, brow furrowed, unwashed hair curling over his eyes. Through the glass, Sancho stares at him intently. Tessa has read that large cats—lions, tigers, panthers—will zero in on animals with infirmities. Watching Sancho, she believes it. The cat is fascinated by Andy, studying his movements with mesmerized rapture.

Tessa puts water on to boil for spaghetti, one of the few foods she can handle. As she stands by the sink breaking lettuce, spraying it twice (she does everything more carefully, more thoroughly lately), Andy comes back into the kitchen. "What's for dinner?" he asks, lumbering behind Tessa, peering over her shoulder.

In ways, the brothers resemble each other. Their tall, broad forms. Their dark, unruly hair. The same slight remains of an accent that to Tessa, who grew up in the North, has always sounded musical and exotic. Sometimes when Andy stands close to her, Tessa feels she's entered an alternate world, where Ben's personality has been sucked out and reinserted—terribly disarranged. The idea makes her stomach lurch.

"Spaghetti," she tells Andy.

He sighs, as if this were the cause of all his trouble, this poor meal Tessa plans to prepare.

"What I really miss," Andy tells her, in a voice as wistful as it is accusatory, "is Southern barbecue."

Then go back to the South, Tessa thinks, but does not say.

.   .   .

Ben doesn't see much of Andy. He works during the day, painting murals on the underpasses of the city bike path. Tessa understands this is a huge commission for Ben, an exciting job. He barely sleeps. He goes to bed early, at eight or nine o'clock, then gets up at three to draw sketches and invent color schemes. Sometimes, when Tessa and Sancho come to bed at eleven, it wakes Ben and he arises then: obviously energized, going downstairs to his studio and working despite the faint light.

Tessa teaches art at the elementary school until two every afternoon. When she gets home, she runs or takes a bike ride—generally the latter since Andy has been with them. It keeps her out of the house longer, and Tessa thinks the smooth motion is better for the baby. She sneaks her bike around the gate of Carriage Knolls, a private neighborhood bordering their own—a steep, paved, and seldom traveled road that winds up into the hills of Boulder Heights. The climb frees Tessa, the pump of the pedals, the nonstop gasp, a four-mile ascent that brings her to the crest of mountain lion country: staring into the thin air over an expanse of houses and brush, reservoirs and tall city buildings. Civilization or the wildness of the front range, depending on which direction she looks. As she takes in voluminous breaths, she feels that she's giving her baby a gift—the cleansing rush of fresh oxygen. The descent is exhilarating: she regulates her pace with the pulse of her hands on brakes, crouching into the wind created by her own speed.

Arriving home to Andy, morosely sprawled in front of the television, Tessa wishes she could somehow transfer what she has just experienced. "I know his problem is chemical," Ben said a few days ago. "But I wish I could get inside his body, get it in shape. I'd get him off the cigarettes, get him running. I can't believe that wouldn't make a difference." Tessa knows that growing up, Ben was always the more active of the two.

Now she sees him clinging to his old perceptions: as if Andy is still the pale, lazy kid who only needs a little fresh air.

Tessa herself wants to shake Andy out of his inertia. Anybody, she thinks, would go insane—hanging around, ruminating, watching cartoons.

"Andy," she says. "It's a beautiful day. Why don't you take a hike around the loop?"

Andy shrugs. "I would," he says. "Maybe I will." He runs a hand distractedly through thick hair, not taking his eyes off the television.

"Did you see anything in the classifieds today?"

"Yeah. I made some calls."

"Andy. Have you been smoking in here?"

"No," Andy lies, his eyes still not turning to Tessa's.

"Look," Tessa says. "It's bad enough that our hill is littered with your cigarette butts . . ."

"Fine, okay," Andy tells her. "Don't worry about it."

Tessa pauses for a moment. She folds her arms and stares at Sancho, who lurks behind the couch: bellying toward Andy in slow motion, stalking him.

"What was that?" Andy says suddenly, angrily. His head swivels, and he glares at Tessa as if she's an accuser, an antagonist.

"Nothing," Tessa says. She steps backward, away from him. "I didn't say anything."

Andy's focus on her is intent, yet oddly vacant. The hairs on Tessa's forearms rise as she realizes he's responding to something outside of this room, this world. Inside of himself. She retreats upstairs, away from him.

"Please explain to me," Tessa whispers fiercely to Ben that night, "why I should feel uncomfortable in my own home."

The door to their bedroom is closed. Tessa has cornered

Ben upstairs early, as he gets ready for sleep—the only time she can speak to him alone. Sancho lolls against the wall, keeping a safe distance from Ben, straining his feline chin toward the night air wafting in through a window screen.

"You shouldn't," he tells her. "But I don't see what he does that's so bad." Ben sits on the bed wearing his boxers and looks up at her, exasperated. Tessa again feels blamed, as if she not only has to tolerate Andy, but is somehow responsible for his being a problem.

She recites a list that admittedly sounds trivial: the slamming doors, the coffeepot left on, the beer bottles all over the house, the cigarette butts outside. "He doesn't lift up the toilet seat," Tessa says. "It's always splattered and wet. And I know he smokes inside. What kind of asshole smokes in a pregnant woman's house?"

"He's not an asshole," Ben corrects her. "He's mentally ill."

Ben, Tessa thinks, alternates between allowing Andy mental illness and allowing him normality: the first as an excuse for his behavior, the second as justification for his presence.

"Then he belongs in a hospital," she says. "We're not equipped to take care of him."

Ben blanches at the word "hospital," as if Tessa has suggested throwing Andy in a dungeon. "What am I supposed to do?" he says. "Kick him out? Where's he going to go? How's he going to take care of himself?"

Tessa frowns, chastened. Feeling selfish, the callous root of Andy's potential homelessness.

"I'll talk to him about the smoking," Ben promises. "Shit." He pulls his jeans back on. "I'm going downstairs to see if I can get any work done. There's no way I'll be able to sleep now."

Once Ben has left, Sancho approaches Tessa. He stops three paces away and sits, staring at her. Tessa stares back, and the cat begins to purr, as he often does, at her mindful notice.

Lonely, Tessa reaches out and gathers him up in her arms, pressing him to her chest. His purring abruptly stops, and downstairs Tessa hears the click of Ben's study door. Sancho reclines, stiff as rigor mortis, abiding the embrace but clearly uncomfortable. He does not look at her but straight up at the ceiling, his mouth open with teeth slightly bared. Tessa can't stand his unhappiness, his polite but aggravated endurance. She lets him go. He leaps across the bed and perches on a high dresser: staring down at her again, recommencing his purr. Tessa lies back on the bed and recaptures his gaze, curving both hands to cradle her stomach. She hears Ben's door open.

"Andy," Ben says. "Put out the goddamn cigarette."

"Fine," Andy says, his voice rife with insult. "I'm putting it out. Don't worry about it."

The sound carries so completely, Andy and Ben might as well be in the bedroom with Tessa. Why would they have considered this deficiency when they bought the house? It was supposed to be just Ben and Tessa, and now the baby, whose room Andy has invaded with piles of dirty laundry and half-filled drinking glasses: the dense, stale scent of an unwashed man. Tessa rests a pillow on top of her stomach as if to muffle the sound of tension, discord.

"Worry about it?" Ben says. "Tessa's pregnant. Don't you get it? You're a guest in this house."

"Okay," Andy says. "Jesus. I'm going outside."

"Make sure you close the door," Tessa calls through the floorboards.

"Jesus," Andy says again. "I have no privacy in this place." As the front door slams, the house itself seems to shudder from its foundation. Tessa moves the pillow from her stomach to cover her face. Still, she hears the quiet, considerate click of Ben returning to his work. If only Andy had something, she thinks. Murals to paint—anything to care about, to do. It might make all the difference.

But then from outside, Tessa hears him: not his specific words, but the stream of them—traveling, disturbingly, into the night, through the scent of pine and wood smoke, occasionally stopping as Andy tries to bite them back, but then beginning again, unbidden. An agitated and rising tone that hollows out Tessa's insides, refilling her with the most primal sense of revulsion and fear. Once, Tessa might have considered insanity subjective: a fine and movable line, arbitrarily assigned. But now, listening to Andy's voice—his word-salad at war with nobody, his uninstigated anger—the line has become thick and definite. Tessa is sane and Andy is insane, as absolutely as he is outside and she is in, he downstairs and she up. She might be able to hear him through this barrier, but what he hears of her gets filtered through his own faulty wiring. He inhabits another country entirely, and Tessa finds herself emphatically xenophobic, panicked by his language, his manner, his customs.

Tessa throws the pillow aside and stands. She creeps into the guest bathroom and empties Andy's pills into her palm, counting them.

Before Andy's arrival, Tessa measured time by her pregnancy, awaiting her second trimester—when the fetus might become less fragile. Now she focuses on the weeks Andy has been with them: nearly three when he refuses to see the psychiatrist Tessa finds, on the grounds that the doctor holds an undergraduate degree from a state university. "Why should I see a shrink," Andy says, "who's less educated than I am? How is that going to help me?"

"How can he be less educated than you?" Tessa argues. "Do you have an M.D.?"

"Hey Tessa," he answers abruptly, in a new tone, urgent and rushed. "I don't know if you're aware of this," Andy says.

"But there's something I need to ask you, so I'm just going to come straight out and say it."

Tessa braces herself.

"Do you know of any good books on the transcendentalists?" Andy asks. "Any really definitive tracts?"

Tessa clenches her jaw. In college, Andy studied literature. But she hasn't seen him so much as touch a book since he arrived. "No, Andy," she says. "No, I don't. Why don't you read Emerson?"

"Obviously I have," he tells her. "Obviously I've read Emerson."

"Any luck with the job search?"

"Yeah, yeah. No problem." Andy falls back to his seat and picks up the remote control. Without warning, Sancho alights on the back of the couch, just by Andy's head, and swats at him—claws fully extended. Andy jumps up, his hand pressed against his cheek.

"Jesus Christ," Andy says. "Fucking cat."

Tessa steps toward Andy. She peers up at his face and sees raised red lines—instantly inflamed, as if the cat injected a mild poison. Sancho has not moved, but keeps his place regally, sitting up straight, tail twitching with static agitation.

"I'm sorry," Tessa says. "Let me get you a washcloth."

As she goes into the downstairs bathroom she hears Andy say, "I don't know why she keeps that cat."

The irony of this statement is not lost on Tessa, and after administering to his injuries, she goes upstairs to the guest bathroom and counts his supply of pills—which has not been disturbed since her last inventory. Through the floorboards, she can hear Andy speaking to himself again: his spill of muddled words, running together, alternately punctuated by quiet laughter and the heavy, depressed exhalation of "oh, boy." She feels a sharp stab of compassion followed by a sense of frustrated bewilderment. Why would he not take his pills? Shouldn't the medication rescue him from his flight of thought, his lethargy, his general confusion? Tessa feels sorry for Andy, she does, her heart honestly breaks for his most awful of predicaments. But she also thinks that if the last place she'd want to be is inside her brother-in-law's brain, the second-to-last place she wants to be is in any kind of proximity to it.

"I saw an ad at Alfalfa's," Ben tells her that night. Tessa has taken to spending the evenings in their bedroom, the closest place to refuge. "A guy who sells Southern barbecue, the sauce and the shredded pork. I might get some for tomorrow night, for Andy. To do something nice for him."

The idea of shredded barbecued pork forces bile up to Tessa's mouth. She bolts from the bed into the bathroom and vomits. Ben follows. He kneels behind her and rubs her back.

"Still bad," he says quietly, pulling her hair away from her face.

"Just sometimes," Tessa tells him. She flushes the toilet and sits down on the cool linoleum, leaning against the tub. Ben hands her a towel, and she wipes off her face. Behind Ben, she sees Sancho step carefully into the doorway—halting at a guarded but companionable distance.

"Andy hasn't been taking his medication," Tessa tells Ben. "I've counted it every day this week, and he hasn't been taking it."

Ben sighs and sits down on the floor with her. He reaches out and gently presses flat palms against her belly—as if addressing both Tessa and the baby.

"I know this is hard," Ben says. "But he's my brother. How can I just throw him out?"

"We made a deal with him," Tessa says. "He had to look

for work. He had to take his medication. He hasn't done either, and still he stays and stays."

"I'll talk to him," Ben says.

"He can't hear you," Tessa says. "I don't see what good we're doing him, keeping him here, while he just rattles around getting crazier and crazier. You don't see it. You work during the day, you work through the night, all you do is have dinner with him." Though she knows it doesn't make any sense, Tessa longs to add: he's upsetting the baby. She feels too selfish to explain how she really feels, her need for the former peace of her life, the deer outside and her cat's gentle, oblique camaraderie. The freedom of her bike rides without returning to Andy's constant and oppressive presence. Now especially, she needs to incubate this child without combating the mood Andy has brought into her house: of impending doom, the heavy curtain of sorrow and hopelessness.

Ben goes downstairs to talk to his brother. Tessa hears Andy swear that he's been taking his medication every day. "Who does she think she is," he asks, "going through my things?"

Tessa tiptoes from the bedroom, down the staircase, and out the front door—closing it carefully behind her so that Sancho can't follow. She sucks in the night air gratefully, the vague chill, the thick pine. She walks to the end of their driveway, taking in the bowing shadows, the sidling light from clear-skied stars. Tessa can see the aspen leaves shiver and shimmer despite the dark; from somewhere close by she hears the ominous alto of a great horned owl. Good spirits here, Tessa has always felt. Even the hazards of this place arise from benign necessity, the circular imperative of the food chain. A kind of excitement pulses in her throat, knowing that behind the trees, the darkness, lurk actual dangerous beasts, the cougar and the coyotes. She wishes she were brave enough to continue walking, down the road, into the woods, taking her chances. A slight flutter, the downward pull of her nausea, reminds Tessa that these chances are no longer hers to take. Still: she prefers to be out here just now, exposed to this night, rather than the bad spirits that lately have taken possession indoors.

The next day Ben brings the pork home after dark, in a sealed plastic bag. It could be any kind of meat, possum or kangaroo, shredded and peppered and unappetizingly gray. Accompanying the package is a Ball mason jar, decorated with a handwritten label. "This is supposed to be fantastic," Ben tells Andy and Tessa.

"You'd better warm it up," Tessa says. "I'll make a salad, but I don't think my stomach can handle . . ."

"No problem," Ben says. He kisses her forehead, then smiles at Andy—determined, Tessa can tell, to forge some kind of truce between his brother and his wife. Stubborn, she and Andy circumvent each other, keeping their eyes to the ground when their paths cross.

While Ben prepares the barbecue, Tessa chops up mushrooms and tomato—feeling happy for a moment at just the two of them, alone in the kitchen, performing tasks side by side. The way it used to be.

Andy comes in for a beer. Tessa tries not to let his intrusion break her improving mood. "Andy," she says. "Isn't it nice that Ben got this barbecue? Did you ever notice how he's always doing things for you?"

"Sure," Andy says, noncommittally.

"I don't mind doing things for Andy," Ben says quickly. "And I like barbecue too."

"Ah, selflessness," Tessa says, breaking a head of romaine in half. Andy returns to the living room.

Tessa sets the table, and she and Ben carry out the food. When Tessa tells Andy that dinner is ready, she sees that the front door has been left wide open.

"God damn it," Tessa says. She walks to the doorway and

calls Sancho. Taking several steps into the darkness, she calls again, louder, to no avail.

She storms back into the house and does a quick inspection—useless, she knows: if Sancho was inside he would not be far from her sight.

She enters the dining room, pale with fury. Andy and Ben are seated, Ben already dishing out food.

"You left the door open," she accuses Andy. "Sancho got outside."

Andy continues to eat, as if she has not spoken.

"He'll come back," Ben soothes. "Sit down and have some dinner. He'll be crying at the door any second."

Tessa takes her seat, unfolds her napkin into her lap. To her surprise, the pork tastes wonderful: meltingly tender, spicy without being hot, the sauce tangy and piquant.

"What do you think?" Ben asks.

"It's delicious," Tessa says.

"It's all right," Andy concedes. "A little vinegary for my taste, but not too bad."

Sancho does not come in that night. Tessa wakes three times, walking downstairs and calling for him at the door. The third time, Ben is already up, working. He comes out of his study and puts his hands on Tessa's shoulders.

"Sancho's gone," Tessa says. "Your brother killed my cat."

Ben squeezes her neck. "Don't jump to conclusions," he says. "Cats are nocturnal, right? Sancho's probably psyched for a little late-night hunting. I bet he'll be back at first light."

But in the morning Sancho is not back, nor when Tessa arrives home from work that afternoon. She throws down her bag and goes directly into the living room, where Andy occupies his usual spot, watching cartoons.

"Have you seen Sancho?" Tessa asks.

"What?"

"Sancho," she says. "My cat. Has he come back?"

Andy shrugs. Tessa's strong and literal desire to strangle him, to step forward and cause him bodily harm, sets her trembling.

"Haven't seen him," Andy says, without a glance at Tessa.

At dusk they scour the hillside, the yards of surrounding neighbors, Ben and Tessa calling Sancho's name. Tessa feels she owes Sancho this search, though she knows with an aching certainty they will not find him. So familiar with Sancho's habits and routines, Tessa understands this great a breach can only mean his permanent disappearance. She is more prepared to find his corpse—some evidence of his demise, tufts of marmalade fur, a spattering of blood—than to see his cantering response to her voice, ever again.

Andy joins them in the search, with the distinct air of knowing it's expected without caring about the outcome. He wanders listlessly, staying close to the house, lighting his endless chain of cigarettes.

"Tessa," Ben says, after an hour or more. He walks toward her, and Tessa sees the light has faded. "It's too late to find Sancho," he tells her. "It's too dark. I'm so sorry, Tessa. But I don't think we're going to find him."

The only thing that keeps Tessa from breaking down, from falling into Ben's arms and sobbing, is the white rage she feels toward Andy. She and Ben both look up to where he paces, occasionally remembering to swivel his head in a searching fashion. They can see that Andy is not silent, that his lips are moving, that he is agitated beyond anything they can imagine, that he is grossly unhappy.

"The poor guy," Ben says.

In the sudden darkness, amidst the rising sounds of

night—the rustle of lurking predators—Tessa's next thought forms so naturally that it surfaces out loud. "If we were a pride of lions," she tells Ben, "or a pack of wolves, we'd devour him. We'd fall on him and destroy him. Tear him limb from limb for the good of the pack. The protection of the family."

Ben turns to her, horror and disappointment visible even in the passing twilight. Tessa begins to cry.

"I'm sorry," she says. "I'm really sorry."

She *is* sorry, and ashamed, and filled with regret. Ben encircles his arm around her waist, cupping her stomach, forgiving her cruelty because of what she carries there. Together, they make their grieving way up the hillside—carefully heading toward the one light, the embered glow of Andy's cigarette, swelling and fading with every inhalation.

scuffling

At first Simone minds terribly, that their mother has locked herself away in the attic. In the late afternoon before their father gets home, after the summer chaos has cooled with the sun, she can hear rustling upstairs, scraping, and sometimes footsteps. Lonely noises, and eerie: making their way through the far reaches of the kitchen, the butler's pantry, the den. Even after they quiet, Simone thinks she can hear their mother breathe, intermittent but endless sighs, like the audible exhalation of this old, ever-settling house.

Her sister Maggie is nearly ten, more than a year older than Simone. They are the only two who care that their mother has for all purposes left. The others, the older ones, barely seem to notice. For three days Maggie and Simone entertain each other on their own. They chase Hound up and down the length of their backyard, avoiding their mother's garden, Simone punching Maggie when she steps on Hound's tail. They play in the garage, dropping marbles into the wall through the hole under the dusty window. They slide down the old coal chute, landing in the basement with bruising thuds. With crayons and markers, they draw on the wallpaper in the rec room, which they are allowed to do, it is their—the children's—room. Maggie and Simone doodle and paint in the space left by their older brothers and sisters, careful (as if the penalty were very grave) not to obscure or intrude upon Sophie, John, Hope, and Conrad's artwork.

Simone and Maggie eat cereal until the milk runs out, rinsing their bowls and stacking them in the dishwasher. They avoid the rooms where children are not supposed to play: their father's study, the four bedrooms beside their own. They follow their mother's rules with near-religious caution, more closely than they do when she is here, thinking they can lure her down—like a cartoon character floating on an aroma—with their obedience.

At night they shut Hound in the kitchen, then go up to the room they share, ignoring Simone's bed and crawling together into Maggie's. Simone stares at the ceiling and listens to the footsteps and movement overhead. She and Maggie are afraid of the attic, whose unfinished and poorly lit rooms stretch the length of their house—carelessly cluttered with stacked boxes and outgrown toys. Before their mother moved up there, probably sleeping on one of the musty, discarded couches, they used to play a game: testing each other, one climbing the narrow steps while the other timed how long she could stand the dusty solitude, the bare bulbs swinging from chains. To Simone the attic air feels heavy with ghosts and loneliness, and she has never lasted so much as a minute—instead racing back down the steps, as if something dangerous were chasing her. In a way Simone admires her mother, brave enough to stay up there alone. At the same time, she dislikes that the attic suddenly seems to preside over the house, which had been such a safe place, but now only exists beneath those stirring and sinister rooms.

Their father tells them good-night from downstairs ("Sleep tight, little girls," he calls, ice tinkling in his glass), and Hope tucks them in halfheartedly, with the superior air of granting favor. Maggie and Simone wish that John, their oldest brother, who has been gone from the house less than a year, were here to take care of them. They lie awake as long as they can (Maggie clinging the way she does), listening for their mother, who must come downstairs to eat: they see each morning that food has been taken. It reminds Simone of waiting to catch Santa Claus, long ago, when they were younger. They always fell asleep before he arrived, and so they do now, every night, before any footfall descends the attic stairs.

On the fourth day their father wakes them. Maggie's and Simone's eyes open in astonishment nearing delight—their father in their room, his tie swinging over them, brushing their chins, his exotic scent of mint and musk.

"Good morning, little," he says to Maggie. "Good morning, littler," he says to Simone. Hope stands in the doorway scowling, her thick knees darkly tanned against John's discarded shirt, which she wears as a nightgown.

"Hope is going to take you to the country club," he tells them. "You'll go with her from now on, while your mother's away."

"Mom's not away," Maggie says, with a punishing tone. "She's in the attic."

Their father presses Maggie's nose like a button. "You listen to Hope," he says. "Don't give her a hard time." He smiles and goes to work. He does not touch Simone.

Hope pulls the covers off them with one angry sweep. "Okay, little girls," she says. "Let's do this."

By the time they get downstairs, where Hope is frying bread, it's clear that despite her pique Hope enjoys her role as

sudden authority—even (or especially) enjoying what she considers her right to feel unfairly burdened.

Hope scoops up the butter-soaked bread with a plastic
spatula and slides it onto plates, which she slams in front of
them. A dramatic and unnecessary gesture: their mother never
serves them breakfast, but makes them get their own. Maggie
eats eagerly, the first piece gone while Simone is still picking
off her crust. Conrad, their younger-older-brother, walks into the
kitchen wearing his bathing suit. He drains the orange juice
carton of its last drops, and while he drinks, the three girls
stare at him: startled daily by his careless beauty—and feeling
strangely apart from him because of it. Maggie and Simone
treat Conrad with deferential awe. Hope, who is older than
Conrad, pretends not to notice his looks.

"Nice, Conrad," she tells him. "That juice was for the
children."

"I am the children," Conrad replies. He takes a piece of
bread from the pan and sits down to eat. Simone feels queasy
from her first greasy bite, and gives the rest to Maggie. Conrad
winks at Simone, a gesture he—at thirteen—can already pull
off gracefully. None of them knows if Conrad realizes the ex-
tent of his handsomeness. He seems to simply assume the
world is an easy place to live.

Hope is not old enough to drive, but her boyfriend is:
Simone, Conrad, and Maggie pile into the backseat of his
car, Simone feeling boundlessly relieved by the familial air of
this activity. She notices, as the car lurches backward, a calico
cat skulking underneath the forsythia bush. She has seen the cat
before; just last week their mother forbade Simone to feed it.
"It wears a collar," she'd said. "It belongs to someone. You don't
want to lure it away from its owners, do you?" Simone watches
the cat now, its long whiskers and flickering tail, and thinks
that she doesn't care about the owners, she only (for whatever

reason) wants the cat for herself. And now that their mother is gone, who's to stop her from feeding it?

Maggie's elbow hits Simone's ribs sharply. When Simone lifts her eyes she can see their mother in the attic window. Already her face has become vague to Simone, it seems she has been gone so long. Conrad and Hope don't notice: the silhouette, wide and grave, way up there, framed by the top story. Maggie and Simone lean together, straining toward their mother as if she were a ghostly celebrity and they her longing fans— their adoration as necessary as their distance.

But then the day is not so bad. Everyone at the club seems to know about their mother, and they lavish attention and care. Maggie and Simone bask in their new orphaned status: nobody can do enough for them. The older girls weave dandelion necklaces, Conrad and his friends feed them honeysuckle, somebody's mother buys them pizza from the patio snack window. When Maggie pretends to faint by the pool, grown-ups swarm around her. Someone tries to call their mother, who of course doesn't answer, but by then Maggie is swimming relays—hopelessly trying with her thick body to keep up with Simone's meatless, eel-like strokes.

Late in the afternoon, wrapped in towels, their long, dark hair slicked off their foreheads, Maggie and Simone recline across the sun-warmed walkway, chalking their fortunes on the steps with broken chards of slate. Maggie suggests writing a list of people they love, in order of preference. Except for Hound, who comes in second with Simone, their lists are identical: each other at the top, followed by John, then Hope, then Conrad, then their father—and last, begrudgingly and out of obligation, their oldest sister, Sophie. In the past their mother has come in after Simone for Maggie, after Hound for Simone.

But today she does not appear on the lists at all, as if she has ceased to exist.

By the time their father comes through the door, carrying a carton of milk and three boxes of pizza, Maggie and Simone are throbbing with sunburn, Simone in too much agony to consider eating. They are both—head to toe, excepting torsos rescued by bathing suits—a deep red bordering on purple, emanating heat, their clothes chafing painfully.

"Damn," their father says. He puts down his load and takes one chin in each hand. They look up at him, too miserable and chagrined to enjoy his touch. "Hope," he calls. "You forgot sunscreen on the little girls."

"Whoops." Hope gets herself a slice of pizza and sashays into the kitchen.

"Damn," their father says again, to himself. "I'll have to get John or Sophie in here from the city to take care of you."

"John," Maggie and Simone chant together. Their oldest sister is sharp angles and unbendable rules, while their oldest brother is pure indulgence. "John, get John, please John, please please John."

All evening Maggie and Simone wait patiently for Hope or their father to take the aloe from the refrigerator (where their mother keeps it). Well after dinner, Maggie finally gets it herself, and they retreat to their room to slather the cold, soothing goop over each other's blistered, stinging skin.

Asleep, Simone dreams she is alone, in her own bed. In this dream, their mother perches beside her, smoothing hair off her flushed forehead.

"I love you best of all," their mother tells Simone. "You are my baby, my littlest, and of all my children I love you the most."

When Simone wakes, she hears voices overhead—one deep, one frail. Not remotely angry, but very intense and huddled. Secretive. Simone peels her body (sticking, painful) out from under Maggie's heated limbs.

She sits up and listens, as if by concentrating she can arrange the muffled rumble into distinguishable words. She doesn't succeed, but realizes: it is not their father who has caused this attic retreat.

Simone gets out of bed. She sneaks down the back stairway and greets Hound in the kitchen. The dog jumps and trembles, overjoyed, his nails clicking, his tags jingling—the most cheerful sound Simone has heard all week. Simone races him upstairs and climbs into her own bed, alone, on top of the covers. Hound jumps up beside her, understanding all rules have been suspended, his long head resting across her legs, his wet gums and tongue cool against her sunburn.

The next morning Simone wakes after her father has left for work. Sophie—who lives in the city, who will start medical school this fall—arrives with groceries and Noxzema. Although she doesn't visit often, Sophie is always quick to reclaim her role as household overseer, declaring what is right and wrong with a certainty that infuriates even Conrad.

After Sophie scolds Hope for their sunburns, she orders Maggie and Simone into a cool tub. She gently dries them off and rubs the medicinal soap into their skin. "Absolutely not," Sophie says when they ask to go to the club with Hope and Conrad. "You need to stay out of the sun today."

The day inside (while the sun dapples and shines) stretches endlessly. Sophie won't let them watch TV, and while she makes tuna fish sandwiches in the kitchen, Simone sneaks into the rec room. With one thick brown marker she draws a portrait of Hound over one of Sophie's old spaceships. While Maggie eats,

Simone scrapes her tuna onto a plate—which she later leaves under the forsythia bush, for the calico cat.

Sophie gains admittance into the attic after a knock and some whispers, while Simone and Maggie play jacks on the hard-tiled floor of the hall bathroom. Between the ball's bounce and the scrape of gathering jacks, they hear Sophie's gentle rap, followed by a coaxing voice much sweeter than she normally uses. They hear their mother's tentative, spectral footsteps. They hear the antique turn of the hooked key. They hear Sophie and their mother, walking upstairs.

Simone bounces the ball so high, it flies halfway to the ceiling, leaving her ample time to sweep her lean fingers across the floor, arranging and gathering the jacks. They must be speaking, sister and mother, but Simone and Maggie do not hear voices. When Simone has won their game, she can tell Maggie is irritated not only at losing, but also at Sophie, upstairs in the attic, as if she knows everything. Maggie locks the bathroom door and takes the dull, rusty scissors from behind the mirror. She holds them out toward Simone, less of a dare than a suggestion.

They sit on the rim of the tub and cut each other's hair, long strands falling jagged across the drain. Close to their scalps, so that Sophie will be too angry to return the following day.

But Sophie only sighs, inconvenienced. She gets the good scissors from their father's desk and sits the girls down on the covered back porch. She drapes dish towels over their shoulders, and uses a damp comb while she snips and evens their hair, curling tendrils behind their ears. Then Sophie brushes off the backs of their necks, blowing wispy, itchy strands with warm breath. When she is done, she crosses her arms and stands in front of them.

"You both look very cute," she soothes, then sighs again. "Simone," she says. "Maggie. I know this is very hard. But you need to realize, it has nothing to do with you that Mom's staying up in the attic."

"What does it have to do with?" Maggie asks, not nicely, but full of petulant skepticism—angry that Sophie should, as usual, presume to know more than they.

"It has to do with . . ." Sophie trails off, and looks out on the lawn. The calico cat picks its way through their mother's garden, toward the bushes by the garage, heading toward discovery of Simone's tuna. "Mom's lilies look parched," Sophie says. She leans against the railing.

"Mom is a little bit sick," she tells them. "Nothing too serious, you shouldn't be worried. She's going to be fine. But she needs an operation, she needs to have her uterus removed. You both know what a uterus is, right?"

"Yeeesss," Maggie and Simone say together, rolling their eyes. Simone instantly jumbles the word "uterus" with "attic," knowing this is wrong but not wanting to confess ignorance to Sophie.

"Okay," Sophie continues. "Well, Mom spent a long time having babies, being pregnant. This may be difficult for you to understand. But Mom, her identity is all wrapped up in kids. Little children. Being a mother."

"Mom doesn't want any more children," Maggie says, enlightening Sophie, her words clipped and precise to override their oldest sister's obtuseness.

"That's true," Sophie grants. "But still. It's hard for her. She feels scared and confused. She doesn't want any more children. But she feels like if she can't have any more children, she doesn't know who she is. Does that make sense to you?"

"No," Maggie says. But Simone, seeing that Sophie is trying to be helpful, nods—hoping that Maggie won't notice. Sophie smiles at her.

"Hey," Sophie says. "I know what. Let's put long sleeves and hats on you two. Then we'll water Mom's garden. She'll look out the window and see us taking care of her flowers, and that'll make her feel a little bit happy."

Digging through the pile of gardening equipment on the basement steps, Simone decides upon the real reason their mother is in the attic. She decides her dream was true: their mother loves Simone, the youngest child, most. And because their mother is afraid of discovery, and very guilty for betraying her other children, she has hidden herself away upstairs.

Simone aims the yellow sprayer at their mother's vegetables. Sophie kneels in the garden, pulling up weeds, while Maggie turns on the hose. The water begins to flow with a creak and a whoosh. When Simone looks up, squinting under the broad, floppy brim of the old denim hat, her head feeling strange and weightless without its curtain of hair, she sees that foreign figure: standing in the window, watching her. Maggie walks across the lawn, looking chubby and awkward in her new pixie cut. Simone drops the hose and lets it snake violently, surrounding each plant with gushing, drowning puddles.

When John appears that evening, after Hope and Conrad get home from the club (Conrad not noticing their haircuts, Hope laughing at them), Maggie and Simone are ecstatic. They tumble down the staircase, shouting his name, leaping together into his arms. Simone wraps her legs around his waist, battling Maggie for position, and buries her face in his neck. She closes her fist into his too-long hair, rubs her sunburnt cheek against his beard. John is the best of every world: possessed of adult size and power, yet always on their side. His hands against their legs scrape, calloused, from curving around the tools he keeps in the trunk of his car—mysterious implements, mauls and levelers.

"Look at you two girls," John says lovingly. "You're a pair of bald lobsters. You're a mess."

Everybody is home: it feels like Christmas. John gives them boxes of Pirouettes, their favorite, letting them eat the cookies before the healthful dinner cooked by Sophie. He gives them sips of his beer, laughing at Sophie when she objects.

"Hey," their father says when he gets home. "What happened to you two?"

"I cut their hair," Sophie says quickly, amazingly—saving them. "It's so hot out."

"Cute." He pours a scotch and carries his briefcase into his study, relieved at finding himself not needed.

John tucks Maggie and Simone into Maggie's bed, pulling the sheet across so tightly they can barely move. He turns off the light and makes shadow puppets on the far wall: a rabbit and a dog, the voices he uses so ridiculous that Simone's and Maggie's laughter drowns out the overhead noise.

Earlier, when Maggie asked John why their mother had moved to the attic, John said, "Mom lived downstairs for a long time. She probably just wants a change of scenery."

The simplicity of this explanation has somehow unburdened them. They feel lighthearted, as if their mother's disappearance is a minor event.

When John leans over to kiss them, Simone grabs his beard and pulls his face close. She breathes her brother in greedily, and feels a sudden surge of anger—that their mother might love anyone, even Simone, more than John, this dear and superior being.

"John," she whispers. "You need to bring up Hound, so he can sleep with us."

John obliges, sneaking down the back staircase and then up with Hound, who crowds onto the bed with Maggie and Simone. They lie back, happy, not caring that John, Sophie, Hope, Conrad, and their father sit around the dining room table—talking, scheming, consulting without them. Everyone accustomed now to their mother: scuffling overhead, the fervent sound of isolation, out of reach, as if she had never been there at all.

In the morning the noise has spread: it's everywhere. Simone roams the house in her nightgown, disoriented by the absence of hair down her back. The rustling continues up above and moves throughout the rooms, now coming from every direction. Simone follows it downstairs, into the front hallway, pressing her face to the wall that borders the garage.

"What?" Maggie says, coming out of the kitchen. Simone starts at the sight of her sister, unfamiliar, red-faced, and shorn. She feels a rising panic—that everything has fallen apart, and will continue to fall apart, now that their mother is gone.

Simone's voice comes out in a crackling whisper, frightened. "There's something in the wall."

Maggie presses her ear obediently, staring gravely back at Simone. She nods. "It's rustling," she says.

They turn together, toward Sophie, who has come to stand behind them.

"It's just a cat," Sophie says.

Maggie and Simone stare back at her in horror.

"John left the garage door open," Sophie explains, "and a cat got in, and climbed through that hole under the window. Now it's stuck in the wall."

Simone feels her eyes fill up with tears. Sophie looks back at her, an amused expression on her face, as if the news she has just imparted did not connote disaster of the highest order.

"I'm sorry," Sophie says ten minutes later, standing in the middle of the garage. The pitch of Simone's and Maggie's concern for the cat seems to have broken her humor: now her voice cracks under the strain of appeasing them. "There's nothing to be done," she says. "Nothing."

Sunlight pours in through the open door. John has not come back yet from driving Conrad and Hope to the club. While Maggie crawls into the coal chute searching for an escape route, Simone stretches her arm through the hole, coaxing the cat with pepperoni scraped from leftover pizza.

"Come on," Sophie pleads. "I'll take you to the club for a swim. We'll leave the door open. The cat got in through that hole, it'll come out eventually."

Maggie and Simone are not convinced. They can hear the cat, its claws scraping against the wall. Occasional meows, desperate: nearly as afraid of its potential rescuers as of not being rescued at all.

"No," Simone argues. "Listen. She *can't* find her way out. That's why she's *crying*. She needs to be *saved*."

When John returns he offers to take a maul from the trunk of his car and break the hole open wide—so the cat will easily see its escape route.

"That's ridiculous," Sophie says. "And irresponsible. The cat can get out on its own. You don't need to destroy the wall."

"Please, John," Maggie and Simone beg. "Chop it open. Please, John. Let the cat out."

"I swear to God, John," Sophie says, "if you chop that wall apart, you're going to pay to have it fixed."

"I'll fix it myself," John tells her.

"Oh, right."

"What's that supposed to mean?"

"I just don't want things in chaos," Sophie says. "For Mom's sake."

"Mom's the one who's caused the chaos," John answers. "Mom's the one who's left the little girls with nobody to take care of them. . . ."

"She's taken care of everyone her whole life. Isn't she entitled to a little meltdown? A little respite?"

"Sure. While her children live on cereal and suffer from sunstroke."

"Give me a break, please, would you, John?" Sophie lets her voice rise, then checks herself and brings it down to a fierce whisper. "What do you know about it, anyway? What have you ever taken care of, in your entire life?"

John smiles slowly, then goes to his car and opens the trunk. He swings the maul over his shoulder and walks back into the garage.

"Dad will kill you," Sophie warns, her voice rising again. "It'll cost a fortune to fix that wall."

"What's money?" Maggie pipes up. "What's money compared to a life?"

"That's beautiful," Sophie sneers. "You're really a genius, you know that, Maggie?"

"Move over, Simone," John says, his voice obstinately maintaining its good nature. Simone steps aside, cold pepperoni clutched in her fist, while John bends his knees. He strikes with the maul once, a great arcing motion. His shoulder blades and muscles move, complex, beneath his T-shirt. Simone flinches as plaster flies—tiny, chalk-scented flecks.

John's second stroke bounces awkwardly, ricocheting to one side and shattering a windowpane.

"You idiot," Sophie shrieks.

"No problem," John says cheerfully. "I'll fix that. I'm very handy, Sophie. You never give me credit."

With his next stroke the wall breaks open, dust rising in clouds like smoke. A crumbling grayness shreds forth from the interior, snowflake diamonds filtering upward through the light. A wide cavity, large enough for Simone—if she needs—to crawl inside the wall herself and fetch the cat.

They step back, the four of them. When John drops the

maul, Maggie and Simone run to him, clinging to his hands as assurance of his heroism.

Sophie stands aside, waiting as the dust settles. From behind the wall the cat meows tentatively, unsure whether it's been liberated or assaulted.

Simone walks back to the gaping mouth and crouches beside it. "Here, kitty," she says, her voice the gentlest singsong she can muster. "We won't hurt you. Here, kitty."

The sound of an animal, rising to its feet, and then a soft padding that seems to come from every direction. By the time its face emerges—orange crossed by black, tortoiseshell eyes blinking against the light—Simone's fear has risen in the form of butterflies, thousands, fluttering beneath her ribs. A feeling that is instantly assuaged as the cat pauses, then steps through, walking regally past her, tail twitching to and fro.

"How's that for gratitude?" John asks, Maggie still leaning against him as the calico cat strolls by, finished here, and out the open door.

John's voice hangs in the air a moment, as the dust had. Then suddenly there is quiet. Not only in the walls but overhead. Simone feels a kind of joy rise inside her: the rustling, the scuffling, has ended.

"Listen," she whispers. "Can you hear that?"

"Hush," Sophie answers. "Let's enjoy it for a minute."

And they do enjoy it—none of them moving, but drinking in the luxurious stillness. The muscles in Simone's face quiver, beyond her control, spasms that feel like smiles.

The world is still spinning, she thinks. The wall will be fixed, the cat will be fine, their mother will come downstairs.

"I feel so happy," she mouths, not letting sound escape her lips.

John, Maggie, and Sophie nod in agreement and solidarity: not wanting, any of them, to interrupt the silence.

the wedding bed

Camille was very much a child of her generation, raised on "Free to Be You and Me." She believed in tolerating anything that didn't cause pain. She believed people of every color had equal worth. She believed in love as the only proper impetus for marriage. Within the ivy-covered confines of home and school, Camille learned from teachers, records, and television that money didn't matter. Only love mattered. So it surprised her how unhappy she felt: moving into the pale, musty house.

"Poverty used to sound romantic," she confessed to Joe, a few months after they married. "At least in connection to love. A bottle of wine and thou. The log cabin in the woods. 'I don't need anything but you.' "

The new house was a far cry from a log cabin in the woods. A blond brick ranch house, circa 1970. Its street in Oakland lay hidden, like an afterthought, behind a frontage road: a truncated stretch of pavement that led to nowhere, bordering a small city park. "This area used to be kind of bad," admitted the landlord, who lived in the lush and expensive hills above Berkeley. "But it's better now. It's being gentrified."

"As if gentrification were a good thing," Camille said to Joe later. But secretly she felt relieved that the neighborhood wasn't considered dangerous. She had wanted Joe to move into her apartment, in the Elmwood section of Rockridge. And he had. They lived there for nearly two months, sharing the tiny rooms with Camille's Persian cat, crawling over and bumping into each other endlessly. Camille hadn't minded. She liked her apartment—the refinished hardwood floors and the coziness of her own good things. She felt safe, surrounded not only by Joe but by the building's business-suited inhabitants, who always seemed to be carrying fresh-cut flowers and dark bottles of wine. She liked the convenient access to College Avenue, its shops and restaurants.

Still, she agreed to move: partly because Joe promised to fix up the new house, and partly because the new street seemed so insulated. Most people traveling the highway or lunching at the park's picnic tables wouldn't even know it was there. Her cat, Penny, would be protected from traffic. The park also offered the promise of feline exploration, not that Penny would take advantage. A homebody, the cat would more likely stick to the large shambles of a back yard, where unpruned branches of apricot and plum trees curved toward the ground, and an ancient, hulking Chevy step van perched on cinder blocks in the driveway. "Makes for a lovely view," Camille noted, dryly, the first night they sat with beers on the cement step outside the kitchen door.

"But isn't it great to have a yard?" Joe said. Camille's old apartment had a terrace that overlooked another building. Joe had lived in a garage apartment, in a neighborhood so seedy, Camille refused to spend even one night there.

The new house—their married house—had two entrances: a front door that opened into the living room, and a back door that opened into the kitchen. Between these two rooms lay a narrow, windowless hallway that led to three bedrooms. Except for the bathroom's mildewed linoleum, every inch of floor space, including the kitchen, was covered by wall-to-wall carpeting: mismatched patterns that clashed when they met at arched doorways. The living room rug swirled navy blue into chocolate brown into orange rust. The beige carpet in the kitchen and hallway had a randomly scattered, heart-shaped design of burgundy, lavender, and forest green. In the first bedroom lay a brown-speckled baby blue shag. In the second bedroom lay a flat nubby weave that years before might have been saffron, but had wilted to a sickly ochre. Another shag, itchy and bloodred, dominated the smallest bedroom, which Camille would use as a study—a place to complete her overdue master's thesis.

Originally they'd decided to sleep in the ochre room; but their first night, three minutes after collapsing on Camille's frameless futon, they noticed the strong, stale odor of cat urine. "Just be sure to keep Penny out of there," Joe said, as they dragged the mattress across the hall into the baby blue room. "She'll think it's a big litter box." He smiled, the vaguely snaggle-toothed grin Camille had always found seductive—exotic in contrast to her world of orthodontia and twice-a-year polishing. "What's wrong with his teeth?" her father had asked, the first time he met Joe. Camille's father, a partner at his law firm in Washington, D.C., believed that bad teeth indicated poor breeding and neglectful parenting. "It points to an irresponsible upbringing," he pronounced, closing his ears to Camille's arguments for egalitarian romance.

Privately, Camille agreed that Joe's upbringing had been irresponsible, and therefore romantic. His college-educated parents had raised him on communes and cross-country trips in VW vans. Joe and Camille met each other in her old neighborhood, forced to share a table one crowded morning at the Buttercup Café. He was working on a house nearby, rebuilding the termite-infested porch. Camille had apologized for the books and notebooks spread across the table, identifying herself as a graduate student. "English literature," she'd said, when Joe asked what she studied. He had been quick to claim his own two years of college. "It wasn't for me," he told her. "I like working with my hands, fixing things. Building furniture." Along with attraction (Joe's eyes were blue like a Siberian husky's, his forearms wiry and corded) she'd felt a tug of envy and admiration. Camille had never built anything. And in her family, abandoning higher education would be considered outrageous, as likely to be accepted as appearing for dinner completely nude.

"How's he going to support you?" Camille's father had asked from his car phone, when she informed him of their impending marriage.

"I don't need a man to support me." Camille paid her way by student loans, clerking at a bookstore on Shattuck, and occasional gifts from her father. "I love Joe," she added firmly, considering the phrase an absolute—an indisputable and sacred bottom line—even to her father, navigating the Beltway in his leather-scented sedan.

Camille couldn't stand to walk barefoot in the new house. She hated the feeling of stale, man-made fiber between her toes. "If there was a fire," she said to Joe, "the carpets would probably just melt. I don't think there's a single flammable strand in this place." She imagined the molten plastic lava, bubbling like witch's brew amidst rising flames. "Hey," Joe said, good-naturedly but slightly defensive. "So it's not the Taj Mahal. How else would we get so much space for such small rent?"

Camille would have traded space for odorless order. "You

and me, Penny," she confided to her cat. "We're the only signs of elegant life."

Penny ruffled and walked gingerly across the living room, leaping and settling on Camille's velvet armchair. The furniture that had more than filled the Rockridge apartment was scattered sparsely throughout the new house, necessity interspersing Camille's good pieces with Joe's ragtag hand-me-downs, his homemade shelves and tables.

Camille's father had presented her with Penny upon college graduation six years earlier. It was a sentimental gift: as a child, she had owned a nearly identical Blue Himalayan High Point. Penny had her breed's characteristic snooty, smushed-up face and long, silky fur. The cat seemed very much aware of her own value: fastidious and vain, she picked her way through life with prim, dainty steps. She bestowed affection sparingly, under very specific conditions. Move the wrong way, pet the wrong spot, and she'd march away, indignant—her great poofy tail held up like a flag bearing a royal coat of arms.

Camille loved Penny the same way she loved Joe: with no thought of what the other might give her, only an abiding longing for togetherness and mutual contentment. But as Penny curled painstakingly into her lap, Camille thought that the new house made her less nostalgic for her Rockridge apartment than the long, curving stairways of her childhood. The chandeliers and antique sideboards. The oriental rugs and well-groomed lawns.

So unlike the ramshackle clamor of this new place, overgrown and brandishing its unruly sprawl. They moved too late in summer to tackle the large garden. Camille worked long hours at the bookstore, wearing the maroon apron she called her "badge of servility." The job stole time she needed to finish her thesis. Joe did work he called "freelance," fixing up other people's homes, so the last thing he wanted to do on weekends and evenings was work on their own. They let the yard grow thick with weeds and brush, overripe fruit falling from branches and mulching into the neglected soil.

Joe took complaints about the new house very personally, so Camille tried to stay quiet. That first afternoon, she'd stood in the kitchen and listed what needed repair. There were bugs in the light fixtures, no screens on the windows, nothing but a chain lock on the hollow front door. Catching a beleaguered glimmer in Joe's eyes, she suddenly felt like one of the housewives he worked for: issuing orders, instructions. Uncomfortable, she'd waved her grievances away with a flick of her wrist. That night, after they'd dragged the futon into the baby blue room, Camille fidgeted restlessly.

"What's wrong?" Joe asked.

"I hate this, sleeping so close to the floor," she said.

"You didn't mind in Rockridge," Joe said. "The mattress was on the floor at your apartment."

In Rockridge, the lack of a frame had seemed to spring from economy of space, the futon on the floor creating a sense of Asian spareness.

"It was a wood floor," Camille said. "It didn't seem so . . . I don't know. So *full*. I feel like my face is millimeters away from God knows what. *Germs*."

She could sense Joe's umbrage in his pause, hear his earnest mental search for a solution. She reached out before he could speak.

"Never mind," she said, moving into his chest, curling her arm around his waist. "I'm just happy to be here. With you."

Camille felt the relief of his smile against her forehead. Their reconciliation moved gently into lovemaking. Afterward, when Joe's breathing had lulled into sleep, Penny tiptoed into the curve of her neck. Camille sighed in gratitude, rolling over to pull the cat to her. The familiar and rhythmic purr, the pulsating fluff of her—it felt to Camille like luxury, and soothed her enough to rest.

A few hours later she awoke to see Penny across the room. The cat sat still as a statue atop a salvaged dresser of Joe's, which they'd shoved against a window. The warped drawers didn't close properly, and Camille thought it cast a sinister shadow, rife with disorder, contrasting the cultivated shape of Penny: bathed in a jellicle light, staring outside so intently, she seemed in a trance. Camille threw her covers aside and went to investigate. There on the window's outside ledge, in the same precise, silent sphinx pose as Penny, sat another cat. Camille started with a too-dramatic gasp, as if facing a human intruder.

This cat was large and short-haired, his coat in the moonlight a muted version of the ochre carpet. Bigger than Penny but extremely wiry—so lean as to be all skeletal angles. His eyes in his gaunt, triangular face looked unearthly huge and pale; they brought to Camille's mind the pictures sketched from claims of alien abductees. Camille picked up Penny and cradled her into her chest.

From the floor, on the futon, Joe stirred. "Cam," he mumbled. "What're you doing?"

"There's a strange cat outside."

Joe mumbled again, this time opening his arms to summon her. Camille carried Penny back to bed, feeling troubled and somehow unsafe. "It's like a little hamster nest," she accused Joe's back. "This pile of blankets on the rug."

She waited for a moment, gauging his mute back. Deciding the silence was rooted in sleep, not anger, she spooned herself around him, thankful and repentant.

Less than a week later, while Camille unpacked their Farberware in the kitchen, she saw the yellow cat again, stalking butterflies in the overgrown garden. Penny, who would not be allowed outside before she was acclimated to the new house, sat on the counter staring. Camille stared too. The cat's leaps resembled nothing so much as flight: the most airborne mammal she had ever seen. Vertical leaps and upward pounces high as a man, so that the cat actually hovered above the moths.

Camille was still in the kitchen when Joe came home from work. "I saw that cat again," she told him, as he walked through the back door.

"Guess what?" Joe said. "I got the job over at Hoshi's. Roofing. Fifteen bucks an hour." He scooped Penny up and held her against his chest: an incongruous sight, the lavish fluff of Penny against Joe's dirty T-shirt.

"Great," Camille said, mustering all her loyalty to smile. And it *was* great. Almost twice what Camille made at the bookstore. Still. Camille had been raised expecting salaries measured by yearly increments, not hourly.

"Yeah," Joe said. "It's great. I wish I had went to him two months ago. We'd be caught up on our bills already."

Camille yanked her salad spinner into two pieces and slammed it into the sink, as Penny twisted herself out of Joe's embrace and thumped to the floor.

"Gone," Camille said. "I wish I had *gone* to him two months ago." She turned on the faucet with a frustrated snap of her wrist. The water came out too fast, spraying her. "Please, Joe. I love you, but you sound like a hillbilly."

Joe laughed. "You mean I sound like a roofer," he said. He kissed her forehead and wiped the water off her face with his sleeve. Camille pushed him away, not sure which annoyed her more: his refusal to care about grammar or his refusal to take offense at her correction.

The next day, after Joe drove his truck to the new job at Hoshi's, before Camille took the bus into Berkeley to work the three-to-close shift at the bookstore, she committed something of a betrayal. She phoned her father and described the new house.

"Sounds like Joe should be right at home," her father said. Camille didn't contradict him, even though she heard in his tone not only pique at the thought of his daughter in such environs, but a kind of gloating, a male pleasure at besting. She hung up feeling sullied, traitorous.

That feeling stayed with her all evening while she sorted books and helped customers. She struggled with her guilt as she snatched off the apron (immediately at closing time, not wearing it one extra second), and as she rode home on the bus. She walked from her stop at the frontage road, cutting through a corner of the park's car lot to their driveway. Joe would be asleep, curled up with Penny, but Camille would crawl into bed and cover him with penitent kisses.

She stopped short by the backyard gate, halted by the human sound of running water.

"Hey," a man said. He stood just beyond no-man's-land—several inches onto pavement belonging to Joe and Camille's driveway. She could barely make out his face, invisible of age, coloring, or distinctive marks. But she easily discerned by his manner, by the much-owned lines of his oversized coat, by the odor of alcohol overpowering even his loud, steady stream: a street person—the natural corollary to the park, something Camille had never considered.

"Hey," the man repeated, as if meeting her at a neighborhood bar. "How's it going?"

Camille hesitated. Should she walk quickly past him? Should she turn and run around the house to the front door? Should she scream?

"Excuse me," she said. "This is my house."

"Hey," the man said again, loudly. "I ain't trespassing. No harm done." He zipped up clumsily, and Camille winced at the intrusive intimacy. When he turned to lumber over to her, she felt assaulted by the disparity in their sizes: the swaggering, unsteady hulk of him.

The back porch light turned on. Joe stepped outside.

"Cam?" he called into the dark. "Is that you?"

Joe walked down the driveway, barefoot in his boxers. In the new light, Camille noticed the yellow cat: sprawled on top of the Chevy step van, looking down like a mountain lion perched on high rocks, surveying his territory.

Shirtless, Joe closed in like safety. His gait was confident and definite—the visible movement of tendon and sinew operated as a warning, making hurry unnecessary. Arriving at the gate, Joe stepped in front of her, crossing his arms over his chest. He dwarfed the man, as the man had dwarfed Camille.

"Hey," Joe said, as if this were their common language. Last Thanksgiving Joe had brought plates of turkey and stuffing to some men who lived in a car near his job site. For a moment Camille wondered if instead of telling this man to leave, Joe would invite him in for a hot meal.

"You need to get along now," Joe said. "And don't come back. Ever."

"Sure, man. No problem. No worries."

As the man retreated backward, to the park, Camille walked quickly toward the house, her elbows locked angrily at her sides.

"Camille," Joe said. "Are you all right?"

"What do you care?" Camille answered. "Not enough to leave the porch light on. Not enough to give me the truck."

"I'm sorry," Joe said, following her into the house. "That was stupid. You take the truck from now on. I'll ride the bus. And make sure you come in the front door at night."

"If someone else hasn't already come through the front door. Some street person. You still haven't fixed that lock."

"I will," Joe said. "Listen, I'll do it right now. I'll go over to Hoshi's and get a dead bolt. I've got a key."

"Thanks," Camille said, kneeling to stroke Penny, who met her in the hallway. "Like I really want to be alone right now." She stood and marched over the offensive carpet, into the bathroom. Joe's face, drawn and painfully handsome, shadowed—burdened with accountability, as if he had been the threatening figure urinating in their bushes.

"I'm sorry," he said again. "I'm really sorry, Camille."

Camille squeezed Colgate onto her toothbrush, focusing her gaze on her own mirrored image. "Never mind," she said, her voice intentionally hard, unreachable. "Don't worry about it."

The following Sunday, in the afternoon, Camille drove Joe's pickup into the back driveway. The truck, spotted with rust, sighed to a halt with a sputter as she turned off the ignition. Joe sat on the cement step, reading the sports page. He squinted at her as she crossed the lawn. The sun shone so thickly, so heavily, it seemed to Camille she ought to part it, like curtains, to reach her husband.

"Hey," he called. "How was work?"

"Fine," she said. "Not too busy."

"Do you know what?" he said. "I think that yellow cat lives in the van."

Camille put her hands on her hips and walked over to the Chevy step van. Sun pulsed densely on her bare shoulders and legs. She braced her sneakered foot against the wide front bumper. "This thing is monstrous," she said to Joe. "It's bigger than a school bus."

"I know," Joe said. "It looks like an ice cream truck for giants."

Camille climbed up the front of the van, scaling with her arms wide. Behind the vast windshield, the yellow cat sat upright in the broad Naugahyde captain's seat, perfectly at home behind the enormous steering wheel. At the sight of Camille, the cat balked: a dismayed double take. He ducked, then vanished through the gaping gearshift box.

Through the glass Camille saw the inside of the van, its strange, apocalyptic mood: a cavernous but halted monument to nomadic life. In the back lay an old mattress covered with stains, its fibrous fill spilling out around rusted coils. The door to an old toaster oven hung open, attached by one remaining hinge. A small metal sink overflowed with building debris— shingles and old boards studded with bare nails. The low bench opposite the sink was covered with cat feces, and throughout the van lay the scattered remains of feline meals—feathers, and fast-food wrappers probably foraged from the park Dumpster. Camille recoiled and jumped down, landing heavily on the balls of her feet.

"Great," she said. "That's just great." She walked over to Joe and lowered herself into his sun-warmed lap.

"What's the big deal?" Joe pressed his face into her neck. He tugged on the end of her ponytail. "I think it's funny."

"The big deal is Penny," Camille said. "How is she sup- posed to come outside? This is her yard. How is she supposed to contend with that tomcat? He's like a miniature cougar."

"Penny will be okay."

"That's what you always say. Penny will be okay. We'll be okay. Everything will be okay."

"Well," Joe said. "It usually is. Right?"

Camille leaned against his chest, still staring out toward the van. "Hey," Joe said. "Know what I did this afternoon? I put two new locks on the front door. Dead bolts. We're sealed in tight." He twined his arms around her waist and pressed his face into her neck. Camille traced the abrupt lines of his tan—halting circles around his clavicle and biceps. She swiveled into his grip and kissed him.

"Thank you," she said, the backs of her thighs sticky against the tops of his knees, their skins attached by summer air.

"Whatever you do, don't feed it," her father said. "You'll never get rid of it."

"I have no intention of feeding him," Camille said, slightly guilty that the idea hadn't occurred to her. "I wonder, though." She watched Penny march into the kitchen and make a habitual check of her own food supply. "Where does he get water?"

"That's not your problem," her father said. "Once you start worrying about where it gets food and water, you're a goner."

Camille hung up and dialed the landlord.

"I wouldn't worry about that yellow cat," the landlord said. "He's been living in that van for years."

"But what about my cat?" Camille protested. "I want her to be safe in the yard."

"That yellow cat never bothered anyone. He's pretty self-sufficient. Eats mice and grasshoppers. Leftovers from the park, that kind of thing."

"Where does he get water?"

"Puddles? The creek, maybe."

Camille pictured the cat leaning over the creek. An unlikely image.

"Call animal control if you want," the landlord offered. "Doesn't make any difference to me."

Camille hung up and looked out the window. The yellow cat lay sunbathing on its back at the end of the driveway. She pulled one of Joe's old garage-sale bowls from the cupboard and filled it with tap water. She carried it outside, placed it a couple yards from the cat, then stepped back onto the porch. Behind her, in the open doorway, Penny sat watching—her feather boa of a tail twitching disdainfully.

The yellow cat rose, immediately interested in the bowl. Keeping one eye on Camille, he stalked the offering athletically, muscular haunches tensed. Arriving at the bowl, he bent over it, then angled a perplexed face toward Camille. What, are you kidding? Water?

"Sorry," Camille said out loud. "You were expecting tuna fish, maybe? Caviar?" She turned back toward the doorway to look at Penny—who had disappeared, probably outraged by Camille's sedition. Her *fraternization.*

The yellow cat reclined, resuming his sunbath beside the bowl. Camille took a few steps in his direction, but he jerked out of his repose and ran to the van: one swift, startled motion. Camille stood there in the drive, vaguely hurt, and distinctly sorry that she'd disturbed him.

"He must have belonged to somebody, at some point," Camille said to Joe that night at dinner. "He knew what a bowl meant, right away. Where would he get that, if not from living with people?"

"Guess it's been a while," Joe said. "He won't let me get within four feet of him."

"My father said not to feed him. He said we'd never get rid of him."

"Feed the cat, don't feed him," Joe said. "I don't think he's going anywhere. Unless you want to call the pound."

"I don't have the heart. Do you?"

Joe shrugged. "Cat's not hurting anybody."

Penny had been outside several times, slinking through the garden, catching and releasing crickets. The yellow cat kept a tactful distance, retreating to the van like a servant allowing the lady of the manor her privacy. Penny regally laid claim to the yard, accepting his deference as her due.

"Do you think he's hungry?" Camille asked Joe.

Joe emptied his salad bowl onto his plate. He shredded the last of his chicken off the bones, placing each piece into the bowl. Camille followed him as he carried it outside.

They stood back. The yellow cat emerged from the van, watching them warily. "Let's go inside," Joe said.

From the window they saw the cat trot to the bowl. He lowered his head distrustfully, then snatched the first bite—inhaling it. He crouched over the bowl and ate with ravenous, jerking gusto.

After he'd made his retreat, Joe and Camille walked out to inspect the bowl, which had been left empty—completely scraped.

"Hungry," Joe said. He picked up the bowl and handed it to Camille, who went inside to fill it with Penny's kibble. Then she carried it back out and placed it under the van.

In the morning Camille carried a jar of Penny's cat treats outside and kneeled to peer underneath the van. The bowl was empty. The yellow cat lay a few feet behind it, licking his paws. He halted, granting Camille a guarded appraisal—not trusting, but slightly less appalled at the sight of her. She placed a treat on the cement just outside the van and stepped aside.

The cat was game, almost obliging. He pulled himself politely to his feet, slouched to the food, ate it. Looked expectantly at Camille, who placed another treat and stepped back—just a little closer than before.

They continued in this way—Penny sitting on the window ledge, a disapproving audience—until Camille sat on the cement step. The eave of the porch cast a thick shadow across the grass, and the cat stopped short at this house-made shade. Clearly considering the dark demarcation of territory too dangerous to cross.

A few days later her father called. "How are you doing for money?" he asked. Camille cradled the phone on her shoulder and dried her hands with a ratty dish towel. Penny wove around her ankles insistently, demanding something: Camille checked the cat's food and water bowls. Both were full. She opened the back door, but Penny refused to exit—wanting something different and chirping in frustration at Camille's inability to determine precisely what. Camille sighed and swung the door closed.

"How are we doing for money," she repeated. "I guess we're fine." Only a week away from fall semester, Camille's student loan check had just arrived, a nice padding to their bank account. Between her job and Joe's, they'd have enough to cover rent, insurance for the truck, the phone bill. But not enough to stock up on *things:* decent rugs, more furniture, a normal car. And not enough to grant Camille the time she needed to work on her thesis.

"So Joe likes being a roofer?"

"It's a good job. Really good. High-paying. And Hoshi—his boss—said he could have lumber for free."

"What's he going to do with lumber?"

"Oh, you know. Build things."

Contrary to her tone, Camille hung up in a sour mood, which increased as she prepared dinner. As she strained to open a jar of marinara sauce, the lid and glass parted, then slipped from her hands. When Joe got home, she was on her hands and knees, trying to lift the stain from the beige rug with a rag and carpet cleaner.

"Look at this," she said. "Who ever heard of a carpeted kitchen? It's so stupid. Why can't we tear this stuff up and put down linoleum?"

"A lot of work, for a rental," Joe said.

Camille stood, frowning. She threw the cleaning supplies into the sink. Joe, she thought, could live anywhere. He would be just as happy inside the van, with the yellow cat. Camille abandoned dinner. She walked to the living room and sunk into her armchair. Penny jumped up on her lap, and Camille closed her eyes: concentrating on the velvet chair, the Persian cat—the softness of what few riches she possessed.

Meanwhile she continued to court the yellow cat. Lately when she offered him treats, he seemed less interested in the food than in her hand. He would move forward to take the treat—then curve his chin downward, rubbing against the air, pantomiming the stroke of a human hand on his head. But when Camille reached out with her other hand, he ducked away.

"Here, kitty," she said. "It's okay. I won't hurt you."

She put the treat down on the cement and backed away. The cat ate, then watched her walk into the house—seemingly disappointed by her retreat.

"The house will be a bitch to heat," Joe said one morning. "We'll have to keep the thermostat low, around fifty-five."

September now. Still warm, still green, but the sun cast a more autumnal light—harvest hues of gold and yellow. Penny had already begun spending more time indoors, as if anticipating the pending dampness, the fog and chill of Northwestern winter.

"Wonderful," Camille told her husband. "Maybe I'll take up knitting. Assuming my hands don't freeze."

"Just knit mittens first," Joe said, and laughed. Camille, on the other hand, did not consider the prospect of a cold house particularly amusing.

"What a pathetic way to live," she said—barely under her breath, loud enough for Joe to hear. As his smile faded, she cast a meaningful glance about the house—the offensive carpets, the still-screenless windows. Suddenly not caring about the insult to Joe, or their life together.

That night Camille came home from work early, parking Joe's truck in front of the house. The porch light shone, barely visible against the lit window—every lamp inside turned on. Camille walked into the living room, expectant, but Joe was nowhere to be found.

From the edge of the park, Camille heard voices. She picked up Penny and walked through the house, to the back porch, and saw Joe: leaning on the fence, a beer in one hand. Making friendly conversation with the same street person Camille had met that summer—who, she noticed now, held a beer bottle identical to Joe's.

Camille stood blinking into the dark, hanging on tight to Penny. The cat's ears perked, startled—listening along with Camille, who couldn't help but characterize her husband's charity as imprudent. This was their home, after all.

Joe's voice carried through the evening air—an easy sound, relaxed and cheerful. The man spoke in answer with the same pitch, the same timbre. She heard Joe laugh. Saw him raise the bottle to his lips in a movement that looked incidental, second nature.

She thought about calling out to Joe, rebuking him. Hadn't he told this very man to go away and never come back? Didn't he realize that this man made Camille extremely uncomfortable, extremely uneasy? Wasn't socializing with him—encouraging him to return, again and again—a slight to Camille, a willful disregard for her feelings?

She thought about saying all these things. Instead she carried Penny inside and crawled into bed—their tumble of floor-level blankets—without washing her face or brushing her teeth. When Joe sat beside her on the mattress, she could feel his cautious peer into her face. She kept her eyes shut tight.

"Cam?" Joe said. "Are you awake?"

Camille made no effort to deepen her breathing. Joe could tell, probably, that she wasn't really sleeping. But she said nothing to him, just kept her face turned away, not responding to his hand on her shoulder, or the beer-scented draft of his breath against her cheek.

The following evening, the yellow cat finally accepted Camille's touch: reminding her of the first time she and Joe kissed outside her Rockridge apartment.

On the back stoop, waiting for Joe to come home from work, Camille perched on the cement step, drinking a glass of wine-from-a-box. She leaned against the doorway and watched the wheat-tinted light spread across overgrown grass.

The cat approached her like prey—steadily, carefully. Guarding himself against possible counterattack with torporously slow movement. Camille stretched out her hand, mimicking his cautious tempo.

"No treats," she told him. "Just me."

The cat craned toward her knuckles, bowing against the air with his eyes half-closed—as if imagining the skin of her fingers against his crown.

"I won't hurt you," Camille said. "Come on."

At last he let his head connect to her hand. Upon contact he did not recoil, as Camille expected, but instead commenced the loudest, most elated purring—deep and tattered in his throat.

He continued pressing his head against one hand, allowed her to stroke his back with the other. In one instant the yellow cat had given his supple, bony body over to complete and delirious contact. Like two people whose first kiss leads immediately to passionate lovemaking, with no discussion, no turning back. Camille felt the same unruly joy that would accompany taming a wild animal: the same surprise and delight as if a raccoon had suddenly crawled into her embrace.

"Well, well," Joe said, when he returned home to find Camille still on the back step, the yellow cat purring blissfully across her lap. "Looks like we got ourselves a new cat."

"Good God," her father said, when she called him from work. "Just don't let it inside. God knows what kind of bacteria it's carrying. What kind of germs."

"It's funny, hearing you say that," Camille said. "I could attach those words to the expression on Penny's face when she sees me petting him. Completely disgusted."

"Smart cat," her father said.

Driving home in the truck, Camille shivered against the cold snap of air coming through the broken back window. I'll have to have Joe tape that up, she thought.

She parked the truck out front. From inside the house, she could hear the heavy pounding of nails.

"What's up?" she called from the living room. "What are you doing?"

"Cam," Joe called back. Camille walked toward his voice, across the swirling living room carpet, over heart-shaped patterns toward the baby blue room. "I wanted to be finished before you got home."

He was finished, nearly. Their futon and thick winter quilt, their soft feather pillows, had been lifted off the carpet by a broad pine base: the widest bed Camille had ever seen. So tall and high, she would need to pull herself up into it—which was why, presumably, Joe now worked building stairs at its foot. Two low steps, so she could easily reach the now-endless expanse of covers. Of warmth.

Joe tossed his hammer aside and threw his arms out, smiling. "A surprise," he said. "Hoshi gave me the lumber. I made it for you. It's your wedding bed."

"It's beautiful," Camille said. "It's the most beautiful bed I've ever seen."

"Nowhere near the ground now," Joe said.

"No," Camille agreed. "Nowhere near."

He swept her up, then, into the new bed. Far above the floor, where they passed the next hour or two, until Penny—using the new steps for her ascent—made a nest at their feet, and the daylight had all but disappeared.

From outside their window they heard a low mewl. Soft at first, then louder. Nearly reaching an insistent wail.

Joe climbed down from the bed, opening the window to the cool night air, and also to the yellow cat, who moved inside easily, winningly. Like a marathon runner taking his last step across the finish line.

Penny arched and hissed. The yellow cat ignored her in his beeline for Camille, and Penny jumped down with an indignant thud: horrified, outraged.

Joe pulled himself up, next to Camille. The yellow cat coiled into her neck, the same loud and thankful purr.

"What about Penny?" Camille asked Joe.

"She'll get used to him," he said. "She'll be okay."

Camille cradled the new cat's thin, angled face and kissed him just above his nose. He returned the favor by taking the flesh of her cheek ever so gently between his teeth: pressing down with a heartbreaking consciousness, just so slightly.

Camille swelled with inexplicable happiness, cuddling into the just-tamed creature. And her husband, who drew her in with his familiar, corded arms. Deep inside the blankets, way up top the wedding bed.

"Okay," Camille said. "Everything's okay. Isn't it?"

"Why not?" Joe answered. "I have everything I need here. Don't you?"

She paused a moment—long enough to bristle Joe's contentment. And because Camille loved him too much to be dishonest, she soothed him with this whispered equivocation: "Penny's not here."

"I have everything I need," Joe said again, firmly—as if he hadn't heard her. And his voice sounded so much like a promise, Camille accepted these words as a gift: believing for one minute that she too had nothing to need, other than the momentary calm, the animal company, the connubial darkness.

"I do too," she promised her husband. "I do."

human contact

I've never been the sort of woman who fan-
tasizes about Marlboro Men. I don't have a
weakness for the strong, silent type who
works with his hands and gets more emotional over sunsets and Jim Beam than the
woman in his life. I like civilized people,
who use correct grammar and have at least a
vague understanding of silverware placement. People who understand the imperative of a college education and well-written
thank-you notes.

Needless to say, I fell in love with Charlie
before he became a cattle rancher. We met at
the Colorado university I attended directly
from a private Manhattan high school. Charlie
was a little bit older, and an English major
like me. He came from a terrific family in
Santa Barbara—very wealthy, with lots of
brothers and sisters who all knew how to sail,
golf, and horseback ride. His voice lilted
with a Jimmy Stewart quaver and he had a
beautiful face—classic features made interesting by huge Modigliani eyes. He played

his Martin guitar at the university coffeehouse, singing along with his sweet, trembling tenor.

Charlie taught me to put aside my New York ways and be polite to waitresses. He showed me how to play three chords on the mandolin. Every night he would sit on the edge of my bed and strum his guitar while I nodded off to sleep. He shortened my name from Elisabeth to Beth, and for the first time I didn't mind the way that sounded. Because when Charlie described his feelings for me (so boundless and unprecedented) I remember thinking, Yes. This is it. Now my life begins.

Toward the end of Charlie's senior year, his father bought a cattle ranch in Northwestern Wyoming. The deal had something to do with the Nature Conservancy—a confusing blend of donation and acquisition. Still a junior, I was positively dismayed when Charlie accepted his father's offer to live in the main house and oversee operations. The ranch was in a town called Lizard Creek. Until then, my idea of provincial had been our college town in Colorado or my parents' summer house on Cape Cod.

Charlie's nebulous liberal arts training and stubborn nature made it hard to talk him out of the ranch. "It's a job offer," he said firmly, when I asked him to stay in Colorado, "something I'm not in a position to turn down."

I didn't remind him that he didn't really need a job, thanks to a generous trust fund set up by his grandfather. We had always talked about moving to New York together after I graduated, and getting jobs in publishing. When I mentioned this, he replied with a noncommittal shrug.

"In the meantime," I suggested, graciously ignoring his sudden turnabout, "you could stay here and teach music. You could get a job in Denver, with a software company. Or you could just hang out and ski."

My brainstorms did nothing to keep him in Colorado, so

I reluctantly agreed to pack my summer clothes and go to Wyoming until September. When we arrived at Charlie's ranch, I looked out across the miles of gray rocks and green hills, the famously big sky. I absorbed the breadth of beyond-bucolic expanse and smiled, filled with relief. It was beautiful, sure. But we were the only people, alone in the middle of thirty thousand acres. There was exactly one store, a gas station forty miles down the road that sold cigarettes, tampons, and potato chips. No sane person could stay in Lizard Creek more than a few weeks.

I immediately hated how animals were treated at Charlie's ranch: like nonsentient chattel, existing only to serve the purpose they'd been assigned. Even the dogs slept outside, crawling under the house for protection whenever the temperature rose or fell. The cats all lived in the barn, and their personalities varied without rhyme or reason. Some may as well have been raccoons, totally wild and uninterested in people, whereas others from the very same litter would run to greet you, mewing for attention.

One cat's primary goal in life was to make it into the main house. Instead of stalking mice, she would stalk Charlie's comings and goings—hoping for a clean break inside. On a rainy morning I opened the front door to find her hanging—spread-eagle—on the screen. She was a funny-looking cat, vaguely cross-eyed with long, matted tortoiseshell fur. I had never seen anything so pathetic, and I couldn't understand why Charlie didn't let her inside. Prior to his incarnation as rancher, Charlie had had a soft spot toward animals—he always stopped to pet dogs, and he would get tears in his eyes when describing Victor, his childhood cat who'd died of hepatitis at nineteen.

"Cats live in the barn," Charlie said now, as if he'd always held this belief. "That's the way it's done out here."

Charlie loved everything about the ranch. He loved getting up at four in the morning to feed cows. "They're your cows," I told him. "Can't you train them to eat at a decent hour?" He loved riding horses all day, accompanied by the mottled little outdoor dogs who barked at the cows' heels and ran in hysterical circles. He loved checking which fences needed to be mended and which calves needed to be moved. He stopped reading, he stopped playing his guitar. I was mystified.

"Don't you feel isolated?" I asked him. "Don't you get bored?"

"Bored?" he said. "Are you kidding? There's so much to do."

I studied his face carefully to see if he was joking.

"We can always have dinner with Dell and Edith if we get lonely," Charlie said. Dell was the foreman of the ranch, Edith his wife. I guessed Dell's age at about ninety-six, Edith's at a hundred and four. They both scared me to death. Edith spent the days in her garden and kitchen, weeding and baking, always with a Virginia Slims dangling from her lips—the result being beautiful tomatoes and flaky pastries that tasted like menthol cigarettes. Dell wore a mechanic's jumpsuit, a cowboy hat, and a permanent scowl. Charlie told me, without a trace of indignation in his voice, that Dell once shot a dog because it couldn't learn to herd properly.

In addition to his work for Charlie, Dell kept some sheep up on top of the first hill. I learned from Charlie that sheep farmers were disdained in Lizard Creek—supposedly because there wasn't a lot of money in it, and it didn't require as much land. I suspected sheep were a tad fluffy for Wyoming: too cute and cuddly to satisfy a real cowboy's proclivities.

•   •   •

I had no idea what to do with myself that summer. To Charlie's clear displeasure, I would sleep until the slothful hour of eight-thirty, when he came in for his midmorning coffee. The first week I tried riding with Charlie and Dell in the afternoon, but this involved specific herding methods that were a world away from my experience with posting and indoor dressage rings. After Dell shouted at me for sending a calf in the wrong direction, I decided to stay behind—rattling around the house, reading cookbooks (the only literature available), and going for aimless walks on Charlie's endless property.

On one of these walks, about three weeks into my stay, I visited Dell's little herd of sheep. As I headed toward their pen I heard a faint but enthusiastic yip of warning. A small, lopsided shed stood to one corner. Sitting next to it, behind the fence, was a fat white puppy.

I couldn't find a gate, nor did I see a way to climb over the fence, the top of which was looped and ringed with barbed wire. So I knelt down and stuck my fingers through the diamond-shaped spaces. The puppy (I guessed her age at about eight weeks) looked at me for a second, a little confused. Then she hurled herself toward my fingers, quaking with joy. She stood up on her hind legs and licked my nose through the fence, wafting puppy breath across my face. She pawed the wire with one-two punches in an effort to get through it and to me. I scratched her belly.

When I stood up and walked away, the puppy ran along her side of the fence, frantic, yipping in a new tone: don't leave me, don't leave me, don't leave me. She worked her plump little body around the obstacle of grazing lambs, stopping short at one of the larger sheep's head. She sat back, foiled and anguished, and let out one desperate plea of a howl.

What else could I do? I turned around and sat myself down in front of the puppy. I worked my hand through the wire and stroked her ears until she fell asleep—her lips curled back in euphoric delight, her sweet breath gathering in my palm.

"You didn't touch it, did you?" Charlie scolded, when I mentioned the puppy. It was noon, and he'd just come inside for lunch. He leaned against the kitchen counter, eating cold Hormel chili from a can and scowling at me. He'd taken to wearing the same kind of jumpsuit as Dell, and looked strangely foreign.

"Of course I touched it," I said. "It's a puppy."

"Oh no, Beth," Charlie said. "Oh shit."

"What's wrong?" I felt a dismal lurch in my stomach. "Does it have some kind of disease?"

"No," he said. "Nothing like that."

Charlie told me the puppy was a Great Pyrenees. Full-grown, it would be as big as a Saint Bernard. The point, Charlie said, was to raise the dog with the lambs and ewes. The puppy was not supposed to have any kind of human contact. The sheep would be its pack. Then, when the dog was full-grown, it would fend off any predators—bobcats, coyotes, cougars—that came to attack the herd. I noticed, with faint disdain, that Charlie now pronounced the word "coyote" in two syllables.

"The dog is supposed to grow up with just the sheep," Charlie explained. "It thinks it's one of them."

"That's the stupidest thing I ever heard," I said. "The dog knows it's a dog. It's never going to think it's a sheep."

"It will," Charlie insisted.

"If the dog thinks it's a sheep," I said, "why would it fight bobcats and coyotes?"

"Instinct," Charlie said. "That dog cost Dell four hundred dollars. Which is a lot of money for him. Now you've probably ruined it."

Charlie shook his head. He sipped his coffee. I saw in his scowl, jumpsuit, and opinions not only shades of the hideous Dell but a distinct reconsideration of his love for me. My throat swelled with panic and anger. Charlie was buried so deeply in his fantasy of himself as cowboy, as rancher. Every time I spoke, the mists lifted and he remembered his true identity: a privately schooled Californian, reared with spaniels and tabby cats who'd all lived indoors—snoozing happily beside the fire and visiting veterinarians yearly.

"I think Dell's wrong," I said to Charlie. "I think it's cruel."

"You don't know what you're talking about," Charlie said. His voice—devoid of emotion aside from cool disapproval—devastated me. "Just don't touch the dog again."

"Charlie," I said. "Don't you love me at all?" Given Charlie's demeanor, the question did not feel like a non sequitur.

"Of course I love you," he snapped, with all the warmth of an irritated schoolmaster. "You're here, aren't you?"

Charlie stormed back outside to perform whatever menial task he had scheduled for the afternoon. The flimsy screen door slammed behind him, leaving me with more to say and nothing to do. I paced the living room, not only angry but bored to stupefaction. My presence on this brutal expanse of land did not constitute, in my mind, a convincing expression of Charlie's love. While I had made an effort at compromise, Charlie had become completely immovable. In the three weeks I'd spent on the ranch, the old Charlie—the one who loved me so dearly and completely, the one who strummed his guitar as I fell asleep—had barely been in evidence. It sometimes seemed like he'd been possessed, changed into another person entirely.

And then I remembered what Charlie had told me about Dell shooting his untrainable herding dog. I wondered, with sharp alarm, if my playing with the fat white puppy would lead to its murder. But when I imagined the barrel of a shotgun pointed at the puppy, the person wielding the weapon was not Dell at all. But Charlie, wearing his horrible new jumpsuit and a determined grimace.

First I packed all my things and loaded them into my car. Then I rooted through Charlie's toolbox and extracted a pair of wire cutters. I walked up the hill, back to Dell's sheep pen, and cut out a square large enough for the puppy but too small for the lambs. I scooped the puppy out of the corral, carried her down the hill, and deposited her in the passenger seat of my car. I returned the wire cutters to their precise original spot, then drove back to Colorado.

The puppy wedged herself between the bucket seats and rested her head on my thigh, staring up at me with adoration. I named her Zoë, wanting to give her not only a name but an umlaut to commemorate her deliverance. I knew that Dell, Edith, and even Charlie would use words like "thief" and "weirdo" when discussing me. But if you asked Zoë, I was nothing short of a hero.

My absconding with Zoë turned out to be a good deal for Dell. He had bought her at a fairly low price because she didn't have papers, and before long it became apparent that she was not really a Great Pyrenees. Full-grown, she stood shorter than a midsize retriever, and a scrawny one at that. A little bit smaller than the average coyote.

But because of me, Charlie wrote Dell a check for four hundred dollars. I did not feel guilty about this. I, after all, was a struggling college student. Charlie had a trust fund gathering dust, his own ranch expense account, and a stack of undeposited paychecks in his wallet—literally thousands of dollars that he hadn't gotten around to cashing, so thick that the billfold wouldn't close.

Back at school, Zoë took Charlie's place as my primary companion. She slept on my bed, not at the foot but curled up beside me with her head on the pillow. She would accompany me to campus, waiting outside patiently while I attended class. I saved her a portion of every meal I ate and bought her the most expensive kind of dog food. Zoë loved to go for runs. She loved to ride in the car. She liked cats. She was brimming forth with goodwill: not a single mean bone in her body. If she barked when a stranger appeared on my doorstep, it was only with the anticipatory delight of a new acquaintance.

Early in the semester, about six weeks after I stole Zoë from Dell, Charlie put aside his outrage and sent me a letter explaining his feelings in mathematical terms. "My love for you equals one hundred times one hundred to the hundredth power," Charlie wrote, "which also equals one hundred with a thousand more zeros. That's a lot. What I mean is, I love you so much you can do anything. And it won't change how I feel about you."

This glimpse of the old Charlie—the sentimental one from California—melted me. I dialed his number at the ranch. The tinny sound of the phone ringing in Lizard Creek made me feel as if I were calling a different decade, a lost way of life from another era. I hung up before anyone answered.

But later, when I woke up at four in the morning and couldn't get back to sleep, I called Charlie. It was his usual rising time, after all. He sounded so genuinely pleased to hear from me, I told him he could call me later that evening. He did, and over the phone strummed one of the songs he used to play for me when we both lived in Colorado.

"I'm not going to apologize for stealing the puppy," I warned him before we hung up. Zoë lay across the couch with her head in my lap, and I stroked her white head. "I really do think I did the right thing."

"Okay," Charlie countered. "But I'm not going to apologize for loving the ranch."

"Fair enough," I promised.

. . .

That Christmas, instead of going home to New York, I stayed in Colorado. Charlie came down to visit. I picked him up at the airport, and when I saw him get off the plane—in jeans and a thick wool sweater, his beautiful face smiling, his battered guitar case dangling from his fingertips—my heart swelled to match the size of his ranch.

Zoë waited for us in my car. When Charlie opened the door, she jumped obediently into the backseat. Charlie tried fruitlessly to brush away the mass of white hair she'd left behind. Zoë leaned forward and licked his cheek.

"Hey," Charlie said. "Do you think she remembers me?"

I didn't tell him this was Zoë's standard reaction to any living human. And I suppressed the suggestion that if Zoë *did* remember him—or the ranch—it probably wouldn't be fondly.

Over the month Charlie stayed with me that winter, I managed to suppress all my snarkier thoughts. And Charlie, I assume, kept his complaints to himself. If this politeness cut into our old intimacy, I can't say that I minded. I just loved being back with Charlie—hearing him sing, listening to him explain how much he loved me. We were both too young, really, to consider the future as a concrete entity: it was easy for me to pretend the ranch did not exist at all.

Winter semester found me walking Zoë and talking on the phone with Charlie. We both tiptoed around my post-graduation plans, which were still conveniently nonexistent as spring break approached. I agreed to spend my ten-day vacation in Lizard Creek, and that's when Zoë was killed by a cougar, the week after a heavy spring snowfall.

Was it my imagination that Zoë recognized the ranch, and

worried that I'd leave her there? When I pulled up in front of Charlie's house and opened the car door, I noticed a distinct hesitation—not her usual happy bounding, but a pause, and a reluctant, stiff-limbed exit.

Charlie tried to make this visit different. He took the week off. The first day, we went for a leisurely horseback ride with Zoë trotting alongside. The second day, we went for a long hike in the Tetons, Zoë running joyous circles around us, Charlie squirting water from his plastic bottle into her wide, doggy mouth.

"Charlie," I admonished. "That's *human* water. Dogs don't need *water*. They're only *animals*. They can dig in the ground or suck bark for water. They can go for miles without . . ."

"Okay," Charlie snapped, unamused. "I get it."

That night, the late-season snow fell. Charlie shook me awake a little after four, whispering some storm-related reason he had to help Dell. "I'll be back late morning," he said, "and we'll spend the day together."

I don't know how long he'd been gone when Zoë started scratching at the door. I tried to ignore her, but her whines and barks were too persistent. I assumed the scraps from last night's dinner weren't sitting well, and I stumbled out of bed to let her outside.

Despite the mountains, Charlie's acres stretched out like Siberia—desolate wind and drifts. Zoë galloped through the snow in the cold and dusky first light. I dozed off on the couch, waiting for her scratch at the door. When I awoke, the sun bore through the windowpane in insistent streaks. I stepped outside and blinked into the glare. If I were to draw a picture of that moment (me in the middle of all that snow-covered expanse and Zoë nowhere to be seen) I would sketch an enormous hand reaching down from the sky. Flattening me into a pancake on Charlie's front stoop.

In my Sorrels, long underwear, and a checkered wool coat of Charlie's that sagged past my knees, I searched definitely for

Zoë and obliquely for Charlie. I didn't want to experience the enormity of this disaster alone. Later that afternoon, when Charlie found her dismembered remains on the first hill—a hundred yards from her original pen—I couldn't understand how I'd missed them.

I can't say for certain what Charlie felt about Zoë— whether he could steel himself to a dog's death, or if his original self fought through and experienced genuine sorrow. But I know that was the moment he began to grieve me. Because as my heart was breaking with bereavement and guilt, I also understood that Zoë was not the only one I'd lost.

We walked in circles that night, Charlie and I. As if the result of our search had been so unsatisfactory, we could not bear to end it. As if by staying outside in the bitterly cold and forbidding night we could revise our awful discovery and somehow Zoë herself would come bounding through the darkness.

Finally Charlie stood behind me and opened his coat, wrapping it around me and buttoning us both inside. His smooth cheek rested against my temple, and I felt so close to him: as if the scent of wood smoke and lanolin had inundated my crib as a baby. The most familiar and companionable sense of calm, even in sorrow.

We stared at the still, frozen shadows surrounding us. The sky was so empty of stars, only two colors existed: white and black. All around us lay the deep and clumsy tracks we had made with our search. "Will we ever feel this way again?" I asked Charlie, my breath hanging visibly in the air. It was so cold, nothing could move—my breath, the trees, nothing. "Will we ever feel this way again, about anybody?"

"No, Beth," Charlie said. His cheek felt strangely warm, and his voice was as steady as I'd ever heard it. "We will never feel this way again."

•   •   •

"This place," I said to Charlie, later, when we came inside. "It's so empty and cruel. I was smart enough to take her away from here, but then I had to bring her back."

"Please," Charlie said. "Don't say anything else." He knew without my telling him that I would leave in the morning.

We made love on the living room rug, without lighting a fire or collecting blankets—as if neither of us deserved the warmth.

In the late-night morning, Charlie woke to feed his cows. "I don't want to watch you drive away," he said, kissing my forehead. I pretended to be able to go back to sleep. I closed my eyes for a good five minutes after the screen door slammed, then got up and started packing.

When I opened the storm door, the tortoiseshell cat was splayed out, clinging to the outside of the screen. Frost sealed the ends of her wild, matted fur into points. When I swung the screen door open, she didn't budge, but let out a low, mournful mewl. I opened my hatchback and threw in my suitcase. Then I peeled the cat off the screen door—her detaching claws crackling like Velcro—and dropped her into the passenger seat.

I did not drive back to Colorado, to college. There, the temptation to reunite with Charlie would be too great. Instead I drove east, at first with no particular destination in mind. As we crossed into Iowa, I named the cat Monique.

Monique was a poor substitute for Zoë, as traveling companions go. Zoë used to sit beside me, watching the scenery, or else settling down to rest with her head in my lap. Monique spent the entire ride underneath the driver's seat, yowling at sixty-second intervals and occasionally climbing onto my feet, inducing terror by interfering with the brake and gas pedal. By the time I decided—somewhere in the Great Lakes region—to head for my parents' summer house on Cape Cod, Monique's shrill, incessant complaints had frayed my nerves so much, I was tempted to let her escape at a rest area.

The cat's tune changed when we got to the Cape. I dragged her into the house, to the detriment of my bare forearms. She alighted on the hardwood floor and looked around with wonder. She raised her eyes to the powder-post-beetle-filled beams, lowered her nose to the musty oriental rug, raised her eyes again, and inspected the dining room table and chairs. She looked back at me and drew in her breath. Indoors. She was indoors. She walked over to me and rubbed against my legs with ecstatic fervor. Her mats of fur felt like tightly coiled cocoons vibrating against my skin. She made a delirious burbling noise I'd never heard before. No tycoon depositing his first million, no starlet receiving her Academy Award, no chemist winning the Nobel Prize, ever felt more blissful, more accomplished. More absolutely and completely *arrived*.

Monique was the only one I knew who felt pleased about my move to Cape Cod. Charlie did not agree with my leaving; and my taking a mangy, half-wild animal on a cross-country road trip compounded his assessment of my mental health. My parents, of course, were appalled that I'd left college halfway through my last semester. They couldn't understand why I wanted to hole up in an empty house at the edge of the world, on a peninsula that would be deserted until the Fourth of July—which was four months away. My father was so furious about the lost tuition money, he wouldn't speak to me, but only relayed messages through my worried mother.

I ignored everyone's anger and complaints. I made a little money pouring coffee at the restaurant up the street (the only one open) for the few ancient locals who lived on the Cape year-round. I brought Monique to a groomer and had her crazy fur shaved down almost to the skin—the only way to get rid of all her mats. Monique didn't seem to mind, at least not as soon as she found herself back at the house, with access to plush chairs, beds, and carpets. Without her fur, she was even more ridiculous—cross-eyed and scrawny, with none of the sleek grace normally possessed by cats. Monique was a klutz. Jumping down from surfaces, she often missed her mark and teetered sideways, as if intoxicated. Instead of leaping onto my bed, she would insert her front claws into the covers and drag herself up—an effort that involved useless kicking of her hind legs. Once up, she was pleasant and affectionate company—still ecstatic over making it indoors, let alone up on a bed. I felt grateful for her gratitude, her funny and slightly bizarre company.

During the day I took long walks on the beach, which I had all to myself. Often I had to fight back rising sobs, thinking how Zoë would have loved chasing the waves. Then I'd climb out onto the rocks (freezing waves soaking my sneakers) and stare out at the hook of Provincetown.

I ate dinner over the sink, or in front of the television. I hung out with my clumsy, bald barn cat. I could read the tide through the cheerful panes of our picture window overlooking the harbor, and not only breathe the misty, salted air, but taste and swallow it. The huge, old-fashioned brick fireplace in the living room and the ragged rabbits darting across the lawn comforted me. I didn't care that the house wasn't winterized, that it lacked insulation, its two-hundred-year-old floorboards rattling like restless spirits with every nor'easter. Some days I never got out of my pajamas.

Charlie called at least once a week. At first we avoided the obvious conversations—Zoë, and the ranch, and my leaving. Then one afternoon Charlie told me he was sorry.

"What are you sorry for?" I asked him.

"I'm sorry about your dog," he said. "I know how much you loved her."

"You don't have to apologize," I told him. "You don't even have to sympathize. It was my fault."

"No, Beth," Charlie said. "It wasn't."

"Thanks," I said, but I knew better. I'd known from the first, the ranch spelled death for Zoë, and still I'd brought her back. "Thanks for thinking that," I said anyway, to Charlie.

After that, he called me nightly. Sometimes we would eat dinner together, over the phone. Sometimes we would drink, me sipping wine and him sipping beer. "Tell me what's different about this," Charlie would say. "Why is it better for you to be isolated on Cape Cod and me to be isolated in Wyoming when we could be isolated together?"

If Charlie had appeared on my doorstep, wearing Docksiders and Nantucket Reds. If he'd agreed to spend a year skiing, or to move to Manhattan, I might have let him woo me back. But Charlie's quavery voice made its way through tinny wires from the land where cougars, coyotes, and ranch hands stalked good-hearted dogs.

I just needed a break from living in the world. I needed some time with myself. I needed to mourn Zoë without anyone reminding me she was only an animal. I needed to escape from everything, especially the idea that Charlie and I might truly be over.

"Then why do you talk to me all the time?" Charlie asked.

"Because you keep calling," I said.

"Why not tell me to stop?"

Because I love you, I thought. Because you're my best friend. Because nobody knows me better.

"I don't know," I told him.

The next morning I woke up startled at not finding Charlie next to me. Startled at finding purring Monique instead of snoring Zoë. So I jumped out of bed and went for a six-mile run, my legs feeling strong and powerful, my body capable and healthy.

I arrived home to find Monique pawing at a baby rabbit, which she had dragged just beyond the poison ivy patch behind the house. The rabbit lay sideways on a stretch of mown grass, and I struggled against the image of Zoë, captured by a feline predator three times her size. I leaned over to see if the rabbit still breathed, while Monique stared up at me with fond pride.

The rabbit, about the size of the cat's head and covered with downy fur, blinked vacantly.

"You shithead," I said to Monique. I grabbed her by the scruff of the neck and, against her loud, astonished protestations, threw her into the house. Then I came back to inspect the rabbit, who did not—as I had hoped—hop away upon the removal of his attacker.

The cat yowled from inside, infuriated. I squatted and ran my finger along the rabbit's narrow spine. His fur felt hopelessly, painfully soft.

Once, when Charlie and I were driving somewhere in Wyoming, we hit a duck. There had been several of them in the road, and Charlie hadn't slowed down—expecting, understandably, that the birds would scatter in time. And most of them had. But this one, a slow-witted duck, I guess, got hit straight on. Charlie screeched to a halt. Behind us we could see the duck, a dull-brown female, slapping its wings against the asphalt—its head craning above a flurry of pinfeathers. Charlie did not waste a second. He got out of the car, leaving the engine idling, and walked back to the duck. He picked it up by its head and swung its body like a lasso: whoosh, whoosh, whoosh, more feathers flying along with a muffled, dying quack. When the bird hung limp, its neck successfully wrung, Charlie tossed it to the side of the road and without dusting off his hands returned to the driver's seat.

This rabbit was much calmer. He didn't even seem upset. With the cat gone, he righted himself from his side and lifted his ears. He quivered his nose the way rabbits do, and stared ahead with an expression that—to me—looked entirely untroubled, undisturbed.

But still he did not hop away. Probably, I thought, he was already dying. The humane thing to do, the brave thing, would be to find a shovel and quickly finish the job. Even as this thought formed, I realized there was no way on earth I could possibly do it. If I had been alone that day, back in Wyoming, I would not have been able to wring the duck's neck. I simply did not have the ability, not anywhere inside of me, to take a shovel and brain this tiny rabbit.

I pulled the sleeves of my sweatshirt over my hands and picked him up. To my inexpert eyes the rabbit did not look seriously injured. A scrape by the side of one ear, a larger scrape—the fur chafed off—near one haunch. In my cupped palms, he seemed as calm and gentle as something you'd find in an Easter basket. I had a fleeting fantasy about taking him inside and nursing him back to health. But the cat lived inside. I didn't see how the rabbit would ever recover from shock, with the sound of that predator so close and persistent.

So I carried him up the road a few hundred yards—far enough away so Monique wouldn't find him, but close enough so that his mother might. I spoke in a soft, soothing voice, stroking his fur—deluding myself that I was any less terrifying to the poor thing than Monique. I walked into a landscaped grove in the yard of a summer house and deposited the baby rabbit on a patch of grass between two trees. Then I went home.

Monique was beside herself, consumed with the epiphany that I was not, after all, entirely benign. If we had been two people, the sounds we made would have amounted to a screaming match: me with harsh words for her sadistic capture of a harmless and adorable creature, her with enraged caterwauls regarding my outright theft. I let her outside and watched as she furiously marched around the yard, searching in vain for her purloined quarry.

"You should have taken the shovel and killed it," Charlie told me that evening.

"What a surprise that is," I said. "Coming from you."

"You're a good person," Charlie said. "But you know what they say about the road to hell."

"I certainly do," I said, looking at Monique—who, having apparently forgiven me, was sprawled luxuriously on the rug in front of the fire.

I can't say I knew absolutely that Charlie and I weren't right for each other. Does anyone ever know such a thing absolutely? After all, I loved Charlie. But I felt with sudden certainty that these phone conversations were a bad idea, a misleading source of comfort.

"Charlie," I said. "Maybe we shouldn't talk for a while."

There was a pause on the other end, filled with static from Lizard Creek's primitive phone lines. When Charlie finally spoke, his voice sounded cold and angry. "Maybe you should make up your mind," he said.

"Maybe I have," I whispered. And Charlie hung up.

I wanted to call him back. Or else I wanted him to call me back: I wanted to hear his voice as much as I wanted to hear Zoë, scratching at the door. But I pulled the phone plug out of the answering machine, and willed myself against dialing.

The next morning my first thought was not about Charlie or Zoë but the rabbit. I pulled on my robe and walked up to the glen feeling sad and guilt-ridden. My spirits lifted a bit when I saw an adult rabbit, peering out from bushes near where I'd left the baby. But as it hopped away I reminded myself: here, the rabbits were everywhere. I tried to remember what kind of animal rejected young that had been touched by human hands.

Sure enough, the spot between the two trees was empty.

Once, another time driving with Charlie, we'd stopped to eat at a little diner in Nebraska—one of those nowhere towns, the kind where you can't imagine people really living. I left my wallet, with three hundred dollars in cash, on the back of the toilet seat in the rest room. I didn't realize what I'd done until the end of the meal. We went to the front counter and asked the cashier if anybody had turned in a wallet, and he handed mine over—credit card and driver's license intact, but all the cash gone.

Charlie paid for lunch, and as we drove out of Nebraska we invented a profile of the person who had found my wallet. We named her Jeanette. We decided she'd been saving for years, working at some low-level job (waitressing, clerking at the five-and-dime), dreaming about getting out of Nowheresville, Nebraska. Her boyfriend was cruel to her. Jeanette would come close to accumulating the amount she needed (we decided a thousand dollars was her goal) but she always wound up just a little bit short. She couldn't get a break. Until today, when she walked into the bathroom and saw my wallet, perched there on the back of the toilet.

She could have taken my credit card, but Jeanette was essentially an honest person. She figured anyone who'd forget that kind of cash probably didn't need it too badly. So she pocketed the three hundred dollars, turned in my wallet to the cashier, and within the hour had packed up her meager belongings and was blasting off to Hollywood, New York, Las Vegas.

"It feels better," Charlie said, "if you imagine the person who robbed you needs the money more."

"You feel less violated," I added, "if the reason you were robbed in the first place was a little bit your own fault."

Any number of fates could have befallen that rabbit. Another cat. A coyote. A fox. It could have died a slow, painful, and frightened death—languishing there in the grove—before being carried off by some lucky scavenger.

But then again. After I walked away, maybe he shook his head and realized (miracle!) that he'd escaped unharmed. And maybe the adult rabbit I'd seen *was* his mother—she'd found him, and rescued him. Commenced taking care of him (doing whatever mother rabbits do) in that hidden patch of brush.

I stared at the empty spot between the two trees. I should have kept it, I thought. Or I should have killed it. I should have done anything besides create this miserable uncertainty.

A heavy wind billowed up from the shore, showering me with a light sea mist. Balanced on my heels, I shifted uncomfortably.

Here I was, after all. Forgiving the cat, who really (in the realm of felines) had done nothing wrong. Enduring the loss of Zoë. Living, once and for all, without Charlie.

I told myself the future was full of hope and promise. I told myself I had done the right thing. "Everything will be all right," I said out loud, as I rose to my feet and headed back to the house—where I would do my best to stay, pretending that strength of resolve amounted to certainty.

"I did the right thing," I said. My footsteps tapped out a tentative rhythm, trying to assuage my remorse. Trying to convince me: I had done the right thing. The right thing. The right thing.

in his shoes

Shy people hate everyone, and Lucy is no exception. Getting dressed for her husband's funeral, she runs a mental inventory of the barely known relatives and friends who will feel compelled to make her the center of attention. The quasi-familiar lips that will blunder their way to her cheek, which she won't know how to offer—forced into an awkward waltz while everyone stares. Two years before, Lucy convinced Paul to elope so she could avoid this very manner of spotlight. Now here she stands: trying to figure out what to wear, trying to wrangle her unruly hair into some semblance of respectability, dreading every eye soon to be upon her. So unlike Paul, who once gleefully paraphrased a description of Teddy Roosevelt in reference to himself: "I want to be the bride at every wedding and the corpse at every funeral."

Sometimes, when Lucy found herself closed-lipped at a party, Paul would take time out from entertaining the crowd to whisper, "Be nice."

"I am nice," Lucy often said later in the taxi going home. "I'm very nice. I'm just not all that friendly."

Paul loved Lucy but disliked her silence. He wanted to show off her wit and intellect the way he showed off his own. "You're so smart," he would say. "You're so funny. But nobody knows it except me."

The sound of Paul's voice is as fresh in Lucy's mind as the scent of his clothes, some of them worn recently. She inhales, as if from this distance—within the narrow threshold of their shared closet—she can re-create his corporeal presence by breathing in its fragrance. Paul would be standing next to her. "Wear this," he would say, pulling out a dress Lucy had forgotten. Or else he would say, "Don't worry. You'll look fine in anything." He might very well chastise her: reminding Lucy she was going to a funeral. That it didn't matter what she wore.

Better yet: Paul would be standing here alone, dressing for *her* funeral. Lucy having died instead, as she very well might have. Paul possessing by far the better instinct, the stronger ability to function in any gathering regardless of how emotional, how awkward, how terrible. Paul being—she had always felt—better suited to inhabit the world in general.

Does anyone wear black to funerals anymore? With a great thrust of her upper body, both arms locked at the elbows, Lucy pushes through the heavy curtain of clothes. Black for funerals is passé. Too blatantly mournful. The last funeral Lucy and Paul attended, the family wore white: a broad and optimistic statement that would be inappropriate in Lucy's situation, given the closed-casket nature of Paul's service. Anyway. Every dress Lucy owns in black or white seems on the short and clingy side. Also inappropriate.

Lucy's mother, now in the kitchen probably wringing her hands, brought her navy suit for Lucy to wear. But it bunches at the waist, and Lucy's only navy shoes are a pair of scuffed clogs that everyone will take for black. "Just wear brown shoes," her mother said earlier. "Nobody will care."

Paul and Lucy live in a midtown apartment that belonged to Lucy's uncle, her mother's brother, who died just before they got married. The past few days, Lucy has watched her mother roam the place tentatively—aware, Lucy thinks, of a preponderance of possible ghosts. Her mother stares at Lucy in a way that seems both frantic and penetrating: as if, not showing expected signs of grief, Lucy might implode at any moment. She supposes her mother would like to place her under an X-ray machine, with the depth and scope of her sorrow mapped out, exposed, and enumerated.

Lucy kneels to dig through the tumble of mismatched footwear. Paul's size twelve sneakers and one pair of good brown cordovans. Lucy's six-and-a-half narrows, which run to sandals, loafers, and boots. Nothing matches her mother's suit. She sinks down and leans against the doorjamb, letting out a deep, air-filled sigh that always annoyed Paul. In swift deference to his feelings, his preferences, she sits and pulls her legs into the lotus position—which Paul, who couldn't even touch his toes, admired. "You're so limber," he would say, gently pulling Lucy's leg back so that her foot balanced easily on her shoulder, behind her head.

But now the simple effort of the lotus exhausts Lucy. Halfway through a deep and irrepressible yawn, she again imagines herself gone and Paul in her place. Dressing for Lucy's funeral, Paul would simply pull one of his two suits from the closet. A white shirt, or maybe light blue. His good brown shoes. It would be his mother in the apartment instead of Lucy's, and she might choose a tie for him. Lucy pictures his long fingers, easily looping and knotting silk. She tries to imagine his expression, tries to arrange it in her mind to appropriate grief.

Would he be crying? In five years, as long as she's known Paul, she's only seen him cry once, when his father died. He wept copiously then, his shoulders heaving. So yes, Lucy thinks. If she were killed, Paul would of course be crying. It would be a relief to the people around him: a signal for them to comfort and touch.

Lucy has never been a weeper. Paul has sometimes remarked that she cries less than any woman he knows. When she does cry, it tends to erupt from frustration rather than sorrow. She is more likely to shed tears over a jammed stapler, or a sealed roll of Saran Wrap, than any particular grief. If she were to cry right now, it would not be over the loss of Paul: but the jumble of fabrics, crammed into the closet like disassembled puzzle pieces. Refusing to offer a solution.

The clothes rest densely on their hangers, not arranged in order of ownership but everything mixed together. Lucy's sleeveless dresses and short, filmy skirts. Paul's chamois and flannel, his corduroys and jeans. Everything of Paul's so much longer, broader, bigger than Lucy's. Still sitting amidst the jumble of clothes, she reaches up and fingers the ragged edges of what Paul calls his party shirt: Hawaiian, rayon, so busy and colorful that nobody notices the sprinkling of mildew alongside the buttons, from the time Paul threw it damp into his laundry pile and forgot it for weeks. In fact, the last time Lucy saw this shirt it was somewhere in the middle of that pile, where Paul—not having learned his lesson—tossed and abandoned it yet again.

Who washed this? Lucy wonders. Her left thigh throbs vaguely under the weight of her right foot. Paul's shirt is its own carnival. Every panel has a different design: tropical trees printed one way, then another. All manner of floral, all manner of varying hues. Lilac, periwinkle, peach, teal, magenta. Squiggles. Slashes. Polka dots.

Lucy narrows her eyes severely, painfully. So that the patterns perform for her—run together in blending, moving for-mations. She pulls Paul's dress shoes toward her and slips her hands inside them. The leather is cool through the felt lining. It feels moist against her palms, hinting at the memory of Paul's warm feet, and Lucy presses into what might be the residue of Paul's perspiration. She would never have done this a week ago, placed her hands where sweaty feet had been. But now she has to resist the urge to lift one shoe and cover her nose and mouth: breathing it in, like an oxygen mask.

Lucy shuffles across the spare hall from their bedroom to the kitchen. Her mother, nervously drumming fingernails against the side of a coffee cup, raises worried eyes. Lucy waits for the reflexive scan, the maternal inventory, and her mother pauses— fingers frozen in mid-drum limbo. She opens her mouth to speak, but Lucy doesn't listen. Instead she imagines Paul, in the kitchen with his mother, on their way to Lucy's funeral. Paul's mother would be crying, probably, as Lucy's mother has been, her eyes these past few days continually bloodshot and red-rimmed.

She thinks her mother has just said something about the shoes. But Lucy—daydreaming—doesn't hear her precise words. Faced without a verbal response, her mother smiles. The same gentle, be-brave smile that lately dominates every-one's countenance.

"Darling," Lucy's mother says. She stands and walks over to Lucy. She places her hands—soft and refreshingly cold—on either side of Lucy's face.

"Are you ready?" she asks. The question has a stretched and wary tone. As if she really means, are you sure?

Lucy runs flat palms against the skirt of her brown dress (a good fall color) and returns an obedient I-am-brave smile.

"Yes," she says. "I'm ready."

Her mother frowns again toward Lucy's feet, an expression that battles further tears. But she doesn't say another word, only slips her arm through Lucy's. They head out the door. Riding down in the elevator, Lucy breathes in rhythmic gulps and counts floors with the light.

She can do anything, and no one will dare caution or comment. Her new, foreign status as widow—the day's star mourner—sets her aside, apart, and above. The realization is so heady and overwhelming, Lucy finds herself leaning into her mother, smoothing her cheek against a silky shoulder. While they stand on the curb, waiting for the hired car to pull up and collect them, Lucy reaches out to grasp a fold of her mother's sleeve. She bunches it into her fist, hanging on, in a way she has not done since she was a very small child.

When she and her mother step out of the taxi in front of Saint Hilda's, they are instantly flanked by mourners, all the people who have gathered at the bottom of the stone church steps, lingering before filing up and going inside.

If Paul were here, he would register emotion for her. He would express—either verbally or with tears—his own sorrow, and compassion for his fellow mourners. Lucy would nod in agreement, allying herself with the correct and expected responses.

Without Paul, she moves obliquely, placing herself behind her mother, wishing she had a larger body to use as her shield. But concentrating on forward movement in the cumbersome shoes is distracting, and blocks out the hands which—Lucy imagines—all reach out in an attempt to touch her.

When Lucy first walked through their apartment to the kitchen, and then from the elevator to the car, she had some difficulty keeping the shoes on her feet. At first she pointed her toes up dramatically so that they slid back toward her ankle.

But she soon discovered that the opposite approach—weighing down heavily with each step and clenching her toes the way she would with flip-flops or Dr. Scholl's—was easier.

The stairs to the church present the greatest challenge yet. Lucy wonders how Paul ever managed walking up and down any staircase with such enormous feet. She finds she has to position her feet at an angle, like a duck, all the while keeping a very close watch to guard against false placement. The climb involves so much focus, Lucy does not notice Paul's family waiting on the landing until she has finally ascended. His mother—who heretofore has kept the most stoic bearing in Lucy's presence—takes quick inventory of Lucy and bursts into tears. Lucy obligingly folds herself into her mother-in-law's arms, patting her back with a there, there cadence.

As she walks down the aisle with her own mother's hand at the small of her back, the cavernous shoes render Lucy's progression a hesitation step. She senses a hush overtake each row as she passes. Lucy reaches the front pew and sinks down beside Paul's sister. With the soles anchored solidly on the church floor, Lucy moves her feet quietly in the shoes, back and forth. Her nylons rustle within the good, good shoes—so much finer than any pair of Lucy's. The deep umber of her tea-length skirt matches exactly. Perfectly.

All evidence to the contrary, she could not possibly be sitting here, at Paul's funeral. It isn't that Lucy is unaware of her grief: its hollow expanse, its tumble of rage, helplessness, confusion, and despair. It's only that she has been denied direct access. In a way, Lucy admires this protective device, which her body performs so naturally, like blinking against strong sunlight. At the same time she hates her reflexive instinct for survival—this insistence on her own well-being—that in its way is responsible for their entire catastrophe.

Lucy folds her hands in her lap. She crosses her ankles and presses her knees together, the way she was taught years ago at the Barclay dancing classes. She musters a faint, beatific smile and sadly furrowed brow—to comfort and deflect the seemingly hundreds of glances flickering toward her—while church music breathes across the altar, and people filter quietly to their seats.

The reception on Riverside Drive, hosted at an aunt's rambling apartment, is packed. When Lucy and her mother arrive, the thick crowd parts to let them through. Lucy, now moving expertly, carries herself through the separating guests as if a red carpet has been rolled. A sofa instantly clears and Lucy is helped onto it, hands out of nowhere commandeering an elbow, a wrist.

"I'm fine," Lucy wants to tell them. But aware that this is the wrong sentence—that she should not, after all, be fine—she keeps quiet and allows herself to be touched. If it were Paul, he would go further than this: folding friends into return embraces.

Three or four guests rush to get her food—as if she were Scarlett O'Hara at the Wilkeses' picnic—and Lucy leans back against the cushions and scans the room. A fantastic crowd, she observes with unexpected bitterness. Paul's death, she thinks, was exciting, igniting prurient interest: and so his funeral amounts to a sort of happening. If he had died from cancer or pneumonia, even in a car accident, the volume of mourners would not be so impressive.

In Lucy's place, Paul would not entertain cynical thoughts. All these same people would be present, for the same dubious reasons. But Paul would only accept whatever comfort they offered. He would never question motives.

Lucy, of course, knows nearly everyone. Over by the potted ferns stands Martha, Paul's most obnoxious cousin. Martha has bony elbows, and one of those voices that carries: Lucy can hear her from across the room, despite all the other conversations. Before they decided to elope, Lucy and Paul argued over including Martha on a small ceremony's guest list.

At the buffet line, Paul's sister is consoled by Brad, Paul's college roommate. Lucy's mother, now standing a good yard away but keeping such an eye on Lucy there might be a thread connecting them, nods at something Paul and Lucy's night doorman says. All of Lucy's coworkers are there, flitting troubled eyes toward her feet. And every last one—all the people who were at the party they attended on that night last week, the night Paul died—stand somewhere in the room, oddly, socializing. John, Kevin, Claudia, Emily—Lucy absorbs their presence at a glance. She feels as if she's biding her time, waiting illogically for Paul's arrival. Lucy has always been shy. But now she thinks it's become worse since she's lived with Paul. By allowing him to function for her socially, she has lost what few skills she ever possessed.

Paul's friend Rick carries a plate heavy with ratatouille and kneels in front of Lucy. He perches the food on her knee so reverently, she almost expects him to bow. Lucy likes Rick. Last year, in a Christmas letter, he complimented Paul on his extravagant performance at a holiday party. "I hope you *never, ever* restrain yourself when the life-of-the-party muse lands on your shoulder," the letter read. Toward the end, Rick added: "Lucy, I admire the way you let Paul be Paul while simultaneously commanding so much presence, and conveying an omniscient wisdom with your silence."

"Thank you," Lucy says, feeling panic and excitement: at the thought of her own presence, without Paul, fading and dying.

She takes the plate from Rick and smiles apologetically at the two or three others arriving behind him, also bearing food. The offerings crowd the coffee table in front of her—spaetzle, roast beef, chicken tetrazzini. Rick hands Lucy a glass of wine, crudely filled to the rim. She accepts it with both hands, immediately sipping away the top layer to defray spill. Spiraling across her tongue and down her throat, the wine tastes clean and buttery, so much so that Lucy finds herself not sipping at all—but drinking long and deep, like water after a long run. Her toes, deliciously encased, tingle.

When the glass is drained Lucy looks up, faintly embarrassed. But the eyes watching her (which, directly or indirectly, amount to every eye in the room) only look solemn and concerned. Not judgmental. Lucy thinks with odd pleasure that she could rip off her clothes, smash good china to bits, swing from the chandelier: and not one expression would waver from its carefully frozen solemnity. Lucy hands her wineglass to Rick, who rises to refill it.

Her mother sits down, carefully guarding a plate she has prepared with Lucy's favorite foods: teriyaki chicken, bow tie pasta, *pad thai*. Lucy senses a pause in the people surrounding her. Nobody wants to leave her sitting alone. But nobody knows what to say. They look at her feet, then look away: as if the combination of Paul's shoes and Lucy's apparent calm represents an impending hysteria that will surpass anything they have prepared for, any usual widow's grief.

"What happened?"

Lucy hears someone's breathless, unfamiliar voice.

"What happened?"

Is it Lucy's imagination that the entire room has fallen silent? All these people waiting for an answer, though they know perfectly well—every one of them—exactly what transpired.

"What happened?" Lucy hears again. Ridiculous. Of the expectant faces now zeroing in on Lucy (thankfully accepting more wine from Rick), a fair percentage were actually there.

It occurs to Lucy that she herself has manufactured this question: pieced it together from the prevailing awkwardness. Maybe someone simply said, how are you. Or hello.

Still: all these people. So watchful and curious. So visibly wanting to hear everything from Lucy's own lips. Lucy presses down on her heels, sliding them backward. She pushes her ratatouille onto the coffee table. She takes another draught of wine.

"What did you say?" says Paul's cousin Martha. "Louder, Lucy. Nobody can hear you."

Lucy levels a deadly disapproving look at Martha, then focuses on her mother. And Paul, Lucy reminds herself. Paul loves me. I can do this. I can speak to this crowd.

Project, Lucy's sixth grade drama teacher used to urge. Speak up, dear, we can't hear you, Lucy has heard a thousand times. Sometimes she thinks her own hearing must be more fine-tuned than most.

But now, in consideration to the watchful silence, Lucy gathers her voice from deep within her diaphragm—suddenly speaking in a voice that could fill Saint Patrick's.

"The dress wasn't really new," Lucy tells them. "I'd had it for a while. A black dress, kind of clingy. I'd never worn it, because I felt too self-conscious. But Paul really wanted me to wear it. And when I put it on, he just . . . he complimented me so much. So I wore it."

"You looked great," Rick says. And then reddens, realizing his words might sound accusatory. But Lucy only nods. A comforting gesture, she hopes, much like the one Paul might grant.

The party was at a brownstone on lower Fifth Avenue, bought by someone's parents for a song—a hundred years ago, Lucy supposes. What must it be worth now? A house like that in New York City?

The guests all nod, relieved by the sound of this familiar litany.

"It was such a civilized party," Lucy says. They had been to so many *un*civilized parties—at railroad flats in Alphabet City, those horrible bathtubs in the kitchen and the scent of urine and cigarettes in the crooked stairwells. At those parties, Lucy worried about getting a cab—the dark interval on the street would feel dangerous, precarious.

"But this was such a good neighborhood," Lucy says, and again her audience seems to agree.

"Well," Lucy says. "There was this man. A slightly older man. He claimed to be somebody's uncle."

"Martin's uncle," Claudia says. "I think he really is Martin's uncle."

"Sure," Lucy says. "That's why it was so easy, afterward, for the police to pick him up."

"So they did pick him up," somebody says. "Thank God."

"Yes," Lucy agrees, politely. "Thank God. Anyway. Martin's uncle, his name was Bill. And he seemed to take a sort of liking to me."

At this, the listeners grow silent—vaguely uncomfortable. Lucy remembers her own discomfort that evening. Bill had been so insistent upon drawing her out, trying to engage her. He was a tall, slender man, with sparse gray hair and an anxious blur to his watery blue eyes. With a loud, jarring voice. Why not be frank? Lucy hated him. But no more so than she would hate anybody—intruding upon her diffidence, interfering with her quiet stance. Lucy tried all possible ways to avoid him: escaping to the bathroom, the buffet, Paul's side. But no matter where she went, Bill shadowed her. And though he struck Lucy as rather too intense, and decidedly odd, she couldn't just tell him to leave her alone. He was fifteen years older, and somebody's uncle. She didn't dare be rude.

"It's amazing," she says, "how politeness can override your own sense of comfort, or even safety."

"You should always trust your instincts," says Martha. "Trust your instincts, and don't worry about being rude."

Of course *she* doesn't worry about being rude, Lucy thinks.

But Lucy, that night, did worry: despite the inordinate attention this man—Bill—paid her. Despite his seeming peculiar,
and what was in fact his own stubborn rudeness: monopoliz-
ing Lucy, who so clearly preferred being left alone. Lucy remembers how Bill's hand fluttered strangely close to her neck as he
spoke—about art, about New York: normal, inane party topics.
Bill made outrageous claims. He had, he told Lucy, a painting at
the MOMA. He'd played first violin with the Philharmonic.
He'd edited *Portnoy's Complaint*.

Paul (never one to be jealous or suspicious) was mostly
on another side of the room, a glass of merlot in his left hand,
his right hand gesturing cheerfully. Lucy heard great bursts of
laughter from his clustered audience. If it had been reversed,
Lucy thinks now: if he had been the one monopolized by a
strange woman. Lucy would have been upset. She would have
intervened.

Then again: maybe not, if the woman had been older, and
odd. Clearly not a threat. Still, she would likely not have been
far from Paul—if only to avoid conversation herself.

"Not that I blame him at all," Lucy assures the crowd.
"Paul was just being Paul. And it was impossible to tell . . .
you know. I mean it was weird, and a little embarrassing. But
who would think we'd be in any kind of danger?"

While she talked to Bill, Lucy peppered her conversation
liberally with the phrase "My husband." She kept her answers
brief and her expression vague, flitting her gaze around the
room, making little eye contact—this the only discourtesy she
allowed herself. Every time she said the words "my husband,"
she would gesture toward Paul: who was broader than Bill,
younger and better muscled. So well surrounded by people. Lucy
felt that attaching herself to Paul afforded her the protection of
everyone in the room.

When Lucy finally placed herself at Paul's elbow (clinging

in a way that was bound to annoy him) Bill would not be discouraged, but positioned himself doggedly beside her, just close enough that she could not tell Paul about his disturbing pursuit.

Paul had been generous to him, to Bill, including him in his gestures and his glances. Until finally Lucy managed to stand on tiptoe, and whisper in Paul's ear: "Please. Please let's go home now."

Nearly an hour later they walked out onto the sidewalk, into the fresh scent of autumn night—dry concrete and reddening oak leaves. Lucy with her hand in Paul's pocket, about to speak, to assuage his irritation, to explain why she needed to go.

They stepped into the street, craning their necks for a cab.

"It's not late," Paul said. "Maybe we should just take the subway."

And then, behind them so suddenly it was like a magician materializing through dry-ice mist: Bill stood there.

"Hey," he said. "Paul. Lucy." As if they were old friends. Paul looked at Lucy and immediately comprehended. He draped an arm over her shoulder—covering the bareness, drawing her close to him.

"Listen," Bill said. "I've got a problem. Maybe you can help me out here."

All three of them hesitated. A gaggle of teenage girls— flushed and giddy with alcohol—passed loudly between them, laughter momentarily brightening the street.

"There's a cat trapped in my car," Bill said when the teenagers had moved on.

Paul squeezed Lucy's shoulder. "I don't quite get you," he said to Bill. "What cat?"

"I don't know," Bill said. "It's the damnedest thing. I go to my car, and I hear this meowing. I look through the window, and there's a cat sitting behind the wheel. How about that?"

Paul and Lucy exchanged glances. It struck them both as very unlikely, that a cat could have climbed into Bill's closed car.

"Why not just open the door?" Paul said. "The cat will jump out. Right?"

"I don't want it to run into the street," Bill said. "I figure with the three of us, we can grab it. See if it has tags, or at least put it down somewhere safe."

Lucy felt briefly comforted by this concern, this expression of kindness. Apparently, so did Paul. He removed his arm from her shoulder and took her hand. Hesitantly, they followed Bill to his car.

"We didn't really want to help him," Lucy tells the crowd. "We didn't really think he even needed help. But there he was, asking us. And he was Martin's uncle. It would have felt too strange, just ignoring him. Too rude. And of course we had no idea."

"Of course you had no idea," Lucy's mother echoes soothingly. "How could you have dreamt what would happen next?"

The next few moments passed in artificial twilight, the actual darkness softened by lit windows and headlights. Bill's car—one of those ancient GMC Pacers that look like an upside-down bathtub—was parked under a broken street lamp, just catercorner from the party's front door. Paul and Lucy peered dutifully through the driver's window. And indeed, just as Bill had claimed, there was a cat: visibly distressed, sitting behind the steering wheel, staring back at Paul and Lucy. Not a stray, obviously, but a house cat—Lucy remembers a narrow collar with a bell. The cat opened its mouth and yowled imploringly, loud enough to be audible through closed glass and tin. Then it raised one paw and banged insistently against the window— a startlingly human gesture, fraught with demand.

"Who knows where he got that cat," Lucy says now. "Maybe it was his cat, I don't know. I don't know what became of it, afterward."

"Claudia," somebody says. "Didn't you find it in the park? Didn't you bring that cat home with you?"

"Yes," Claudia says quietly. "She was easy to find, with that bell. She didn't go far. Nobody in Martin's family . . . nobody seemed to want her, and she didn't have tags. So I brought her home."

"Really," Lucy says. "Good. I'm glad." And she *is* glad. She remembers the cat dispassionately, its muddy green eyes and patchwork brown-orange fur. Lucy thinks when she is finished with this story, she might approach Claudia: ask her if she could have the cat, to keep herself. She imagines curling up with it on quiet evenings, sipping tea and watching television. The cat, after all, is the other survivor. Lucy wonders if it knows what happened. If an animal could recall an incident, and speculate on its outcome.

"Anyway," Lucy says, gathering breath for the denouement. "Obviously, he had planned out the entire thing. To go to this party, and target somebody—maybe even a married somebody—and do this thing. It could have been anybody that he chose."

Meaningful, measured, and guilty silence from the several possible anybodies present.

"But it just happened to be me. And Paul."

"Lucy," Bill said. "You go around to the other side of the car, in case the cat gets through us and heads into the street. Paul and I will open the door and try to catch the cat when it jumps out."

Lucy glanced at Paul for confirmation. He shrugged. She turned from him and began to move around the front of Bill's car. She did not see, but heard the slice—not a gurgling at first, but a clean kind of whoosh, a cool and sharpened noise. She swiveled her head to see Paul's instinctive grasping, both hands rising to his throat, covering the gash as blood pumped through his knuckles.

Up to that moment, there is nothing Lucy necessarily regrets. She could not have known what Bill had planned. She could not have imagined that Paul was in any kind of danger. But then, after Paul was hurt. While Paul was dying. Lucy's knees moved instantly into a running position. She heard the knife clang noisily to the pavement. From that instant—until the entire thing was over—she had a single focus. The front door of the brownstone. It became a glaring porthole, an entryway to the rest of her life.

If only Bill had cut *her* throat. Paul, Lucy felt certain, would have retaliated. He would not have thought of himself, of his own survival. His only concern would have been Lucy: protecting her, rescuing her. Punishing her attacker.

But Lucy concentrated on her own safety. Not once in the ensuing moments did the door move from her sight. Not when Bill lifted her with one arm around her waist and dragged her to the passenger door. Not when he opened the passenger door, his fingers digging into her stomach, gripping tightly against her struggle.

Lucy saw Paul, sinking to the curb on the other side of the car. She saw the people on the sidewalk, clustered and horrified, several of them grabbing cell phones and dialing frantically, but none of them daring to interfere even to help Paul—whom Bill had apparently finished with. It seems amazing to Lucy now, and very nearly hateful: that she was able to lift her own limber legs and position them impossibly, bracing them on either side of the door, the arch of one foot curved against the edge of the windshield. Lucy saw the cat escape, diving underneath her—its spine brushed against her raised buttocks as it darted from the car. She heard its light-footed dash across the street and into the park. While Bill persisted, trying to shove her through, into the car, making no headway against her stubbornly, brutally locked legs.

"You have these dreams," Lucy tells the crowd. "Don't we all have them? When something horrible happens, and you need help, and you can't find your voice. But it was like my voice found me. I wasn't aware of it, consciously, trying to scream. It just came out of me. These loud, deep shouts."

Lucy looks around at the listening faces, pausing at the people who had been there.

"I remember," Kevin says.

The brownstone door opened, and as a river of party-goers stumbled out, Lucy kicked her legs straight with a sudden thrust. She and Bill fell backward onto the street. Lucy heard the bugling sound of wind knocked out of Bill: loud, honking clutches for air. She used her elbow to lift herself off of him, and ran not to Paul: but through all the people, toward the doorway, and into the brownstone. She made her way to the bathroom—familiar from her many trips, trying to escape Bill—and locked herself inside.

Paul would have gone immediately to her. He might have taken off his shirt and wrapped it around her neck to stop the flow of blood. He would have spoken to her, stroked her face. He would not ever, under any circumstance, have left her, bleeding on the sidewalk, while he fled to safety.

Lucy knows from reports what happened next, how nobody had gone to Paul until Bill pulled himself into the car and drove away. Paul lying alone on the sidewalk while Lucy huddled—entirely unharmed—between the toilet and the sink. Seconds later the ambulance arrived, and Lucy heard a pounding on the bathroom door, accompanied by the loud pronouncement:

"Police. Are you okay in there?" Lucy flung the door open and threw herself thankfully into the officer's arms.

"And then they let me ride in the ambulance with Paul," Lucy says. "And he died on the way to the hospital."

For the first time she clears her throat—hoarse now from unaccustomed projection. She senses from the weight of the silence that something more is expected. Her mother, still holding the plate of food, seems to be waiting. So do Claudia, and Emily, and Rick. Paul's mother and sister. Very likely, Lucy thinks, they expect her to cry. To sob or weep. But Lucy knows that if she cries now—if she lets herself emit one single tear— she will never stop. The unreality would end, and the only way for Lucy to arrest the ugly, convulsive sobs would be to smash a wineglass or china plate, using an elegant shard to cut her own undeserving throat.

So instead Lucy takes a cool, dry breath and offers this: "I feel bad about it," she says. "I feel bad about running to the brownstone, instead of going to Paul."

This, apparently, is the correct phrase: everyone begins to speak at once, soft and fluid, as if comforting a startled animal. "You were in shock." "Of course you were panicked." Even Paul's mother says, "There was nothing you could have done."

Their assurances rise, running together like a kind of ovation. Someone gives Lucy a new glass of wine. Her mother strokes the hair away from Lucy's eyes.

Lucy smiles in thanks and then stands, extricating herself from the crowd. She makes her way to the buffet table. As she walks, she finds with relief that her feet do not expand to fit the shoes. But the shoes themselves shrink to encase her feet. They cling to her arches and soles as if tailor-made, allowing her effortless and thoughtless movement across the room.

Lucy prepares a plate. She chooses the foods Paul would like. She pours him a glass of wine.

As if somehow this offering will change things. As if she

will not be required, after all, to pursue this survival, and continue past this day—with no one but herself for company.

The party noises continue, voices discussing the tale Lucy has told, the details she has bestowed. They whirl around her like dust kicked up by gale force winds. A sound like a roar, the dull thunder of applause.

the politeness of kings

I fell in love with Dante the night he told
me about breaking bottles off Stone's Bluff.
Before his father died, when he and his
younger sister Christina were children, their
family owned a house on Cape Cod with five
bedrooms, sitting right on the water. Dante
and Christina would collect bottles, the
deepest and brightest blue they could find,
and during winter visits smash them to pieces
on the rocky point adjacent to their property.
In the summer, cobalt sea glass would wash
up onshore. "The most beautiful stuff in the
world," Dante said. "More beautiful than sap-
phires or lapis lazuli!"

It was our fifth date in just over a
week—Dante having called me every day
since I first agreed to go out with him. This
time he'd invited me for dinner at his apartment, and we lay stretched out together on
his couch, my body folded in his arms. Unusual for me, to be so physical so soon, but
Dante had just cooked a crown roast of pork

stuffed with wild rice. Rich food plus a third glass of wine had rendered me helpless.

"My mother still has some of it," Dante told me. "Dad died without his affairs in order. We had to sell everything. All we have left from the Cape house is the blue sea glass. The big ones look like gems, like they should be the centerpiece for a princess's tiara."

"Didn't your mother get angry?" I asked. "About breaking bottles on the beach?"

"No!" Dante spoke so emphatically, he almost rolled off the couch, which was too small for both of us. "She approved. She encouraged it!"

A small, childhood part of me thrilled: that a *mother* would encourage the willful breaking of bottles. My mother used to order me out of a room if anything broke accidentally—as if just the sight of broken glass could cut fingers and toes.

"Mom loved the sea glass too," Dante said. And then added, as a clear show of faith in my character: "So would you, Anne."

"Maybe you'll introduce us," I said. "She can show me."

Dante squeezed his arms around me tightly, joyously. So tightly, in fact, I felt the air rush out of my lungs and heard my vertebrae crack. But not wanting to discourage further displays of affection, I kept complaints to myself.

In my family "rude" was the code word for bad, unspeakable, or loud. "Gracious" meant good, worthy of respect, or tactfully unmentioned. Dante's family amazed me with their lack of pro-scription. We took our first trip from Boston to his mother's house in Greenfield before I told Dante I loved him, and before I thought we were ready for familial introductions. "Christina and I visit my mother at least once a month," he said, "and I can't stand to be away from you for one hour, let alone forty-eight."

When we arrived his mother, Marie, ran onto the lawn to greet us, a cloud of Shalimar preceding her. My own mother wore Chanel No. 5, only at her pulse points: an understated scent that never stayed in a room after she'd left. Marie folded me into a welcoming embrace as if I were her long-lost child. She had lobster and corn on the dining room table. "In Anne's honor," she said.

The extravagance made me uncomfortable, and not just because it presupposed a future to our very new relationship. I knew the family history, how Dante's father had created the illusion of wealth by juggling loans and mortgages. For the past fifteen years Marie had lived on a modest insurance settlement, struggling to make payments on her little house. Dante fantasized about being able to take care of her when his architectural restoration business had some success. He worked with a partner who handled finances and sales, reconstructing old historical homes slated for destruction. Dante took the buildings apart beam by floorboard, then rebuilt them in a new location. "If the business ever makes real money," he would say, "I'm going to buy Mom's house so she won't have to worry anymore. It'll be like when Dad was alive."

That first night, Marie presented a rich Sacher torte for dessert, coincidentally my childhood favorite. She refused to let me clean up after dinner. When everyone had gone to sleep, Dante's sister Christina arrived from New York. I lay awake staring at the champagne flute—filled with blue sea glass—which Marie had placed on our bedside table. It sparkled even in the dark: specks of light glinting like a deep-sea treasure trove. I listened to Christina stomp through the house, clanging dishes and slamming doors. Dante grumbled beside me, barely disturbed.

The next morning the mess from dinner still exploded, untouched, in the kitchen. While Marie's obese Bengal cat hauled itself onto the counter and picked through lobster shells, I noticed that Christina had grazed the remainder of last night's meal before stumbling to bed. I opened the refrigerator and saw the milk bottle, its cap tossed aside and lost, chocolate caking the rim where she'd chugged without wiping crumbs from her mouth. I felt like I'd ventured into a foreign land without rules or expectations. A place where a person could get drunk, overeat, belch, and insult—only to be met by laughter.

In those first few months of dating Dante, we made four visits to his mother. I had grown up at dinners where the reprise was "excuse me" and "would you please," phrases almost never uttered at Marie's table. Their family meals consisted of warring anecdotes. Objections were never suppressed or saved for later, but immediately voiced, often resulting in bellows and tears. Usually Dante and Christina drove the arguments, but occasionally Marie would enter the fray—loudly pointing out Christina's ingratitude, or weeping over criticism of her green bean casserole.

Dante was Marie's clear favorite, and his sister found extravagant methods of redirecting her attention. Striking, redheaded Christina would make dramatic references to her own good looks, or else burst out with a song of her own composition—usually after her sixth or seventh drink. Dante himself had almost no interior dialogue, but erupted with every thought from "Isn't Anne beautiful?" to "Christina, you're making an ass of yourself."

"She was a sweet baby," Dante often said of Christina, whether or not she was present. "But after the first year she started talking. It went downhill from there."

"Oh, Dante," Christina would sneer, imitating Marie's adoring tone. "How clever. You're so *wonderful*."

My behavior amidst all this never really changed. The easiest method of negotiating my own family had always been silence, and I couldn't alter a lifetime of being seen and not heard. When they traded insults, I pretended not to hear. It irritated me that Christina and Dante never helped Marie clean up, but I always loaded the dishwasher without a word. And I never told Marie that her beloved cat, who was so fat I could have balanced a coffee mug on its striped back, activated my asthma, which had been dormant since high school.

Marie called the cat Madame Grey. She fed it flaky albacore with a fork and allowed it to lounge on clean place mats stacked on top of the dining room table, which we ate from hours later. She spooned tiny piles of catnip into corners and onto window-sills. "Anne, honey," Marie advised, "Madame Grey loves to be scratched under her chin. If you want to make friends." I couldn't bring myself to ask that the cat be put outside: instead I'd retreat into the bathroom at discreet intervals, clutching my inhaler and a bottle of Visine.

Like most cats I'd encountered, Madame Grey sensed my discomfort and took every opportunity to inflict herself on me. During family meals, while she rubbed against my legs, I did my best to ignore her and respond to what went on at the ta-ble: laughing, gasping, or nodding sympathetically. But I never contributed to the actual noise. "Anne has such beautiful manners," Marie would declare at the end of a meal through which I'd been largely silent. "No wonder she's so good at her job."

I worked at a PR company, smoothing over unpleasant situations for large corporations. When a company received bad publicity, for striking workers or any kind of lawsuit, I mediated between stockholders and the press.

Christina leveled angry blue eyes at her mother. She was a waitress in an upscale Manhattan restaurant, and probably made more money than I did. But she clearly considered Marie's praise of my profession a veiled insult to her own.

"You should see Anne heading off to work," Dante praised, oblivious to his sister. "Perfection!"

I smiled modestly, but it was true. Perfection was part of

the job. My appearance had to be impeccable, exuding competence and reason. What a relief to be at Marie's dinner table, where I could earn points just by quietly absorbing the chaos.

The first time Dante asked me to marry him, I said no. The thought of a wedding, with my painfully proper parents in a receiving line alongside Marie and Christina, let alone seated together at the head table, seemed like the convergence of two opposing universes.

"But I love you," Dante said. "I adore you."

"We've only known each other five months," I soothed. "Let's give it a little more time."

There were times Dante's unconditional and ardent love made me feel distinctly unworthy. I decided to bring him to my father's sixtieth birthday party in Connecticut, to meet my parents, as consolation; and also as a kind of test run. I warned him not to expect anything like his own family.

"What do you mean?" he asked.

"Nothing," I said. "We're just a little . . . quieter."

At my father's party there were place cards, uniformed servers, finger bowls, port, and after-dinner cigars (smoked only by the men). Although there was a good deal of laughter, none of it came in response to anything that could be called inappropriate. Dante, handsome and relatively reserved in his one good suit, made a lovely impression. I think my mother was particularly touched by the protective way he kept to my side, a hand always hovering at the small of my back.

"This is splendid," Dante said to me at one point, in a whisper loud enough for everyone to hear.

"Don't be too impressed," I said later, alone with him in the hall. Dante rolled the cigar my father had given him between two fingers. "It's not like they do this every night."

After dinner, exhausted and full of good champagne, we

headed toward the separate bedrooms my parents had assigned us. "That's only a nod to propriety," I told Dante. "They know we'll sleep together. They just don't want to *talk* about it."

But Dante was spellbound by all the gentility. "I think your parents really like me," Dante said. "I don't want to do anything that could upset my future in-laws."

I didn't object to this premature phrasing. Dante gave me a chaste good-night kiss and closed the door to the guest room, leaving me alone on the plush, velvety carpet.

Several hours later, feeling the nocturnal effects of Veuve Clicquot, Dante ventured into the labyrinthian hallway to search for a bathroom. He stumbled loudly through my mother's dressing room, into my parents' bedroom, and switched on the light.

When Dante shook me awake to explain what had happened, this is the scenario I envisioned: my parents, eyes wide with groggy astonishment, staring over covers pulled to their buttoned, pajama-clad necks—while Dante swayed over them, sleep crusted in his eyes, wearing nothing but a pair of paisley boxer shorts. I burst out laughing. Dante buried his face into my pillows, mortified.

The next morning I got dressed and went downstairs to the kitchen, leaving Dante in my bedroom. Nobody would ever know a party had been prepared there the night before. Every surface sparkled. The stove glistened so pristinely, it might have just been installed. My mother stood at the counter, pouring coffee. My father sat at the table reading *The Times*. Like me, they were already dressed for the day.

"Good morning, darling," my mother said. "Would you like some coffee?"

"Yes, please," I said.

"Did you sleep well, sweetheart?" my father asked.

"I slept wonderfully, thank you," I said. "And you?"

"Wonderfully," my father said.

"Wonderfully," my mother agreed, handing me a steaming mug. I sipped the coffee, looking from my mother to my father. I knew that the three of us could sit quietly in the kitchen until the world spun to its close. My parents would live out their entire lives without ever breathing a word of Dante's intrusion.

A moment later Dante burst into the kitchen with his arms outstretched—opening the door with such force, I worried the knob would chip the paint on the opposite wall.

"I am so sorry about last night," he said. Dante was unshaven, a wrinkled T-shirt and sweats hastily pulled over his boxers.

My mother smiled. "Don't be silly, dear," she said. "Nobody can negotiate that hallway."

"I beg your forgiveness," Dante boomed. "My intrusion was inexcusable. Please don't hold it against me!"

"Well," my father said. "That's perfectly all right."

"Please, don't give it another thought," my mother said.

Dante sunk into a chair, visibly unburdened, unaware that his profuse apology had to be far more embarrassing to my parents than his original trespass. But they did not exchange the barest flicker of a glance.

We had to leave right after breakfast. Dante was in the midst of a sentimental project, moving a house from Plymouth to Cape Cod. He and his partner had bought a small plot of land just down the beach from Dante's childhood summer home—a lovely location, overlooking the town harbor. The house, built in 1723, had its original posts, panels, beams, floorboards, and fireplaces. Usually Dante rebuilt his houses in the suburbs of Boston. But from the moment he saw this one, he knew it belonged east rather than north. "I'm telling you," Dante kept saying. "It wants to be by the sea."

On the drive from Connecticut, Dante forgot his embarrassment to focus on more pressing issues. "Marry me, Anne," he said, as we merged onto Route 95. "I love you. I love your parents. They're so elegant. So polite!"

"I love you too," I said, sidestepping his question. As a test run, our visit had had debatable results.

"I'd like to throw a party like that," Dante said. "My mother's sixtieth birthday is coming up in June."

Through the window, the bare winter branches gave way to early spring buds. June seemed terribly close.

"It's the kind of thing my father would have done," Dante said. "Things were different when he was alive. Not so perfect as your parents. But not so out of hand. There were manners when my father was alive. Money and manners."

Usually when Dante mentioned his father, he described a wheeler-dealer who built his family's security on an attractive but shaky structure. I suspected time was allowing him some liberties with the past, but I put my hand on his knee—as if comforting him not only for the loss of his father, but for the deterioration of decorum. Dante grabbed my hand and kissed it.

"We should at least live together," he said.

Within three days of my father's party, Dante moved all of his belongings into my apartment. Exhausted from the relocation of both his life and the Cape house, he suggested a visit to Marie's. "Christina will be there," Dante said, "and Mom's house always relaxes me." I packed a weekend bag without questioning the accuracy of that statement.

At Marie's that Friday, we all expected Christina at dinner. But, as was her general habit, she arrived well after midnight without having phoned to say she'd be late. Instead of dozing through her noisy entrance, Dante leapt out of bed and intercepted her in the living room. "Christina," he bellowed. "You're not a teenager anymore. You need to get here at a reasonable hour!"

Marie, probably woken by Dante's bellow rather than Christina's arrival, got up and tried to calm things down.

"Dante, sweetheart," Marie said. "Relax. So Christina's late. She's always late."

"That's exactly the problem," Dante said.

"So what? Why does it matter?"

"It matters," Dante said, "because punctuality is the politeness of kings."

"The what?"

"The politeness of kings."

From the bedroom, Dante's syllables sounded clipped and emphatic, as if this were a common and self-explanatory phrase. His use of the word "politeness" made me wonder if this was some oblique form of courtship, and I found his self-defeating rally for etiquette strangely touching.

Christina laughed bitterly. "Oh," she said. "And I guess that makes Dante king. Hail King Dante."

"Don't provoke your brother," Marie warned.

"Like he's not provoking me? You always take his side!"

While every one of their childhood grievances was aired at high volume, Madame Grey found her way through the open door of Dante's bedroom. At first I only saw her bushy tail, bobbing like a banner of my impending misery. When her fat body landed on my chest, I pushed her off the bed, but she immediately jumped back up. I started to wheeze, my airway shrinking. When the family moved safely out of earshot (taking the argument outside to wake the rest of the neighborhood) I grabbed Madame Grey around her engorged middle and tossed her into the hallway like a bowling ball. Breathing in my inhaler, I understood how a junkie must feel, injecting heroin into an opened vein.

•   •   •

The next morning we all sat together at the breakfast table as if nothing had happened, eating scrambled eggs and toast. Dante announced his plan for Marie's birthday party: to throw it at the house he was renovating on Cape Cod, before it went on the market.

"The Cape," Marie said, delighted. "How wonderful! It'll be just like when you were kids."

"It's just like when we were kids now," Christina said. "Everything Dante does is *wonderful*."

"Oh, Christina," Marie said.

"When we were kids," Dante said, "our father would not have accepted this kind of behavior."

"Sure he would have," Christina said. "He'd have agreed with me. Dad always agreed with me."

Dante snorted in outrage.

I ate my eggs in silence. Inwardly, I thought that I had uncovered the myth of catharsis. It was true that in my own family, grievances—never aired—might broil and linger. But really, the same could be said of Dante's. For all their high-volume honesty, nothing was ever resolved. I sniffled as Madame Grey settled heavily on my feet. I still loved the way words came out of Dante's mouth, without editing or worrying about how people might react. I always guarded my thoughts so carefully, and backtracked endlessly after speaking, sifting through my speech for mistakes and possible offenses. But I knew, for example, that if we spoke to Marie about Madame Grey and my asthma, nothing would change. There would be shouts and tears, hurt feelings and—eventually, from either side—an apology. The cat might spend a few hours outdoors. Then somebody would open a door, and Madame Grey would begin the cycle again, once set in motion destined never to stop: clamorous fight after thunderous dispute, adding to my allergic misery.

I would stick to my inhaler as remedy.

Back home a few nights later, I sat on the couch, reading articles about an equipment leasing company we represented, who'd fired an employee with HIV. I needed to come up with some image-smoothing maneuvers, and took notes on everything from funding AIDS hospices to extending the man's insurance. Dante interrupted me with his checkbook. "Look at this balance," he said. "I've been thinking. Now that we're sharing one rent, maybe I can afford to keep that old Cape house myself."

"But you haven't paid any of your bills yet," I pointed out. "After you do, that balance won't be so impressive. You can't afford a summer house. You don't even own a primary house yet."

Dante frowned at his checkbook, as if it were a more reliable source of information than I.

"Anyway," I said. "I thought you wanted to help Marie. Wouldn't buying a house for yourself delay paying for hers?"

"Mom could live at the Cape!" Dante said. "She misses it so much. She could live there, and we could visit her."

I fought to keep from rolling my eyes. While Dante often mentioned how much he missed Cape Cod, Marie never did. All her friends lived in Greenfield.

"That doesn't sound like a very practical plan," I said.

An odd sort of cloud came over Dante's face, and I decided to postpone the argument. "Hey," I said. "The house isn't even finished. Why talk about it now? See how the restoration goes. How the property looks. You can worry about it then."

· · ·

When the renovations on the Cape house were complete in May, Dante had to make it temporarily inhabitable for the party just one month away. He worked with such passion, finishing the details. He came home late every night, his long day topped off by hours of battling traffic, to find me sitting at the kitchen table poring over Marie's guest list. It was as if we'd both taken a second job. On one of these nights—while I took notes for a morning meeting and Dante addressed envelopes—Christina called.

Dante had decided not to include Christina in planning Marie's party. This, he thought, would avoid the inevitable outbursts when she began shirking responsibility. But a part of me believed that once we sent out the invitations, Christina would start offering assistance. After all: most of the guests were people she'd known all her life, relatives and family friends. She'd naturally think of people she could give rides to, or an extra stash of linen we could use.

"Hey, Anne," Christina said. "I was wondering. Have you guys thought about what you're getting Mom for her birthday?"

"Getting her?" I said. Dante's hand froze over his intricate calligraphy.

"Yeah. I thought we could all go in on something nice."

"Well," I said. "I guess . . . we were thinking . . . this party? I think that's going to be our present to Marie."

Dante snatched the phone, his chair wobbling as he stood.

"Are you insane?" he yelled at his sister. "Do you have any idea how much work Anne and I are doing?"

He rattled off a to-do list so impressive that a funnel cloud of fresh anxiety formed inside my body: the invitations, the hotel reservations, the liquor, the food, the enormous preparation of the house including finding beds, chairs, couch, and tables. "It's like we're putting on a wedding, plus building a home for the newlyweds!" he thundered. Then he fell quiet as Christina spoke. While I couldn't make out her precise words,

I could tell that Dante's outburst had not fazed her in the slightest.

"Really?" Dante said, his voice suddenly normal. "Yeah. Uh-huh. Well, that's a great idea. Okay. Good luck. Love you too." He hung up and resumed his lettering.

"What was that all about?" I asked.

"Christina." Dante shook his head with fond disapproval. "Can you believe her? Absolutely oblivious! But she's going to buy this feather cat bed, with iron rails. Mom will love it."

"That reminds me," I said. "Do you think you could make up a reason for Marie not to bring Madame Grey to the Cape? It would make this whole occasion much more pleasant for me."

"Don't worry," Dante promised. "I'll take care of it." He picked up his envelope and blew lightly on the drying ink. Then he added, "Don't let Christina contribute a dime to this party. If she gives so much as five bucks to pay for beer, she'll want credit for the entire affair."

In the morning, Dante gave me a stack of invitations to mail. Sifting through them, admiring Dante's printing, I was surprised to discover an envelope addressed to my parents.

"Look," I said, showing Dante the invitation as if it would be as much a surprise to him. "You're inviting my parents?"

"Of course! They're family. We're all one family. Right?"

I slid the letter back into its stack. Dante, wearing his usual work uniform of jeans and ratty T-shirt, poured us coffee. For a second, I had a removed vision of the two of us, together in the neat little kitchen that used to belong only to me. My necessarily perfect navy suit, with matching unscuffed pumps. And I thought that Dante and I also matched, in our own way.

I looked at Dante's face. He smiled at me with effusive,

adoring approval and handed me my coffee. I thought that I could search the world over and not find someone who loved me so much, let alone so vocally. Of course I wanted to marry Dante. I just didn't want our *families* to marry.

"Your parents will love this party," Dante said, kissing my lips. "It'll be elegant and tasteful. Just like them."

The weekend of Marie's party, when it finally arrived, shaped up beautifully. Dante had done a superb job on the house. Its picture window framed the harbor. Its overhead beams, burnished by nearly three hundred years, happily breathed in the salt air. Dante had finagled an antiques dealer into loaning us furniture. The dealer, he explained, would let him keep everything until he sold the house, in the hope that the buyer would purchase the furniture as well. The caterer set up the deck with folding chairs and round tables. There would be a full bar and a surf and turf menu. I had gently steered my parents toward a little bed and breakfast, and clear skies were predicted into the week.

The morning before our families arrived, Dante and I took a walk along the beach to see his childhood home. We struggled over the slippery rocks on Stone's Bluff, Dante periodically reaching out a steadying hand. "This," he said, "is where we would smash the bottles."

Their old house was beautiful: cedar-shingled and dark-shuttered, standing squarely above the sea. It looked perfectly conceived and constructed, as if it had stood there for the last two centuries and would remain the next thousand. I understood why Dante mourned the place so. We observed it from a hiding place, crouched behind rocks and reeds. Dante grumbled about changes the new owners had made. "That trellis is abominable. Tasteless! And there used to be a porch," he said, pointing to a door that overlooked the ocean. "Dad would sit there in the morning. He'd look out at the sea and drink his coffee." He turned away from the house and stared toward the water. "In a perfect world," he said, "my father would be alive and his finances would be stable. The party would be at this house. And you and I would be married."

I ran my hand consolingly through his hair. "Your new house is beautiful," I said. "And the party will be lovely."

"I wish you would marry me," Dante persisted.

"Well," I answered. "Maybe I will."

Dante smiled. The grin was huge and happy but—as his only reaction—surprisingly understated.

We walked back to the beach and collected sea glass for hours. We found green, white, amber, and dark brown. But no blue. I rolled the smooth, damp glass between my fingers— marveling at the patience of the tides, the time it took to polish the once-jagged edges to this graded, harmless beauty.

The night before the party, my parents arrived with appropriately gracious compliments for the house. "What a lovely job you've done, Dante," my mother said. "It's just beautiful."

"Yes," my father agreed. "Everything looks fantastic."

Their approval made Dante glow like a June bride. And for all my fears about Marie, Christina, and my parents meeting, their first encounter went smoothly. Marie did not attempt to hug either my mother or father, but shook hands with warm reserve. Dante cooked a Portuguese fish stew, which we ate in the dining room. Through the picture window we watched a fishing boat unload a tuna at the harbor, the giant fish swinging from a hook over the pier. Aside from a narcissistic toast by Christina, referencing the beauty Marie's genes had bestowed ("Thanks for the bones, Mom"), Dante's family behaved more or less normally. And my parents ignored Christina's bragging so inscrutably, I thought that our families might be more compatible than I had supposed.

My only complaint was Madame Grey. Dante had forgotten to ask Marie to leave her at home, and the cat wound herself persistently around my ankles.

"Madame Grey just adores Anne," Marie gushed to my parents. Then she raised her glass. "To Dante," she said. "For bringing our family back to the Cape."

Over the saucer of sea glass I had placed as a centerpiece, we all clinked drinks—as Dante beamed and his sister glowered. I held my breath (already in short supply, thanks to Madame Grey), but Christina miraculously let the moment slide.

"Are you all right, darling?" my mother asked when I walked her and my father to their car. "You look a little . . . tired."

I knew my eyes were red and puffy. I tried to gulp in the air—crisp and clean of cat fur—but my throat felt swollen and scratchy. "It's the cat," I admitted, suddenly hoping my mother might give me permission to address—politely but firmly—the issue of Madame Grey.

My mother rustled in her purse, then handed me a packet of Benadryl. "Take this," she said. "It will help you sleep."

That night, I tossed in and out of an antihistamine fog. The house, with its bare walls and floorboards, had outrageous acoustics. I could hear every creak and movement from every corner. I could hear Christina humming in the upstairs hall. I could hear Madame Grey roaming from room to room—pacing, crouching, plotting her pounce on me.

While Dante slept peacefully beside me, his breathing

smooth and simple. As untroubled by Madame Grey as he had been by our families meeting.

The next morning, while Christina strolled down the beach or disappeared in the car to visit childhood haunts, Dante and I prepared. We helped the caterers set up the barbecue and the lobster bake, cleaned the house yet again, made last-minute runs to the liquor store and the bus station.

The day itself was a gift to Marie—clear and warm, with a delicious offshore breeze. As the party began at midafternoon, she stood out on Dante's deck, looking nowhere near sixty, greeting her guests. Behind her the harbor posed like a painting, the sailboats and schooners swaying on calm water, the dinging of their masts so musical that Dante decided not to bother with the new CD player. I would have felt completely happy if I hadn't been battling an asthma attack thanks to Madame Grey's persistent stalking.

When my parents arrived, my mother joined me at a corner table. "Feeling better?" she asked. I lowered the sunglasses, which camouflaged my red-rimmed eyes.

"Stay outside," my mother advised. "You'll be fine."

Christina joined us, splendid in bright red lipstick and a silk sarong tied below her bare arms. She tipped back a champagne glass, looking beautiful enough to get away with her boasts about bone structure. I slid my sunglasses back into place.

"The party is lovely," my mother said to Christina. "You kids really did a wonderful job."

"Thank you," Christina replied. "But after all. It's not every day your mother turns sixty!"

Someone let Madame Grey outside, and she wound her way through my bare ankles. "Darling," my mother said, notic-

ing my instant wheezes. "Would you please get me a gin and
tonic?"

I took the opportunity to steal into our bedroom and insert
a fresh canister into my inhaler. Dante sidled in behind me and
closed the door.

"It's going really well, don't you think?"

"Fabulous," I said, then sucked in the medicine greedily.
Dante wrapped his arms around my waist and kissed my neck.

"Just think," he said. "If I owned this house and you married me. We could come here all the time."

I glanced across the room, at our reflection in a gilt mirror
loaned by the antiques dealer: Dante cloaked lovingly around
me, his face positively lit—as healthy and pleased as mine was
swollen and pathetic.

I imagined, in that moment, a different kind of inhaler:
one that I could breathe in, that would suddenly allow me to
speak my mind. A canister charged with courage and harsh
words and maybe even action. I'd inhale, then tell Dante to
face the fact that he could not afford this house, let alone all
the antiques that were making it so inhabitable. I'd admit to
being on the verge of needing epinephrine. Then I'd load
Madame Grey into her cat carrier, drive up to Provincetown,
and let her loose among the crowds of tourists, where she'd
never find her way back.

When I returned, I'd tell Dante: Yes, of course I'll marry
you.

He looked so happy. I thought of the party, the white
tablecloths and the luxurious menu, the fantastic breeze and
the cool blue harbor. I thought of his father, long gone but still
mourned, and the childhood summers so dearly missed. My
throat—freed by medication—expanded with something like
love. I turned in Dante's arms and kissed him deeply: hoping
my lips would articulate an empathy for his longing, approval

for what he'd accomplished with this party, and an unqualified maybe to his proposal.

When I left the bedroom, several steps behind Dante, I found Madame Grey waiting for me in the hall. I scooped the cat up around her fat middle and hauled her to the upstairs bathroom, where I closed the window, pulled the shade, and shut the door behind me.

At dinner Christina sat with my mother and me. Every time a guest complimented her on the party—the food, the house, even the weather—she replied with a proud, slightly slurred thank-you. I was relieved that Dante sat safely out of earshot, across the deck, holding court at Marie's table while she beamed adoringly.

As the sky darkened to evening, the toasts began. First a spattering of simple sentiments by family friends, wishing Marie the happiest of birthdays, complimenting her youthful appearance and the beauty of the Cape, the house, the day. A few praised the efforts of "the children" for planning the party.

Dante gave a beautiful speech, loving and sincere. In the midst of his applause, Christina stood (resplendent if wobbly in her sarong) and slunk to the center of the deck. "And now, Mom," she announced, lifting a freshly filled glass, "I'm going to sing you a little birthday song." Behind the trail of her speech, from somewhere up above, I heard a faint feline moan.

The birthday song, on its own, might have been a touching and personal gesture. Christina's voice, while distinctly untrained, had a pretty kind of lilt. But when the song ended, she did not respond to applause by returning modestly to her seat. She held the floor and launched into another. The guests shifted, wanting to return to their meals and conversation.

Christina prefaced song number three with a short toast.

"Thank you for coming," she said to the guests. "It means the world to Dante and me that you could all attend our party!"

Dante frowned furiously as Christina started to sing again. He whispered to Marie, who stood up. "Thank you, Christina," she said, interrupting midnote. "That was lovely. I can't thank my children enough for this wonderful evening!" Marie toasted amidst applause, not noticing the severe cloud crossing Dante's face. He stood up and walked over to Christina, who hadn't budged from center stage. He grabbed her elbow and whispered instructions. Christina yanked her arm away. Marie's smile began to look strained. I looked across the deck to my father, and then glanced at my mother. They both fixed their gazes cheerfully on Marie, as if nothing unusual were happening.

"I don't know what you're talking about," Christina yelled.

"I'm talking about you taking credit for my party!" Dante exploded. "Anne's and my party!"

While the other guests cleared their throats or spoke to each other in low, disapproving voices, my father discreetly got up from his chair and walked inside the house. My mother busied herself dabbing a napkin at an imaginary stain on her sleeve.

"Jesus Christ, Dante," Christina shouted. "You make it sound like I didn't do *anything*."

"You didn't!" Dante shouted back. "Not one single thing! Not one penny. Not one errand! Not one thing! If Dad were alive, you would *never* get away with this."

"If Dad were alive, we'd be on the beach," Christina said. "Not at this piddling little *shack*."

Dante grabbed his sister by the shoulders. For one horrible moment, I thought he might actually hit her; but after a minute he simply released his grip. I could only watch, wondering what to do. Wondering why, despite nearly an hour away from Madame Grey, my eyes still watered and my breathing still labored.

Dante announced to all the guests, by way of explanation, the exact dollar amount he had spent on the party. My insides roiled, but my mother didn't so much as bat an eyelash.

"Dante," Marie exclaimed, easily cheered. "You shouldn't have!"

Christina burst into tears. "God damn you!" she screamed at Marie. "It doesn't matter how beautiful I am! You'll always love Dante more!"

To my surprise, I saw a smile cross my mother's face. Of course she suppressed it, suddenly taken thrall by a bent tine on her dessert fork. My father had not reappeared.

So here we sat: Dante's family dynamic on parade, my worst fears realized. And my parents displayed no reaction at all. I thought, as I had the night before, that my family and Dante's might actually be a perfect combination—his behaving as wildly as they liked, mine flawlessly ignoring them.

I watched my mother, biting back her smile and studying her fork: sailing the unsteady waves of acrimony by staying silent. I wanted to ask her if she admired Dante's family for their unrestrained outbursts. I wanted to ask her if she ever wished she could get away with similar boasts and accusations. At the same time, I thought how *easy* her silence made everything. No wonder Dante and Marie love me, I thought. Perhaps I don't need that inhaler after all.

"Anne," my mother said. She nodded toward Christina, who had dissolved into a chair with petulant and drunken sobs. "Why don't you take Dante's sister for a walk to the beach? She looks like she could use some air."

"Okay," I said, not pointing out that there was plenty of air on the deck. And then added: "Mom? Are you . . . all right?"

"Of course, darling," she said. "Don't worry about me."

I kissed her cheek, and walked obediently to Christina.

· · ·

We were halfway down the road, Christina humming and sniffling, when Dante called to us from the edge of the lawn.

"Hey," he said. "Where are you two going?"

We stopped walking. Away from the lights of the party, in the newly minted night, his form was barely discernable. "We're going for a walk," I called back. I could imagine Dante's face: weighing his anger at Christina against his reluctance to be left out. "Want to come?" I asked.

"Sure," Dante said, and trotted up the road to join us. From the house, I heard the party noises returning to normal: clinking glasses and laughter. Dante took my arm, snubbing his sister. As the three of us walked toward the beach, I noticed I was no longer having trouble breathing. The ocean air filled with honeysuckle, beach plum, and rugosa rose. My lungs expanded, joyfully accepting the clean, fragrant oxygen.

We walked across a sandy parking lot, past a carload of teenagers in a dented Impala. A match lit the inside of the ancient sedan, illuminating bare, freckled shoulders and wisps of uncut hair. Laughter tinkled through their open window.

Except for two more teenagers, making out in the high lifeguard's chair, the beach was deserted. We walked out toward the surf. Christina's rosy face looked drunkenly calm, the pink flush of tears still lighting her cheeks. I kicked off my shoes and tested the water, rendered gray—a black-and-white photograph—by the absence of sun. The bay was still except for the most gentle waves, and I expected the water to be forbiddingly cold. But to my surprise it felt warm, if not warmer, than the evening.

"God," Dante said, pulling off his pants and splashing in to midcalf. "It's like a bathtub."

Christina and I followed, abandoning our sandals and walking toward the low-slung sky. As she waded in to her waist, Christina's sarong skimmed and spread across the water, behind and around her. I took tentative steps through the splashing waves, stopping to watch the two of them swim before I reached deep enough water. The seascape gaped like a desert or the view from an airplane: endless and immense.

Watching from the edge of the tide, I noticed a fountain of light: small sparks like fireflies, spraying up whenever Dante or Christina moved. I ran my hand across the water, and when I lifted it, the same string of sparks dripped from my fingertips.

"Christina," I called, because she was closest. "Look."

I gathered an armful of water and tossed it above me. The lights twirled up, intermingled, then fell back down in a shimmering spray. My hem fell just above the top of the water, and I thought about submersing myself, fully clothed, never mind the good party dress. Diving in through the glinting, barely there waves.

"It's the phosphorescence," Dante called. He pulled off his shirt and ran back toward me, the phosphorescence crackling around him like so many sparklers. He thrust his clothes into my arms. Christina pulled off her already soaked sarong. "Here," she said to me. "Hold this."

"Say please, Christina," Dante said, but nicely, with a hint of impending forgiveness. He dove into the water headfirst, staying under so long that I felt the vague stirrings of worry before he emerged with a delighted gasp, thousands of lit droplets cascading back into the water. Christina, completely naked, bent forward from the waist, moving her arms as if swimming a stationary crawl, and sent the water upward in splashing bursts.

I thought about walking out of the water and dumping their clothes on the beach. But I remembered the teenagers, and worried about Christina's expensive if ruined sarong. I felt the bulge of Dante's wallet in his pants pocket. And also I was mesmerized: enchanted by my own easy lungfuls, and the sparkling water all around. Dante and his sister, swimming so easily, and so much without care. Spilling up light, manufacturing this magical fireworks. Like something shattered and falling, somehow more dazzling than its original form.

Dante splashed back to me, lit water running from his hair and shoulders. He gathered the clothes out of my arms and threw everything back toward the beach. The garments stretched and spiraled through the air. His pants floated down to the sand, just shy of the waves. His shirt and Christina's sarong alighted on the water, spreading out like jellyfish. He unzipped my dress, pulled it over my head, and tossed it to join their flotilla of clothes.

He took my hand and led me through the waves. I kicked up my feet one at a time, creating the vaguest disturbance. The lights rose and fell, and I watched their slow, delicate drip. "Isn't this magnificent?" Dante asked, quietly for him. "Don't you wish you could be here all the time? Whenever you wanted?"

The question, of course, was loaded. But then again: I did wish that. Never mind the drama. The financial ruin. The embarrassment. Never mind that we all knew this truce— created by summer night and glowing organisms—was only temporary.

"Marry me, Anne," Dante said. "Marry me."

The phosphorescence dripped and splashed from our fingertips like scattered crown jewels. Maybe I would marry Dante, and we would buy the Cape house and then lose everything. Maybe we would war and battle, destroying relationships, breaking apart, then coming back together.

"You win, Dante," I said, the words coming easily as my breath: while the party, and Madame Grey, and our families— even Christina, just a few yards away—receded. "You win."

His whoop of victory exploded with the lights, which spiraled and crashed around us, breaking into brilliance against our bodies. I laughed, and kissed him, the warmth of our chests colliding underwater. Knowing that after some time we would have to arrive back on shore: just where we'd been originally. A version of ourselves, worn down but somehow made better, more beautiful, by the passing time and tides.

by his wild lone

1. Mia

My little sister grew up to be a tall, broad
woman. But as a child, before adolescence,
she was the tiniest, most fragile fairy creature
you can imagine. Mia's bones were made
of finer stuff than the rest of ours—hollow,
like imported ivory. When you picked her
up, it felt like she measured in ounces rather
than pounds. She walked with a skip that
originated in her slender knees, so springy
that her feet barely touched the ground. It
seemed a miracle that she'd even cast a
shadow.

I usually don't have faith in my childhood memories. "Oh, Natalie," my mother
always said, if I mentioned an event she
didn't recall, "you must have dreamed it."
But I do know that once on a Cape Cod
beach the wind lifted Mia up off the sand.
My brother Mark corroborates this: he was
twelve, I was ten, Mia was six. The three
of us stood on the beach late in the day,

heading toward sunset, watching a stormy evening roll its way to shore. Dramatic, swirling winds and a thick, persistent mist. Heat lightning above our heads and across the melting horizon. Gust after gust assaulted us, but one felt like it came from below rather than above—like it had traveled across the waves horizontally, hugging the water and then the sand, to rise up inches from our feet in a full-force gale. And it lifted little Mia as if she were a sail or a parachute, her blond hair floating like a mermaid's, her body folding into a U and billowing upward into the air so that Mark and I each had to grab one hand and pull her back to the ground.

For a long time afterward, that storm seemed to live inside Mia. Before, she had been manageable and eager to please. Not exactly docile, but certainly not at all wild—which is what she became after the wind took her. She could no longer be trusted or controlled. Anything lost or broken, anything gone amiss, could always be traced to Mia. At the same time, when my parents attempted to punish her, she would turn up startlingly attractive, flashing an electric and remorseless grin several times bigger than herself, her tiny, blue-eyed form surrounded by a mischievous, glittering patina.

Before the storm, when Mia was well behaved, I loved her in the patronizing way of older sisters—remembering her mittens and tying her shoes, cultivating my own importance through small, tending tasks. After the storm, I stopped holding her hand when we crossed the street, or correcting her when she recited misinformation. Even Mark—twice her size and age—admitted to feeling a little nervous around Mia. But in a funny kind of way, we loved her more. In this particular phase, she possessed an intimidating sort of glamour: not the kind you see on the cover of magazines, but the kind witches use, to change form or to dazzle.

But Mia's store of electricity seemed to run out as she grew, and her personality returned to its original quiet. By fourteen she stood five foot eight with a substantial body mass index. She wore bras. She menstruated. She deferred to boys, to our parents, and to her teachers, eventually distinguishing herself by being the only girl in history to go away to college and stay faithful to her high-school sweetheart. Everybody loved Clay, and Mia returned home to marry him almost immediately after graduation. Their three children arrived in quick succession. Mia was a disorganized mother, but a loving one. Compassionate, selfless, always juggling everyone else's needs—running a house full of cats and children with a scattered, lenient sensibility. A likable woman, even an admirable one. The first person you'd call if you came down with the flu and needed soup or extra blankets. But still—and a little sadly if you'd known her as a child: surrounded with the dull light of day like the rest of us.

As an adult, Mia retained a taste for the odd and romantic: she loved stories with tragic endings. She loved myths and fairy tales about characters—especially cats—who transformed because of events, nightfall, or weather. But in her daily life, we never saw so much as a spark from that original storm until years later: the autumn Walter Engel lost control of his car at the corner of Sea Street and Vine, careening into the old post oak and catapulting Mia facefirst through his windshield.

At the time of Mia's accident, she and I both lived in the Cape Cod town where we'd spent our summers as children. I'd moved there from Vermont two and a half years before, wanting to be close to my sister on the heels of my thirtieth birthday and a humiliating divorce. Our old summer home had originally belonged to my mother's family, and she'd kept it after her own divorce from our father. She loaned it to Mia and Clay when Oscar, their first child, was born—temporarily, so they'd have a free place to live until they got on their feet financially. Which never happened. Clay worked as a teller at the local bank, and Mia wanted to stay at home with the children—who drained what little money Clay managed to earn. My mother attempted a few summers living with Mia, Clay, and their multiplying brood, but couldn't stand Mia's method of running a household, which was no method at all. Mia was the kind of mother who paid more attention to tears and tantrums than to dust and clutter. Mom finally threw up her hands and relinquished the place altogether. A year later she remarried and moved to Florida.

I lived footsteps down the road from Mia and Clay, in a weathered old Cape that sat above the beach where we used to play. At home I had no one but my Border collie Scout for company. Thanks to our family's local connections, I had landed a cushy job working from home, editing a column called "Special Memories" for a Cape-based magazine. The job was supposedly full-time, and paid me accordingly, but it rarely took more than one day a week. The magazine expected me to read each of the hundreds of letters sent in by readers, detailing life's particularly precious events, and choose one or two to run each week. Instead I'd wait until the end of the week and spend one morning reading twenty or thirty of the submissions. If this smaller pool didn't yield anything, I'd borrow a cute anecdote from one of Mia's children and attach a pseudonym. It was very easy, and left me plenty of time to spend with Mia and her family.

My mother's old house overlooked the marina, a picturesque but bustling view: I found the ocean sights and acoustics of my new place much more soothing. And when the shore-side winds knocked out my power, I could walk down the road and camp out at Mia's. Oscar, Juliette, and Deirdre (Mia's children) provided me with hugs and unconditional love whenever I needed them, and helping Mia made me feel useful and productive—especially when it came to six-year-old Oscar.

Deirdre was barely two, naturally attracting plenty of lavish attention, and at three Juliette was a pretty and confident goody-goody, constantly correcting her siblings and asserting her own superiority. But Oscar had always been a sensitive, needy child—colicky as an infant, and so precocious as a toddler that you had to watch what you said around him before he was a year old. I loved Oscar—that particularly strong and poignant love inspired by awkward children. Whenever I picked him up at the Waldorf school, the sight of him made my heart constrict: Oscar blinking through thick glasses, an empty backpack strapped to his shoulders while he clutched an unwieldy stack of books and loose papers in his arms. Mia had named him after Oscar Wilde, and even before his classmates had a chance to torture him ("Oscar the Grouch," "os-SCAR"), he seemed burdened with angst worthy of his persecuted namesake.

When anything went wrong for my sister or myself— when Juliette was stung by a bee, when Mia ran out of milk, when I heard news of my ex-husband Geoffrey and Lacey, his new girlfriend, or when I stepped on a rusty nail and had to be rushed to the Med Stop for a tetanus shot—we were in shouting distance of each other. At the same time, I always had my own home for escape, away from the chaos of children and the fluff and swirl of Mia's cats, whose names she had chosen with her usual romantic pessimism—Heloise, Abelard, Icarus, Persephone, and Ophelia.

The Friday night Walter Engel crashed his car, I was at Mia's house in seconds. I pulled into the driveway to find Oscar pressed against the front bay window, sobbing hysterically through his myopic squint, two cats winding themselves around his ankles.

My dog Scout reached him first. She leapt up onto the windowsill, sent the cats leaping for safety, and covered Oscar's swollen face with rapid dog kisses. In my own agitated state, not knowing how bad Mia's accident was, I felt relieved to have

Oscar to comfort. I scooped him out of Scout's clutches and rocked him, his tears gathering in the hollow of my collarbone.

Oscar and I sat up for hours before Clay called from the hospital in Hyannis, his throat chafed with shock, his deep voice reduced to a shaky whisper. Mia hadn't worn a seat belt, and shot through Walter's windshield like a cannon salute.

"She's in a coma," Clay told me. "The doctor rates it as a seven on a scale from one to ten."

I called my mother in Coral Gables, my brother Mark in Boston, my father in Jackson Hole. They all arrived the next day. Since I couldn't leave Mia's kids or bring them to the hospital, I was the last one to visit her. On Monday afternoon I finally made it to the hospital, my arms full of books from Mia's shelves. Considering her trip through the windshield, Mia looked remarkably all right. It was an eerie relief to see her lying there, looking peaceful and unbloody despite her broken cheekbone and the wires in her jaw.

Every day that week, while my mother, father, Clay, and Mark rotated watching the children, I sat by Mia's bedside and read her books aloud. I read her Japanese myths where vampires took the form of cats, and Chinese myths about cats warding off evil spirits in the night. I read a fairy tale called "The King of the Cats," where the family pet disappears up the chimney, and four different versions of "Puss 'n Boots."

I read her "The Cat That Walked by Himself," the Just So Story where a cat tricks a cavewoman into giving him the benefits of fire, hearth, and milk, but never really allows himself to be tamed. I'd bought this particular book for Mia several years before, when I was still married. Sitting by her bedside, I found myself reaching for it more often than any of the others. Not that it helped: Mia seemed to wither away by the hour, appearing more dependent on life-sustaining machinery with every passing day. "I am the Cat who walks by himself," I read, hoping the words might impress her subconscious with their autonomy, "and all places are alike to me."

The person who put in the most consistent bedside hours, aside from me, was Walter Engel. Clay, after all, had the kids, and occasional trips to check in with the bank. My parents had to rotate their shifts in order to avoid each other, and Mark had to travel back and forth from Boston. Walter had been given time off from his job at a resort hotel, and in the midst of familial comings and goings he paced Mia's room—his eyes watery and bloodshot, his curly blond hair in anguished disarray, his tall, bent figure filling up the room more often than I would have liked. Such a sad and broken emergency ought to be private, I thought. I assumed Walter's vigilance sprang from guilt—his being the driver, the owner of the car, and the relatively unscathed fellow victim. Walter's injuries were glaringly non–life-threatening: a broken wrist and a nasty cut over his eye. But he'd worn a seat belt, and compared to Mia was in great shape—and deep trouble, his blood having registered an alcohol level of .13.

None of us suspected anything scandalous between Mia and Walter. They'd known each other since their first swimming lessons at Squire's Pool. And while Mia generally spent evenings with her children, it wasn't unheard-of for her to go to an occasional party, or out for a drink, while Clay stayed home and watched the kids.

Also, everybody thought Walter was gay. He liked to wear outfits: matching socks and T-shirts, his gorgeous hair combed specifically—tousled or slicked—to jibe with jeans or chinos. More than once I'd heard him refer to a sweater or coat of Mia's as "a beautiful piece." True, he often spoke of girlfriends and conquests in a contrived, overly boyish manner, but we ignored this as so much closeted bluster. There was no real reason to think of him and Mia as anything but old childhood friends.

When Mia started to wake, ten days after the crash, her behavior seemed more or less as one would expect: groggy, vague, drifting in and out of consciousness. The doctor promised a full recovery, and we all felt enormous relief. I went home and slept for the first full night since the accident, then got up and put my column together. When I arrived at the hospital that afternoon, my mother pulled me aside. "Mia's been saying strange things," she told me.

"How do you mean?" I asked.

"She's been saying things that seem terribly odd to me."

"What kind of things?"

Mom rolled her eyes, unwilling to elaborate. I shrugged and took a seat beside my sister.

"Hi," Mia said. She waved from her elbow, a forlorn gesture. I was struck by how spindly she'd become after ten days of feeding tubes. She looked pale and very thin, her blue eyes strangely colorless. Even her freckles looked gray. Somehow, her hair had grown at an accelerated rate during her coma. It looked much longer and wilder than two weeks before.

"Hi," I said. "How do you feel?"

"Not so good," Mia said, as clearly as she could with her broken jaw. She jerked her head delicately toward Mom, who stood by the window arranging Walter's gladiolas in a cobalt blue vase. I thought they looked beautiful, but my mother frowned and muttered, "Who brought these funeral flowers?"

"She's driving me insane," Mia whispered, which seemed normal enough. I noticed that she didn't ask about Oscar, Juliette, and Deirdre. But she'd just emerged from a two-hundred-and-forty-hour coma, so I didn't question her parental devotion.

Mia smiled in a pleased, dreamy way. Then she turned her head and looked directly at me, her long, unwashed hair clinging to her scalp.

"Natalie," Mia said, clicking her syllables through the wires fusing her jaw. "Would you please ask the nurse to bring me some mouthwash? I need to give Walter another blow job."

"Excuse me?" I glanced back toward the doorway, where Clay stood chatting with a doctor.

Mia sighed with faint exasperation and laid her head back down on the pillow. "I need to give Walter another blow job," she muttered, and turned her dreamy stare out the window.

The doctor assured us this was not unusual. Lots of patients who'd suffered head injuries went through a stage of sexual fixation. Of saying wildly inappropriate things. It would pass, he promised. We should all try to gloss over it.

But it was hard to ignore Mia's placidly graphic remarks. In the middle of a perfectly normal hospital conversation— about the food, or Mia's luck in getting a private room—she'd interject in the same slightly garbled tone she'd used to complain about the Jell-O. "That reminds me of the time Walter took me from behind," she said to Mark, my father, and me. "Out in the parking lot by Nauset Beach. Do you remember?"

"Sorry," Mark said. "I don't think we were there." I jammed my elbow into his ribs. My father looked like he might cry.

Sometimes Mia described innocuous impersonal acts. She made a comment about monkeys and parakeets in pear trees that might have been poetic if only she'd omitted the phrase "sucking off." Mostly, her comments involved detailed sexual acts executed by Walter and herself. An occasional doctor or celebrity would enter the scenario, but—we all noted—never her own handsome husband. One morning in the cafeteria Clay said, "It would be nice if I could get in on this action occasionally. I'm starting to feel neglected." Mark and I laughed in a burst of relief that Clay's general confidence afforded him a sense of humor about even this.

Because we still didn't suspect anything between Mia and Walter. Despite the fact that he'd blush furiously if he happened to be in the room—which he often was—when she made these comments. We attributed it all to some subconscious connection between the accident and the sexual act. When they finally unwired Mia's jaw and pronounced her fit to go home, none of us had any right to be shocked when she announced she'd be moving in with Walter. But we all were.

Like the rest of my family, I'd always been fond of Clay. He was a sweet man, an attractive guy, a great father. Still, if Mia had left him for any other reason, my allegiance would have naturally fallen with her. She was my sister, after all.

But in this circumstance, I couldn't help but sympathize with Clay. In my own marriage, I'd been equally unsuspecting. It took Geoffrey four months to tell me about his affair with Lacey, one of his graduate students at Bennington. Mia told me I should have seen it coming—an insight I understood much more clearly after her accident. And I had known that Geoffrey and Lacey were close. I even knew the two of them had gone camping together. They went for a six-day hike on the Appalachian Trail, with my clueless blessing.

Like Clay's misguided naïveté, the reason I never suspected anything between Geoffrey and Lacey had more to do with prejudice than trust. Her fondness for long walks notwithstanding, Lacey weighed more than two hundred pounds. She had a quick wit and extensive knowledge in her (and Geoffrey's) field, especially impressive for a student. She dressed surprisingly well, and I forever found myself complimenting her outfits. I understood

why Geoffrey liked her. But love her? I never for a moment believed my husband capable of attraction toward someone so simply huge. When Geoffrey first told me, I thought he was joking.
I honestly laughed. And when the conversation took that surreal
turn—in the moment I began to believe him—I felt a level of
anger I don't think would have been present had it been one of
his many nymphet or homecoming queen protégées. "Are you
kidding me?" I'd screamed at Geoffrey. "*Lacey?* The woman is
enormous."

Enormous or not, Lacey lifted my husband quite handily.

Now, I couldn't help but compare my original attitude
toward Lacey to Clay's toward Walter. Clay had been so nice to
him, despite his role in Mia's condition: he welcomed Walter
by his wife's bedside, and never questioned his overly dis-
traught, grief-ridden demeanor. I myself had included Lacey in
party plans and dinner invitations. How she must have laughed
at me—offering her leftovers, loaning her books and scarves
and CDs—while she disguised her salacious relationship with
all those extra pounds of flesh.

By the time they discharged Mia from the hospital, more than
a month after the accident, Mom and Dad had already returned
to their respective homes. Mia gave me a list of things she
wanted from her house. I felt a sisterly duty to help her, regardless of my disapproval, but I was astonished by her list.

"Mia," I said. "There's no kid stuff here."

"I don't need any," Mia said. "Clay's taking the kids."

"For now?"

"Probably forever," she said breezily. "I think they'll be
happier with him. Don't you?"

I stared at her. With the wire removed from her jaw, Mia
looked approximately like herself in a spooky way—her left

cheekbone just slightly higher than the right. No scars at all, but she had lost an enormous amount of weight. As she folded pajamas that were now several sizes too big into an overnight bag, it was impossible to look at her without being conscious of her bones—pointing through the skin of her elbows, wrists, and knees. Her old jeans, which had been snug, hung off her hips like something borrowed from a burly boyfriend.

"What about your cats?" I asked her.

"Walter doesn't like cats," Mia said.

I took a mental inventory of Mia's cats and children—as if her assignment of all those ill-fated namesakes had foreshadowed this appalling abandonment. "Mia," I said. "Are you telling me that you're just deserting your husband, your pets, and your *three beautiful children* for a man who's obviously gay?"

"What do you mean?" She zipped up her bag and sat on the bed, drained from the effort of folding and packing.

I raised my eyebrows, and Mia laughed. "Believe me," she said. "Walter is not gay."

I raised my hand in a please-don't-tell-me gesture. "He's a man, Mia," I said. "A gender famous for having sex with sheep. Plastic blow-up dolls. He doesn't have to be heterosexual to have sex with you."

"Look, Natalie," Mia said. "If you're not going to help, then just don't. I can get the stuff myself."

"Sure," I said. "It will give you a chance to see your children." I had a vision of my sweet sister when I'd stepped on that rusty nail. She'd rushed over with all three children, carrying Deirdre in a Snugli at her chest. She'd assigned Oscar and Juliette age-appropriate tasks to keep them busy; and she'd washed out my foot with touching gentleness, wrapping it cleanly and expertly, moving with such grace that her baby in tow seemed just an extension of her body.

"Mia," I pleaded. "Think about what you're doing. This is not you."

She didn't reply, just closed her suitcase and snapped it shut. I tossed her list onto the bed and tried to leave the hospital room, but bumped into Walter in the doorway. I took a second to glare at him, and noticed that his clothes—baggy corduroys, faded Rockports, and a handsomely frayed Shetland sweater—were exactly right for collecting an illicit lover from the hospital.

"Don't worry," Walter said to me, as I tried to storm by him. "I'll take good care of her."

Mia stared at Walter with that dreamy, emotionless gaze. Like someone who'd been hypnotized. I had to remind myself that their relationship had started before her trip through the windshield, that it was not purely the result of trauma and lost brain cells.

"Look at her," Walter said, a similarly vacant film glazing his eyes. "Isn't she beautiful?"

I looked back at my sister. A funny stardust light gathered under the fluorescent ceiling bulbs, illuminating the uncombed frizz of her hair like a halo. She looked strangely electric, and I had to agree with Walter.

But not aloud. I elbowed past him and marched myself down the sterile, muted hospital corridor.

11. Abelard

Of course it astounded me most that Mia would abandon her children—one of whom, Deirdre, was in that best developing phase, just starting to talk and be her own unique self. But I also couldn't believe Mia would desert her cats. It was one thing when she thought Clay would be at the house taking care of everybody. But two weeks into their separation—when it became clear that this was not coma-induced dementia but the new structure of their lives—Clay announced he would not stay in our family's home. When he said that he would of course take his children but the cats were Mia's problem, she employed her new approach to all responsibility: she shrugged it off.

"Remember the Just So Story?" she said to me. "It doesn't matter where the cats go, really. One house is as good as another."

"Mia," I said, annoyed that she would use that story to justify herself. "These are your pets."

"How much of a pet can a cat really be?" Mia replied. "Remember how the cat walks? 'Through the Wet Wild Woods, waving his wild tale, and walking by his wild lone.' That's the thing. Cats will accept what comfort they can get, but when it comes down to it, they'll always take care of themselves."

I wasn't about to let my mother's house be overrun with Mia's confused, abandoned cats. And I couldn't entreat Clay, who had more than his share to deal with. So I collected them myself. I gave Persephone to the astrologer at my magazine. I brought Icarus and Ophelia to Boston, to Mark's, and he gave them to coworkers. Icarus, I heard, settled in nicely with a family in Newton. But Ophelia escaped from her North End apartment, never to be found. After Cape Cod, the city must have felt like another planet, and I had the saddest image of her wandering through foreign streets, rummaging in the Dumpsters of Italian restaurants, trying to find her way back to Mia, who, she had no way of knowing, had for all feline purposes ceased to exist.

I took Heloise and Abelard—not that they were the pair their names would imply. Both neutered in this instance, Heloise had no use for Abelard, and vice versa. They kept to opposite ends of the house, not disliking each other but showing a decidedly unromantic indifference. Heloise had been Mia's first cat, predating all the children. Fat and docile, Heloise made the move to my house splendidly, not even bothered by my dog Scout. Having no interest in going outside, Heloise tamped a permanent nest for herself in my down comforter, where she'd spend the day, staring out to sea as if waiting for some lost sailor to return. And the night, purring loudly at the pleasure of my company.

Abelard was another story altogether, both in his transition to my house and his mysterious origins. A stray who one day just appeared, Abelard started out half-feral, and remained so with everyone except for Mia. No matter how many years he lived in the same house with Clay, he still fled at sudden movements, and he never went near strangers, or any of the children.

But Abelard loved Mia. He shadowed her on and off during the day, jumping in and out of the window she left open for the cats, always watching for the rare moment when Mia's lap would be free. Then he'd leap into it, suddenly completely tame, purring with rapt, creaky ecstasy. He would rub his face against hers with the most obvious adoration—particularly sweet because he'd lavish it on her alone. I couldn't believe Mia would leave him behind.

Neither, apparently, could Abelard. He paced my house like a caged panther, yowling intermittently throughout the day and night, waking me at intervals like a newborn infant. When Abelard first found Mia, he'd been sleek and rangy. Now, although he still moved with that stealthy, jungle-cat grace, years of ready access to food had given him a gently swaying paunch. In daylight his coat looked washed with a sooty brown tint. But at night Abelard looked deeply black— so dark, the only discernable features on his face were his startlingly round eyes, which generally registered frantic distrust when turned on me. Once, long before leaving her children and cats, Mia told me that ancient Egyptians believed cats stored sunlight in their eyes. "That's why they see so well at night," she said, pointing out Abelard's unearthly iridescent eyes.

"Just give him some time," Mia said now, when I told her of her once beloved cat's misery. "He'll get used to you."

If I pleaded, Mia would dispense terse caretaking instructions for cats over the phone—but she never came by, to visit me or them. There really wasn't much advice Mia could give to help Abelard, whom I didn't want to let outside. "That's ridiculous," Mia said. "The cat was a stray. Who knows how long he survived on his own? What do you think's going to happen?"

I ignored her and kept him in. Abelard was so obviously waiting to bolt to parts unknown. As long as he was inside, I at least knew that he was safe.

Clay carried his new burdens with stoic forgiveness. He rarely said a negative word about Mia, was in fact more inclined to make derogatory comments about himself as a husband. "I guess I was kind of boring," Clay told me one evening, when he picked up the kids from my house. "Mia missed out on a lot of romance. I guess Walter gives that to her."

Before Mia and Walter became a couple, Clay had thought, like all of us, that Walter was gay. But afterward, he never breathed a single aspersion toward Walter's preferences. This impressed me immensely, particularly given my own experience with cuckoldry and divorce. When Geoffrey left me, I had spewed and railed against him endlessly. And "obese" was the least of the words I'd assigned to Lacey.

But Clay wouldn't allow himself to descend to that level. Instead he organized his life. He moved into a small house on a busy street in Scargo—less expensive than our cloistered neighborhood, which was so seldom traveled, I could leave Scout outside, untethered. Clay consolidated his hours at the bank to four days a week. He put Juliette and Deirdre in the same morning preschool, and he pulled Oscar out of his private Waldorf school and enrolled him midterm in public first grade. Before making this switch, he changed Oscar's name to Jake. "The poor kid's had enough to bear," Clay said. "He's going to start a new school with a clean slate and a normal name."

With Clay as primary caretaker, the fanciful chaos that had ruled the children's life seemed to vanish. He had specific and unbending rules, which the children would recite with novel glee. "No sugar before dinner," Juliette told me, faintly incredulous, turning her little nose up at a Popsicle. Clay's new house was clean and orderly. "It's so much easier to find things," Juliette said. "Mommy's house was always such a mess."

Mia and I each took care of the kids two afternoons a week, dividing up the days Clay worked. I was amazed by the change in Oscar—or Jake, as he himself was quick to remind me. "It's Jake now," he'd say, with palpable relief. When he arrived at my house Jake would scoop Heloise into his lap, his cheeks rosy with the glow of normality. "Nobody teases me at this school," he told me, pushing his glasses up on his nose. "It's really working out." He'd throw his backpack—full of appropriate school material—into a corner, then play with his little sisters, or curl himself on the couch with Heloise and a book several times above his expected reading level. Sometimes he'd help me with my column, either by choosing a letter or recalling something sweet Juliette or Deirdre had done. I'd never imagined a child could so obviously flourish in the voluntary absence of his mother. It was almost as if with Mia, the children had absorbed and emulated her chaotic, emotional style. With her gone, there was no reward for misery and gushing tears. They could heave aside romantic disorder in favor of neat rooms, tightly run schedules, and general contentment. Everything exactly where it belonged—with the seeming exception of Mia.

. . .

Living in Walter's one-bedroom apartment over the Scargo ice cream parlor, which was closed for the off-season, Mia seemed a ghost of her former self—but a happy ghost. Initially her new life confounded me. It seemed to revolve exclusively around Walter. He had lost his driver's license in his post-accident plea bargain; Mia decided not to get a job so she'd be free to drive him to and from work. Because she couldn't afford new clothes ("I'll probably just gain the weight back, anyway"), she wore her old ones cinched and belted—hanging and draping off her bony figure in a strangely flattering way.

She used Walter as a blanket excuse for all her actions. When I implored her to take Abelard, she shrugged helplessly and said, "Walter doesn't think cats belong in the house."

"But he's pining for you," I begged.

"It's the whole litter box issue," she sighed. "Walter says they're crawling with disease."

When Clay asked Mia to give Juliette's fourth birthday party, she said that ever since the accident, groups of children gave Walter headaches. "Walter's tired of taking care of things," Mia explained to me later.

"What has Walter ever taken care of?" I asked.

"Oh, you know," she answered, waving her hand vaguely. "Things."

Slowly I realized: "Walter" was her new code word for "Mia." At first I assumed Mia had decided to leave Clay and the children because she imagined herself overtaken with a new and greater love. But on speculation, I realized I'd never heard her say this. In fact, Mia didn't see a whole lot of Walter, who worked long hours at the hotel. The drive back and forth to his work amounted to the bulk of their time together. Other than the two afternoons with her children and occasional visits

from me, Mia—after years of immersion among living things—
spent most of her time alone.

One chilly morning, heading out of autumn and toward
winter, Mia and I took Scout for a walk along Scargo Beach.
While Scout joyfully herded shorebirds and waves, Mia admitted that if it hadn't been for the accident, she probably would
not have left Clay.

"I think the thing with Walter would have just come and
gone," she said. She huddled in her winter coat, more affected
by the cold now that she'd lost her body fat. "No one would
have known, and when it ended life would have just gone back
the way it was. Before, I don't think I could have stood leaving
Clay, because of what people would say. What people would
think of a mother leaving her children." She pushed her hair
behind her ears and squinted toward the ocean. "It's funny,"
she said. "Things don't really bother me since the accident. I
think about the sexual things I said in the hospital, and I don't
mind at all. The old me, before the accident, would have been
mortified."

We climbed up on the jetty. Scout jumped down and
splashed through the water. A little way out on a cluster of
rocks, three fat seals rolled off their lazy perch and into the water. Their dark, big-eyed heads bobbed, observing curiously,
waiting for us to leave.

"I've been feeling like a child lately," Mia said. "For instance right now. I'm completely enjoying this moment. I'm
not worrying about Oscar at school, or whether Deirdre's getting toilet trained fast enough, or whether some cat has peed in
a corner. I'm just thinking about how beautiful it is out here,
how quiet. I feel the same way when I'm with my kids. I can
just enjoy them, and understand them. I think it makes me a
better mother."

"You think living in a different home and spending two

afternoons a week with your children makes you a better mother?"

"Well," she said. "I'm happier spending time with them. It's not out of obligation anymore. Now I really feel joy when I see them. And they seem happier. Don't they?"

I had to admit they did. Mia smiled, languorously serene. In her huge clothes, with her lank hair and makeup-less face, she should have looked wan and unbeautiful. But she didn't, any more than the eel grass—faded to wheat after its summertime green, but catching the sunlight just the same.

That night the wind kicked up fiercely. These were the times I still hated Geoffrey: alone in the dark on my wind-battered bluff, everything extraordinary about my house suddenly frightening. Last winter, on a night like this I would have walked down the road to Mia's. Now I cursed both my sister and my ex-husband as the lights flickered.

I walked into the kitchen to search for candles. The room went black for almost a full minute while I reached into the silverware drawer and fumbled for wax amidst the metal. When the lights came back on I turned, facing the window, and let out a startled gasp. Abelard sat on the sill, as utterly dark as the room had been. Against the blackened window, his outline was barely visible except for his round green eyes, which seemed to hang in the air like the Cheshire cat's smile.

Abelard thumped down and floated to the kitchen door, letting out a yowl so plaintive and mournful, it turned my spine to velvet.

I never would have let Heloise out on a night like this. But Abelard in that moment seemed perfectly suited to winds and ravages. Darkness and wildness: his origins, his homeland. So I opened the door. Watching his tail poof and disappear into the night, I felt a strange amalgam of admiration and dread.

. . .

The lights restored themselves uneventfully, but my sleep was restless. I kept waking to listen for Abelard. Several times I went downstairs, opened the door, and called his name. The wind howled reproachfully, like a moving force field the cat couldn't possibly cross.

"You give the cat too much credit," Mia said the next morning, when I called to report his disappearance. "And then you sell him short. There's nothing emotional about him wandering off. It's territorial. Meanwhile, he's perfectly capable of catching mice and so forth. If he gets hungry—if he has half a brain—he'll find his way back to your house."

"So in the meantime, what am I supposed to do?"

"Just don't worry about it."

But I did. I worried throughout the day, so much that I tried to distract myself by starting my column early. As I read insipid letters about first teeth, Santa Claus, and thirty-fifth wedding anniversaries, I kept an ear cocked toward the door. But no sound.

In the afternoon, when the children arrived, Jake—formerly Oscar—suggested walking by the old house to look for Abelard. "Don't worry," Jake reassured me as I loaded Deirdre into her stroller. "Abelard is one tough cat."

Juliette took my hand, and Jake led the way. He walked ahead of us, calling for Abelard and making meow sounds. He looked like a little man, very confident and in charge. I felt a small, involuntary pang. Sometimes it seemed like Jake was a completely different person—assertively taking the place of dear, neurotic little Oscar.

When we rounded the bend, Deirdre gave a little whoop of joy at the sight of her old house. There sat Abelard, comfortably settled in a patch of sunlight near the fence. He stood at the sight of us—this little army from his past—and hesitated, deciding whether he felt pleased or displeased by the reunion.

Abelard bristled, in the same lazy, obligatory way the seals had rolled off their rocks. By the time I parked Deirdre's stroller away from the street, he'd bolted into the bushes.

"There," Jake said in his clipped, precocious way. "You see, Natalie? He's perfectly all right."

We walked back through the marina so the kids could look at the boats. Jake identified various fishing boats for me and the girls, but I only half listened. The sight of Abelard, whole and healthy but wild and alone, had filled me with an odd combination of consternation and relief.

Back at my house, Jake and I made coq au vin. "Yuk," Juliette admonished, pointing at our block of salt pork. We ignored her, and at six o'clock, when Clay came to collect the kids, we had just lowered it to a fatty simmer. Deirdre lay asleep on the couch, Juliette watched a video. Clay poured himself a scotch and sank down next to Deirdre, stroking the soft perfection of her two-year-old cheek.

At dinner, Clay and I drank half a bottle of wine. Over the children's heads, we spoke in broken code about our respective divorces. "Sometimes," Clay said, "I still feel B-L-A-M-E, and self-righteousness. Other times, I feel like I've been given this gift, to start from the beginning, to . . . I don't know, to be a person who . . ." He glanced around the table cautiously. Jake listened to every word with alarming intensity. "You know what I mean," Clay said.

I did. I felt it too sometimes, that strange happiness, though I'd have been loath to admit it when my divorce was new. The feeling at night, suddenly stretching diagonally across a queen-sized bed; or just before leaving the house, automatically searching for pen and paper to jot down my whereabouts, and realizing with great liberation that I didn't need to.

But other times—like that night, after Clay left: the small bits of freedom paled in comparison to the emptiness of a house—an emptiness whose surface even the jingle of Scout's collar and the hum of Heloise's purr couldn't scratch. I kept thinking of Abelard, picking himself out of the sunshine to escape from me and the children, his own family. The image of loneliness, of misguided independence, made me too antsy to sleep. I pulled on my coat and walked in my slippers down the road.

Stepping outside, I felt embraced by crisp, frigid air and the sound of the fulminating ocean. The low-tide stench of salt and skate egg thinned to a vague perfume against the dry-leafed chill. I remembered one of Mia's stories: a black cat saves a woman by telling her that late-night hours belong to fairy people, who become angry when mortals invade their time. But I felt strangely protected. Heading to my childhood home, passing the other locked and vacated summer houses, my steps were buoyant with melancholy freedom.

The spot where Abelard had been that afternoon now stood empty of both cat and sunlight. Calling him, I circled the house twice, peering under the porch and into the bushes—as if I could possibly have seen that sooty black cat against the night's cover.

From the marina, boat masts chimed their haunting, wind-driven music. As I walked by, I saw a feline specter saunter across the dimly lit parking lot. I matched my footsteps to his, and slunk to the edge of the lot, where I whispered his name.

He stopped, curious, visibly assessing the situation and weighing his options. I sat down on a stack of old pilings, and Abelard came to me—a gesture of courtesy, fulfilling his obligation toward an acquaintance on a dark night. He climbed up beside me to sit, alert and companionable.

Then I pounced on him. I scooped him into my arms, pinned him against my chest, and gathered the scruff of his neck into my fist. Surprisingly, he didn't make any noticeable protest—no noise, not even much of a squirm. I started the walk toward home.

Every yard or so, Abelard tried to twist himself out of my arms and I would tighten my grip, my breath quickening. I walked with an irrational sense of urgency, determined not to let go, no matter how much he wriggled. By the time I got him inside my house and dropped him to the floor, my arms were so tight I could barely unfold my elbows. I shook them vigorously and heard Abelard from the kitchen, alighting to his bowl on the counter and crunching into his food. I felt great relief that he didn't seem traumatized to be back. And I felt heroic—for having captured and carried him in my arms all the way home.

Later, in bed, I awoke to a brush of fur and bone against my face. I thought at first it was Heloise. But when I opened my eyes I could tell—by the fact that I could hardly see him in the dark, and by the unaccustomed rotor of his purr—that it was Abelard.

"You know," Mia said a few days later, when we took the kids to an exhibition at the Model Train Club. "I always left a window open for my cats. Even in the winter, I let them come and go as they pleased. A cat's nature is nocturnal and independent. There's something violent about what you do. Locking them in the house at night, always keeping track of where they are."

"I'm trying to be responsible," I said. "Taking care of *your* cats."

"They're your cats now," Mia said. "I'm only trying to

help." She ran a finger across a miniature track as an engine approached, and shivered. "Ooh. A little shock." She drew her finger back and shook it. "Jake," she called, decidedly nonmaternal. "Check this out."

On the drive home, the kids crowded in back, an alert Jake perched between Juliette and Deirdre, who slept in their car seats. Mia rolled down her window, letting in a cold, salty gust. Jake yelped in protest. "Sorry," she said. "But I'm going to miss the clean ocean air. I always think this is the best time of year here."

"Miss it?" I said. "Why would you miss it?"

"Didn't I tell you? Walter and I are moving to New York."

If it hadn't been for the kids, I would have pulled over. I would have grabbed her by her collar and shaken her so that her skinny bones rattled in her billowy clothes.

"Mia," I said instead, forcing calm into my voice. "How can you possibly move to New York?"

"Walter got a job at a hotel in Gramercy Park," she told me. "I'm really excited about it."

I cast a desperate glance toward the backseat.

"Oh, it's all right," Mia said. "They already know."

I turned into the parking lot of Millstone Liquors and turned off the ignition, my hands trembling. "What are you doing?" Mia asked. "Do you need to pick something up?"

"What am I doing? What am *I* doing?" I could hear my voice rise to a hysteria reminiscent of Geoffrey's and my breakup. "You can't go to New York," I said, feeling like I might cry, but battling against it in deference to the children. Mia just sat, her face blank as usual, crossing her arms heartlessly in front of her chest. From the backseat, Jake leaned forward and put his little hand on my shoulder. "It's all right, Natalie," he said. "She'll come to visit. New York's not that far away."

"Four and a half hours by car," Mia sang cheerfully. "Do you want me to drive home?"

"You have three little children," I whispered. "You have a husband."

"*Had* a husband," Mia corrected me. "And the children will be fine."

"We will," Jake reassured me. Behind his glasses, his eyes were wide—not with anxiety, but with pleasure at his role as consoler. "We'll be just fine, Natalie. Walter's going to show us the Statue of Liberty. You can walk all the way to the top."

I started the engine and pulled back onto the road. Mia dug a sodden lump of Kleenex out of her pocket and offered it to me—a pale echo of her old, motherly gestures. "No thank you," I said. And then added, in a vicious whisper, "I don't see how you can do this."

"I don't see why you care so much," Mia said. She rolled down the window again, the gust making all of us—even Deirdre and Juliette, in their sleep—shiver with the sudden chill.

"To tell you the truth, it's kind of a relief," Clay said over our next dinner. Jake and I had made eggplant Parmesan. "This way, everything will be more cut-and-dried. I won't have to see her all the time. Not to mention W-A-L-T-E-R."

"Well," I said. "If it's any consolation, every time I see him, I think she must be . . . you know . . . to have done this whole thing."

"Thanks," Clay said. "I always thought the same of Geoffrey."

We clinked wineglasses. Clay looked older these days, like someone who knew the world a little better. And I felt a deep kinship with him—deeper, really, than anything I'd felt toward Mia in the last few months. So much so that I didn't say a word when, as Jake and I cleared the table, Clay opened the door and let Abelard out into the night.

"Daddy," Juliette scolded. "Natalie doesn't let Abelard outside."

"That's all right," I said quickly. "I'm sure he'll be fine." I reached out and touched Clay's hand, absolving him.

Abelard did not return that night, or the next, or the night after that.

"You've got it all wrong," Mia said, in response to my frantic phone call. "You think the cat *needs* you. But to him, you're just a luxury. The warm house, the canned food, the kibble. It's all nice, but it's all expendable."

Mia's coldhearted comfort did nothing to convince me. In the next week I spent a lot of time walking—from my house to Mom's, through the marina, into the back yards of surrounding homes. Every squirrel or rabbit's rustle infused me with hope. All night long I listened for the sound of a cat begging entry.

Meanwhile, there was Heloise: perfectly nonproblematic, lounging comfortably, staring out to sea, accepting affection and food whenever it was offered. And Scout, who would bound out the door but stick close to the house, completely reliable, delighted to be a pet in that pure dog way, brimming with love. Both these animals profoundly tame. Despite their presence, Abelard somehow occupied me more: my odd sense of culpability for his fate—combined with an exquisite vision of his nocturnal travels, and his effortless passage through the night.

After ten days I gave up my walks; but periodically I would drive by the house, slowing in case I glimpsed him emerging from the bushes. And one afternoon, there he sat—in his old patch of sunlight, his tail twitching. His household paunch vanished, he looked like the same rangy self he'd been the day he first appeared to Mia.

I pulled into the driveway and got out of the car stealthily, leaving the door open, not making any loud noises or sudden movements. Abelard stared, unblinking. As I approached, he stood and stretched. I bent to pet him and he arched into my palm—happy to see me, not protesting as I collected him in my arms, carried him down the hill, and deposited him inside my car. Driving home, I felt the same triumphant euphoria of his last capture.

Scout greeted us as we pulled into the driveway. I picked up Abelard and stepped out of the car, kicking the door shut behind me. At the sight of the dog, Abelard became an electric package of fur, bristling and squirming out from my grasp.

I should have grabbed him by the scruff of the neck. Better yet, I should have just let go—Scout wouldn't have hurt him, and Abelard might have dashed into the house for safety's sake. But instead I tried to cling, with the same senseless clutch I'd used carrying him home from the marina. The cat transformed into a near-liquid being, slithering up toward my shoulder, trying to give himself leverage for a leap out of my arms, which I tightened around his shrunken middle.

Abelard struggled his upper body free just enough to turn on me. In the instant it became clear to him that I would not release my grip, he sunk his teeth and both front claws into the back of my skull. I heard his hind claws ripping my jacket— thankfully thick enough to protect my chest. I let him go.

An odd film rolled in my head, an outward vision of the incident—how chaotic and preposterous it must have looked, the cat turning so suddenly vicious, employing its every weapon against me. Scout jumped up to lick my face, but I pushed her away and ran toward the house. When I opened the door, Abelard scooted over the threshold and disappeared underneath a chair.

I left Scout barking outside and fled to the bathroom. My face looked stucco-white, and I felt an odd sense of shock—alternating between nausea and dizziness. As if my body were composed of pixels rather than flesh and blood. I couldn't see the wound no matter how I tilted my head toward the mirror, but when I pressed my palm to the curve of my skull, it came down wet with blood.

"Jesus Christ," Mia said. We stood together in the bathroom, me leaning over the sink, Mia parting my hair so she could assess the damage. She'd arrived within minutes of my phone call, and when she walked through the door, I realized it was the first time since her accident I'd seen my sister's new self in an old place. My mind flooded with visions of other times she'd been in my house: the former, larger Mia, surrounded by children. I wanted to sit her down, to feed her, to keep her.

"Does it hurt?" she asked. And though it did hurt—in an achy, puncturing way—the worst part was feeling assaulted. By the cat, whom I'd been trying to help. By this woman, this girlish slip of a woman, who'd taken over my dear and predictable sister.

Mia rinsed out a washcloth and pressed it against my head. "You should really see a doctor," she said.

"Just clean it out," I said impatiently. "My tetanus shot is up-to-date. We know he doesn't have rabies. Let's just clean it out and try to forget about it."

"I wish you could see it," Mia said. "Remember that myth about Japanese vampires and cats? That's exactly what this looks like. Two deep little puncture wounds—a vampire bite. And all these scratches. He really savaged you."

"To tell you the truth," I told her, "I feel savaged more on an emotional level."

Mia laughed. "You would," she said.

I watched her at work in the mirror, cleaning out my injury with her old expertise, using hydrogen peroxide and Neosporin, gently affixing a gauze bandage and then covering it all up by pulling my hair back into a ponytail. "We should clean this out again tomorrow," Mia said. She handed me three Tylenol tablets and a glass of water, and we walked into the living room. Abelard's tail twitched on the rug from underneath the chair.

"What am I going to do with that cat?" I asked my sister.

She shrugged. "Forget about him. Or keep him anyway. What else can you do?"

Then Mia did something she hadn't done in the longest time: she held out her arms. I collapsed, my head pressed into her bony neck, her slender arms wrapped around me. And I cried like a girl from one of Mia's fairy tales. As though my heart would break.

Later, after Mia had gone and dusk had fallen, Scout had resigned herself to the back stoop, and Heloise lay curled up in the easiest easy chair. The wind raged outside—the kind of night when indoors felt especially in: safe and warm and sealed. Abelard emerged from his hiding place and slunk to the front door. He didn't make a vocal request, just placed himself at the threshold and looked back to me.

If I didn't open the door, but insisted on confining him, the cat would eventually find some way out. Up through the chimney, like the King of the Cats. Or maybe he would transform into a different sort of creature—a vampire, walking out on human legs. While I wreaked the havoc owed someone who battles against what's best left to fate and nature.

I lifted myself, still feeling battered, and walked obediently to the door. Abelard slipped outside, noiseless, his form black as coal, black as ebony, black as black can be. I watched him disappear into the bleak, gusty, salt-scented night. Not believing, really, in any force beyond the tangible, the detectable, the visible.

But still. I couldn't help but notice, despite the glow from my porch light, and all the silhouettes cast by surrounding trees: the cat proceeding into the wild, without even the company of his shadow.

stealing baby's breath

Leafing through the paper one morning, deep into her own uneventful pregnancy, deeper still into her own happy marriage, Amelia sees an ad in the classifieds, in the pet section, accompanied by a photograph of a startled long-haired cat. She can tell, despite the black-and-white reproduction, that the flash caught the animal's eyes and turned them red:

> *Beloved family pet needs new home.*
> *Patches is thirteen years old, declawed,*
> *very loving and affectionate. We must give*
> *Patches up, because we're expecting a baby*
> *and he has shown signs of jealousy.*

"Look at this," Amelia says to Chris, her husband. She slides the paper across the breakfast table.

Chris puts his near-empty cereal bowl next to his feet. This is the only way of enticing their cat Bast to set foot on the floor. She prefers traveling from the top of high kitchen cabinets to pieces of furniture to windowsills to mantels—propelling her feather-light form above, rather than upon, such mundane surfaces as wood floors and carpets. Nowhere to be seen seconds earlier, Bast floats down from somewhere to lap away milk. Chris leans forward to look at the paper. He is a broad, athletic man, and Amelia enjoys any excuse to watch him—like now, with his dark head bent, his eyes obediently skimming. The kitchen window faces west, offering up pale-gold autumn and the Rockies' spectacular front range; but to Amelia the mountains pale compared to the view across the table, the sight and form of her husband.

"Please," Chris tells her. "Don't get any ideas. This house will be full enough very soon."

"I know," Amelia says. "It's just so heartless. People who would name a cat Patches, declaw it, then give it away after thirteen years. People like that should not be allowed to reproduce." She does not add that yesterday she found Bast curled up in the new bassinet—making herself comfortable on the handwoven baby blankets—but inwardly wonders if this constitutes an expression of prenatal jealousy.

The baby kicks, a downward jab toward her bladder. Amelia struggles to her feet, wincing, and says, "Caroline's a little hostile this morning."

They know it's a girl and have already named her. "Why pretend we're living in a different century?" Amelia said, after the second or third sonogram, and Chris agreed: waiting until the birth to find out the baby's sex seemed pretentious. And knowing the baby is a girl—referring to her by name—makes her seem already a person: Caroline, loved and specific, a member of the nuclear family they've created together.

As Amelia waddles toward the bathroom, Chris retrieves the cereal bowl and strokes Bast. "Not to worry," Amelia hears him tell the cat. "Your position in this household is safe."

· · ·

Every morning until Caroline is born, Amelia flips to the classifieds to see if the ad still runs. And it does, right up until her caesarian, and four days in the hospital. Two weeks at home when even with the help of her mother, who flies in from Connecticut, Amelia feels too battered and overwhelmed to think about showering, let alone reading the newspaper. When she finally gets around to checking, Patches is no longer advertised. Amelia wishes she'd kept the phone number, or memorized it. So she could call, and ask: Did you find a new home for your cat? Or have a change of heart? Or did you simply hand your "beloved" cat over to the animal shelter and probable euthanasia?

Amelia would never part with Bast, not under any circumstances. She and Chris named her after the Egyptian cat goddess, and the cat conducts herself accordingly, with a deity's confidence and sense of entitlement. Amelia can tell that somewhere in Bast's illicit lineage there was a Siamese: she is spare and weightless, with pale blue eyes against a grayish-white coat. She is regal, demanding, and insistent—forgetting or dismissing her Humane Society origins. Windows must be left open, food must be shared. No preventative measures can be taken against the prey—alive and dead—that she carries into the house, to eat or catch and release on occasionally dusted surfaces.

A secret part of Amelia admires those people, the former hosts of Patches, for being able to put themselves—their furniture, their offspring—first. They must be ruthless and meticulous, flossing daily and always removing the skin from chicken breasts. Amelia imagines the mother decorating a nursery: wearing darling maternity clothes and an expectant glow. Hanging colorful mobiles, and hand-embroidered portraits of Humpty-Dumpty and Mother Goose.

Amelia wants things to be nice for the baby, but can't attempt perfection. She doesn't believe in happy childhoods.

Childhood, in Amelia's experience, is a time of groping uncertainty—of confusion and dependence, a vehicle with inoperable brakes and steering wheel. Happiness comes later, with adulthood and the mastery of proper controls.

Before Caroline's birth, Amelia wore Chris's clothes around the house, sleeves and pant legs thickly cuffed. Her pregnancy was not planned. When it first made itself apparent, she felt, on some level, assaulted. "I can't stand something of this enormity being sprung on me," she confided to her friend Erin, a busy doctor and the mother of two little boys. At thirty-two, Amelia did not have all the time in the world, but she did have time. She hadn't decided whether she wanted to have children at all—let alone whether she wanted to have them *now*.

There were earlier days, of traveling, of dreadfully little money, when including a baby would have been simply inhumane. For three years before they married and moved to town—while Amelia went to art school and Chris waited tables at the Harvest Restaurant—they lived in the mountains, in a house up Left Hand Canyon. A secluded place whose aging absentee landlord charged a ridiculously low rent, the house was idyllic in the summer. Chris and Amelia pulled their secondhand mattress onto the long, screened-in porch, which sat yards away from a burbling mountain creek. They would fall asleep wrapped around each other, listening to the water's restful music. Amelia loved waking up on that porch: sunlight pouring through the screen like a thousand tiny spotlights, the creek singing and her forehead pulsing with delicious heat— the flip side of fever, a euphoric clarity.

But the house hadn't been built for winter habitation. Once the high-altitude cold swept in, staying warm became a full-time occupation. Chris bought and installed an old woodstove, but he never got the draft right: the room filled with smoke whenever they opened it. Their hair and clothes always smelled thickly of wood fire, the scent following Amelia to school and Chris to work. Amelia kept a stool handy so she could remove the battery from the smoke alarm, whose high-pitched alert became as familiar a sound as the telephone ringing. Even with their constant vigilance, the woodstove heated the house unevenly. Amelia complained of perpetual cold. She used to daydream about warmth the way a starving person must about food.

Bast lived her kittenhood in the mountain house, and during those winters they could precisely determine the warmest spot in the house by the location of her curled, snoozing form. Perhaps the Left Hand Canyon house was the origin of Bast's fondness for heights. She may have learned an aversion to cold ground, chasing instead the rising arc of heat.

No, they could not have had a baby then. But now: Chris's job in Denver, as a technical writer, carried excellent insurance. Amelia had regular work as a bookbinder. The rare-book store where she clerked gladly gave her time off, promising to send restoration work her way. She had ample equipment to work from home, including a seven-foot standing press and the smaller nipping press, both from the late 1800s and made of solid cast iron—prized and useful antiques. Two weeks before Amelia's due date, Chris moved the presses out of her study and into the living room to make room for the baby: everything prepared and organized with time to spare. They were adults, already married two years. Financially secure, emotionally stable. So what if Amelia never exactly crossed the line, heard the chimes she imagined should ring, signaling that precise moment, indicating her own absolute readiness?

"If you wait for the perfect time to have children," advised Erin, who had breast-fed during her residency, "you're going to be waiting forever."

·   ·   ·

The birth was brutal, eight hours of hard labor culminating in an emergency caesarian. Fibroid tumors precluded an aesthetic bikini incision, leaving Amelia with a raised vertical scar screaming down the middle of her abdomen. She'd seen the movies and TV shows ad nauseam—even a film of an actual birth, years ago in a biology class. When they gave her Caroline (the false excitement in their exclamation "It's a girl," as if they hadn't already known) she was able in her painful fog to mimic the appropriate expression: of wonder, relief, joy. Of counting fingers and toes, cataloging miraculous health. My baby.

But staring at Caroline's scrunched and angry face, little fists balled in indignation, little mouth gaping and toothless (wanting something, everything, from her) Amelia searched for what she could recognize of herself or Chris. Finding nothing, she felt frightened and queasy. Not that she didn't love the baby. She did, instantly, a definite response, the knee jerking forward after a doctor's tap.

Still. There had been moments of discovery in Amelia's life, of recognizing her own potential for happiness and fulfillment: the time in high school when she won a statewide drawing competition. The first time she sold a book of her own design, her own printing and etchings. The time on a camping trip in Arizona when she and Chris decided to marry. Amelia knew that this meeting of Caroline, this first glimpse of her daughter's corporeal form, should number among these moments. How could she ever admit to anyone that it did not?

When Erin dropped by Amelia's hospital room in the midst of her rounds, she said the maternity nurses would offer to take Caroline to the nursery for the night. "But you don't have to," Erin said. "You can keep her with you."

Later, when the nurse came by, after Erin had left, and

Chris dozed in the bedside chair, Amelia handed Caroline over gratefully—feeling a slight but bearable trace of longing as she watched her new baby being carried away.

She reached out to touch Chris's sleeping hands, then closed her eyes and dropped her head into the pillows: not realizing these were the last moments of freedom she would ever have.

"I just feel so shitty," Amelia tells Chris on her third morning home. He hands her a Percocet and a glass of water. While Chris has already dressed and eaten breakfast, Amelia lies in bed. Her mother collected Caroline an hour ago, after the day's first feeding, saying, "Sleep while you can. You won't be able to when I'm gone."

Amelia has strict doctor's instructions not to walk up and down the stairs more than twice a day. This imprisons her in her bedroom and the nursery while her mother prepares meals and cleans the house, tends the endless loads of laundry, the continuing cycle of baby garments—blankets and burpies and onesies—all too cutely named, and soiled by leaky diapers that don't quite seem to fit. Any clothes touched by feces must be soaked and washed separately, first in a bucket of Clorox and then through the machine with special baby detergent. All the downstairs details weigh heavily in the midst of Amelia's physical upheaval. She feels trapped not only by her own wrecked body, but by this stream of urgent, infinite minutiae.

Bast sprawls out beside Amelia, one paw curved across her eyes to block out daylight as if she too is exhausted from tending the baby. Amelia can hear her mother cooing and singing in the hallway. Last night Caroline woke up four times to nurse. Each time, Amelia hauled her still-great bulk out of bed, irritating the fresh, aching wound of her belly. Post-delivery, she still experiences vaginal bleeding, her supply of hospital-grade sanitary napkins depleting rapidly. She is woefully constipated. It seems a cruel joke that Caroline should rely on such a hugely malfunctioning body. As Amelia struggles with breast-feeding (sore, cracked nipples, a tugging pain when Caroline sucks) she privately longs for her mother's era, her own infancy of formula and sterilized bottles.

"I just had major surgery," she says to Chris, after she swallows the painkiller. She indicates, as proof, the bouquet on her bureau sent by her father, an arrangement of rosebuds and baby's breath. "If you'd had your gall bladder removed on Tuesday, would you want to spend the weekend getting in and out of bed so a baby could suck on your breasts?"

Chris rests one hand on Bast and the other on Amelia's stomach—the way he did when she was pregnant. He looks entirely like his daily self in a coat and tie, and for the first time his appearance irritates Amelia: how inequitable that the journey to parenthood has left his physique so unscathed. Chris has no sutures in his belly, no excess weight imprisoning his original form. While Amelia is warned against the staircase, Chris can run and bike and hike—all the things they both did before Caroline, whose birth has rendered Amelia an indoor person, living almost exclusively within these walls. She longs to get outside again, alone: to climb Bear Peak, to run around the reservoir. Even to walk around the block. She pushes at Chris's arm. "Don't do that," she says. "It hurts. Anyway, there's nothing in there now. Nothing but fat."

"You're not fat," Chris says. "You're beautiful."

"Please," Amelia says. "Would you just go away now? Thank you, but please. Just go to work. I'll see you tonight."

"I'll have your mom bring Caroline in," Chris says. He kisses her forehead.

"She's such a good girl," her mother coos. Caroline nestles her head in a searching motion, rooting for a nipple. As her mother scoops the baby onto the bed, Amelia feels a surge of pride. Caroline is pretty and agreeable—easily quieted by holding or feeding. Burping as if by magic, responding almost immediately to the gentle thumps on her tiny back. Amelia runs her finger across the baby's forehead: soft skin, soft skull, soft smell, soft being. Examining the contours of Caroline's face, her fingers and form, her shortsighted eyes, seems endlessly fascinating to Amelia: activity enough to span hours and hours.

Her mother picks Bast up, off the bed, and drops her to the floor. The cat bristles, and alights in an instant to the bureau. There she remains throughout the morning, occasionally chewing on the flowers, but mostly staring down at Amelia and Caroline, her tail jerking with a restless, indignant twitch.

Amelia will never be able to take care of the baby with her mother's natural ease, and she will never look like herself again. She isn't sure which bothers her more. Her mother has always been reed-thin, and she used to torment the teenage Amelia— constantly commenting on her size, her food intake, her shape. As if her lack of moral fortitude, of human worth, could be measured by degrees of fat. Looking at old photographs, Amelia is angered and confused by this memory: the pictures evidence a smallish girl, round-faced and certainly not skinny, like her mother. But not heavy, not at all *fat*.

Now Amelia feels ruined, the peace she'd made with her body overturned—as if her mother's admonitions are finally justified. Huge, ungainly breasts. A stomach that looks just slightly less pregnant than before the delivery. Numbers on the scale she would have associated only with men. Years of sit-ups desecrated by nine months and one clean slice. Even the color of her stomach has changed, to gray and dimpled oatmeal, the coup de grâce being the hideous scar, raised and red and ravaging. Irretrievably marring that expanse of her body which had been, in retrospect, most beautiful: the barest cuppable bulge, rose-hued and silky. Since Caroline, it's like a huge package, a parcel that she carries with her wherever she goes. It sprawls into her lap when she sits.

When Amelia's father calls she speaks to him briefly, then hands the phone over to her mother—imagining that the voice in the other room is discussing her own distorted form. Amelia's mother has often boasted that after her two pregnancies, she returned home from the hospital weighing a mere five pounds over her starting point.

"I don't think these diapers are right for her," Amelia says to her mother later, changing Caroline to find that they've once again leaked onto her clothes—and the changing pad and the burpie, so they'll all need to be laundered. Amelia wonders how she'll ever be able to do this herself, once her mother leaves. "Are diapers like jeans?" she asks. "You have to try different brands before you find a good fit?"

Her mother laughs. "Oh, Amelia," she says, not in a way Amelia likes, but with a tone that emphasizes Amelia as novice and herself as seasoned expert. Then, as if proving this point, her mother nimbly moves aside as Caroline emits a projectile poop with startling gusto: spattering the opposite wall, the charming wicker baskets holding baby wipes and talcum powder. Amelia moves gingerly, still very conscious of her body's trauma. Uselessly she dabs a baby wipe at one of the baskets.

"You're not thinking of keeping that," her mother snaps. And then amends, with a nicer tone, "Those grooves are impossible. You'll have to throw it away."

Despite this scolding, Amelia feels a surge of warmth—watching her mother clean and diaper Caroline. She realizes, and appreciates, that as an infant she herself received identically loving, devoted care. But she also discovers a powerful sense of loss: how the same love and devotion drained away, diluted by complexity and personal failings, with each passing year of her childhood. Amelia had failed algebra. She'd loved art instead of business, cats instead of dogs. She'd chosen the West over the East, denim over silk. She'd gained five pounds and forgotten to comb her hair. She'd disappointed in myriad ways on myriad levels—changing from an open-book baby into a flawed, specific person whom her mother had difficulty recognizing.

Especially during the first few years of her marriage, but sometimes even now, Amelia has recurring nightmares of losing Chris—his love, his companionship, his favor. Watching her mother's pure adoration for Caroline, she understands the root of these dreams: Chris's love for her echoes the unconditional acceptance Amelia must have had as an infant. Her nightmares reflect the fear that Chris too will discover her—as awkward, cowardly, or inept—and love once again will melt away.

Amelia's love for her own infant is like a muscle, an internal organ, that operates as independently as her liver and kidneys. Will that change as Caroline grows into her own separate entity? Will Amelia learn to disapprove of, or dislike, her daughter's characteristics, her habits, her tastes?

Sometimes at night, stunned by exhaustion, Amelia will sit while Caroline vigorously drains the last bit of energy from her body. The baby sleeps in Amelia and Chris's bedroom, but to nurse—so Chris can sleep—Amelia takes Caroline out of her crib and carries her into the makeshift nursery, formerly her studio. Tearing herself away from the warmth of Chris's sleeping form—after a mere hour or two of sleep for herself—is a painful business. Before the baby, Amelia would lean into Chris when she stirred in the night, pressing her cheek into his until he groaned in contented protest. She remembers how sleep intensified with the two of them together—their undercover world of radiating heat and subconscious companionship. Now that she is tuned in to the baby, sleep has become a lonesome and sporadic occupation. Sometimes, sitting in the rocking chair with Caroline nursing, Amelia feels so overcome with weariness that she slams her fist against the wall in frustration—startling the household and the calming baby.

Then Bast appears, on top of the changing table. The cat swats at the colorless faces on the mobile, and chatters complaints that Amelia's lap is full of Caroline. "You shouldn't let that cat in the baby's room," her mother has admonished. And she's right: twice, Amelia has found Bast snoozing in Caroline's empty bassinet. And she's noticed the barest track of kitty litter on the changing table. During her pregnancy, Amelia was violently warned against kitty litter—the risk of toxemia, of staph infection.

But she can't bear to lock the cat out. Bast is used to having entry into any room she pleases. The cat is company to Amelia, makes her feel less put-upon for being awake at unnatural hours. So Amelia sprays the mat on the changing table liberally with disinfectant and puts down a clean cloth diaper.

Sterile conditions for babies are a new evolution, Amelia thinks. How many babies have her old iron presses seen? All of them, or at least most of them, must have survived. Before antibacterial cleansers, and the notion that everything important in a person's life should be subsumed upon the bearing of a child.

On her mother's last night, the four of them gather in the dining room, with Caroline strapped into her portable car seat and perched on one of the stiff-backed chairs. Chris makes a roast chicken—the one meal in his repertoire. Once her mother leaves, Amelia will have to cook again, as well as change nearly every diaper, soothe nearly every cry. She will have to be home endless hours alone.

Chris pours Amelia a glass of wine, her first since discovering she was pregnant. "Don't have more than a glass or two," her mother cautions. "Remember, everything you eat, she eats."

"Didn't you drink while you were breast-feeding?" Amelia asks. "I thought you all did everything back then—drinking, smoking, amphetamines."

"I didn't breast-feed," her mother says. "It wasn't encouraged then. I drank when I was pregnant, but I never smoked. And of course I never took amphetamines."

Amelia sips her wine, which tastes fantastically cold and crisp. "Anyway," Chris says. "It's been so long since you've had anything to drink. You should definitely take it slow."

"I wasn't planning to guzzle down the bottle," Amelia says. "I'll just have the one glass for now, if you two don't mind."

Her mother grimaces and passes Amelia the salad bowl. As Amelia takes it, Bast flies in through the window, carrying a live mouse. The cat lands soundlessly on the sideboard and releases the rodent. She lets it scuttle toward escape, then pounces.

Amelia's mother scoops Caroline out of the car seat and carries her to the doorway, cradling her away from the cat, as if the rodent might fly across the room to sink disease-laden teeth into the baby. Amelia has a sudden image of her mother: in the sixteenth century, in the midst of the Black Plague, desperately shielding a baby from rats. Back then, Amelia thinks, she would have considered the cat an ally.

Now her mother curves one hand over Caroline's little ear and hisses at Chris. "Get it out of here," she says. "Get that thing *out*."

As Bast lets it go, the mouse squeaks and skitters toward the edge of the sideboard. Seeing Chris's predatory approach, Bast reclaims her quarry with impressive ease and sails back out the window, which Chris slams closed. Amelia imagines Bast's indignation, outside: turning her head in astonishment to see her window—which has always been cracked open even during snowstorms—shut.

Her mother straps Caroline back into her seat. "You can't have that anymore, you know," she says. "You can't have a cat bringing mice in the house, not with an infant here."

"I don't know what we can do about it," Amelia says. She spears a piece of radicchio with an abrupt jab of her fork. "Bast has always had windows open for her. If we close them, she'll yowl all night. I really don't think I can take that, a chorus of baby and cat yowls. I'm barely sleeping as it is."

Her mother turns to Chris, as if he's the only other reasonable adult. "We had a cat, when Amelia's brother was born. We were living in Manhattan then, so it never went outside. But when I had Kevin, my mother started telling me these stories."

"Superstitions," says Amelia, who has heard this before.

"Of course, superstitions," her mother agrees. "She told me that children who played with cats would become stupid, and that every cat has three hairs of the devil in its tail. And if you left a cat alone with a sleeping baby, the cat would steal its breath. Of course I knew this was all ridiculous: but I had so much time awake at night. I couldn't help thinking about what she said, and soon every time I looked at that cat I would just feel frightened. So I gave it away."

"Poor thing," Amelia says.

"I was only thinking about my baby." Her mother's voice is mostly matter-of-fact, but Amelia can hear too the trace of defensiveness. And superiority.

Later that night, after everyone has gone to sleep, after Caroline's first nursing, just as Amelia crawls back into bed. She'd opened the window again, for Bast, after Chris and her mother left the dining room. But this sound comes from outside: a horrible sound, not new, but somehow now especially chilling. Something screeching, wailing, in agony. Something bigger than a mouse—a rabbit maybe, or a squirrel. Sounding almost human in its anguish, begging for torture to cease.

Amelia stares at Caroline, inches away, asleep in her crib. Her friend Erin never put either of her boys in a crib. "It seems cruel," Erin said, "to make a baby go from sleeping in the womb to sleeping behind bars. All alone. It's unnatural. Babies belong in bed with their mothers."

The screeching goes on and on. Amelia worries it will wake Caroline, who sighs in her sleep. A dear sound, wet with mother's milk, it works on Amelia like a finger—pressing itself into the hollow of her being, leaving a permanent indentation. While the sound of Bast's cruelty inundates the room, sickening the very air. Chris stirs, and pulls a pillow over his ears. Much as she'd like to take similar measures, Amelia worries she might fall asleep and not hear Caroline when she cries.

So she lies awake: listening to the wretched, finished animal—trapped in its overlong killing. Until Amelia very nearly whimpers, forming a pleading mantra in her mind: make it stop, make it stop, make it stop.

"Chris," Amelia calls. Their first night alone with the baby, Chris is downstairs in the kitchen, shredding leftover chicken into sandwiches. "Could you come up here?"

When he appears in the doorway, she holds up Caroline's soiled diaper, an item that would have revolted them mere months ago. Now they huddle over it as if the contents contain a cryptic message that must be decoded.

"Is it supposed to be this runny?" Amelia asks. "Could this be because of my laxatives? Or do you think she's sick?"

From their many new supplies, Chris digs out the expensive digital thermometer. While Amelia consults baby books,

Chris presses it against Caroline's underarm and clicks: "Ninety-nine point three," he says.

"That means it's really a hundred point three, if it's under her arm," Amelia says, reading. "She has a fever."

Chris hands Caroline to Amelia and takes the book. Amelia presses her cheek against Caroline's forehead, trying to measure coolness or warmth.

"We'd better call the pediatrician," says Chris, his voice suddenly quavery.

"Why? What does it say?"

"It says she might need a spinal tap. To rule out meningitis."

In mere seconds, mild worry succumbs to catastrophe. One day alone with the baby, and already Amelia has failed. She holds Caroline against her chest, the small but perfectly working heart beating against hers, and in her mind begins to negotiate: I will never leave the house again, I will stay this size forever, I will give Bast away. I will never sew another book, or even draw another picture. Only please, please, let her be healthy.

From their bedroom they call the hospital and have Erin paged. She reassures Amelia that a spinal tap is not as serious a procedure for an infant. "But first," she says, "I'd get a rectal thermometer. They're much more accurate."

Chris runs out to the twenty-four-hour pharmacy. The new thermometer (sixty-four dollars less than the digital) yields far less frightening results: "Ninety-eight point eight," Chris says triumphantly, extracting the thermometer from perfect, sleeping Caroline.

Amelia bursts into tears. Chris carefully lays Caroline on the bed and gathers Amelia in his arms. "It's okay," he soothes. "Are you all right? Caroline's fine."

As she cries against Chris, Amelia feels a residual quiver in his body, left over from the horrifying words "spinal tap," "meningitis." And while she knows her tears spring mostly from relief, there is always the less valiant part of her: frightened that the world might hold her to her bargaining.

Caroline only cries when she needs something, but her needs are endless. She needs to nurse, to be changed, to burp, to nap. To be bathed, kept warm, strapped in, strapped out, rocked and cuddled. Amelia has heard of colicky babies who cry unceasingly round the clock, and thinks if Caroline were that way, she would simply lay herself down and die. Perhaps Caroline has some primal instinct, an internal register of exactly how much her mother can bear, and dares not make demands beyond that tolerance. As it is, Amelia has nothing left for her work and nothing left for her husband. "Are you okay?" Chris keeps asking. "You don't seem like yourself."

"I'm just *tired,*" Amelia answers, unable to banish the annoyance from her voice that has nothing to do with him and everything to do with sleeplessness, with restlessness, with being trapped inside her house and body. She barely worries about how this irritability might affect Chris: her old nightmares about losing him have given way to dreams about Caroline— disappearing, sinking, Amelia losing hold of her: a horrible, slipping, helpless plunge, a desperate search through fog, brambles, and rushing water. Emerging empty-handed, and not quite knowing if this lack delivers or devastates.

Waking, Amelia's fantasies no longer involve her career. She used to daydream about acclaim and respect, her work on display in art museums and selling for thousands of dollars. Now when her mind drifts, it conjures nothing but the porch of their old Left Hand Canyon house. Sunlight pouring through the screen. Chris having left for somewhere, and no noise except the creek. No baby, no husband. Not a single human being at all for miles and miles. Only Amelia and maybe Bast, stretched across the familiar bed with no intrusions looming.

During the day Amelia has plans for what she'll accomplish while Caroline sleeps. She can't bear to go near her equipment for gold tooling: the hot brass fillets and gouges suddenly ring with danger even with Caroline in another room. Amelia has a drawer full of linen thread and flaxen cord, she has a good supply of fine, marbled paper. She might sew sections of a book, assemble at least, if she can't create. But while Caroline sleeps Amelia finds herself either holding her—frightened to jostle and disturb—or simply too tired to move. The first two weeks after her caesarian, while her mother was here, Amelia was not permitted to drive: as restraints are lifted one by one, she feels imprisoned by simple exhaustion, and everything Caroline needs.

Once upon a time, Amelia was her own life's protagonist. She remembers an exhibit of her work at the local library: how people praised her, asking questions about the etchings, and the equipment she used. She wore a black dress that today she'd have no prayer of fitting into. She felt lithe and capable. Sometimes while Caroline naps, Amelia tries to capture that moment, that feeling, in her mind. But all she achieves is the old porch—calm, sun-filled, rife with water's music, and empty of responsibility.

When Caroline is four weeks old, Amelia straps her into the car and drives to Chautauqua—a beautiful and sprawling city park, formerly one of Amelia's favorite places. Amelia feels almost well enough for a flat, gentle walk. She has a Snugli, which she can use to carry Caroline on her chest. She pulls into the pebbled lot, turns off the ignition, and stares up: at the Flatirons, the mountains, and the many trails splitting and forking across and into the hills. Through the open window, the scents and colors of fall surround them—mulching leaves and the quivering yellow aspens.

She glances into the rearview mirror and checks Caroline's

sleeping form, making sure that the brim of her hat hasn't moved—in case sunlight can make its way inside. The baby's white skin looks like the most vulnerable substance imaginable, as if it might smoke and melt if Colorado rays make contact.

Amelia does not budge from behind the steering wheel, her hands upon it slick with sweat as she considers the uneven ground: riddled with pockets that could sprain ankles, or pitch Amelia forward on top of Caroline. Beyond the better-traveled trails, bears and mountain lions dwell. The chances of glimpsing one—let alone being attacked—are infinitesimally small, but now even that barest dram sickens Amelia.

She imagines herself from the outside: a woman, sitting in a locked car, staring out at a beautiful, awe-inspiring tableau. A year ago she would have pitied the person huddled there, shielding herself from the world around her. Shaking her head, Amelia remembers a line from Wordsworth: "Little we see in Nature that is ours." How distanced she feels these days, from everything she used to love.

That night Amelia has only slept a few minutes when Caroline cries. In her painful first moments of wakefulness, she takes Caroline back to bed with her and falls asleep while she nurses. Minutes or hours later, she awakes to a scratching sound. Caroline's eyes are closed, her lips resting against the top of Amelia's breast. While Bast digs around the baby, frustrated, trying to reclaim her usual spot. Amelia sits up slowly, returns the baby to her crib, and settles back down. Bast nestles in where Caroline had been, stitching herself into the crook of Amelia's arm—under her elbow, over her shoulder.

All the measures in place now to protect babies, Amelia thinks. If anything happened to Caroline due to Amelia's flights of attention, Amelia would probably be subject to legal proceedings in addition to her own grief and guilt. Amelia strokes Bast, purring beside her. Nothing in place to protect this cat, she thinks. In the same book that yielded Bast's name, Amelia read that ancient Egyptians punished cat killers by death, no matter whether the act was malicious or accidental. She remembers a few years ago, an incident in the Midwest: teenage boys broke into an animal shelter and bludgeoned dozens of cats to death. Their punishment was nominal, based not on the level of their cruelty but on the monetary value of the cats. The only sacred animals in our society, Amelia thinks, are children.

Chris's breath mingles with Caroline's and her own—a funny kind of downbeat added by the wheeze of Bast's purr. It's a form of narcissism, Amelia decides, this deification of children. The insistence on kid gloves and velvet handling. Smack a toddler and face abuse charges. Withhold lunch and be accused of neglect. Amelia imagines walking out of her house, leaving Caroline alone—safe and sleeping in her crib. The vision is instantly intruded upon by imaginary police cars, sirens blaring: racing up to the curb, trapping Amelia and forcibly escorting her home.

Amelia lets her hands curve gently around Bast's throat. The purr's engine hums against her palms, vibrating. Of course she would never hurt the cat. But strangely, she likes knowing she's allowed to. Knowing that any care she gives Bast is not in any way mandated, but purely of her own volition.

Lying in her crib, Caroline works her little mouth as if nursing. She must be dreaming, Amelia thinks, marveling at her daughter's gently limited scope. Caroline looks perfectly contented with her dream-breast, and Amelia thinks: what a patient person she is. Back in college, Amelia took a literature class, the American Renaissance, with a handsome, blue-eyed boy who stuttered horribly. At the beginning of the term,

Amelia had admired him: his insistence on speaking despite the painful struggle. But as the weeks wore on—when the clock had jumped past departure time and the boy still worked over spitting out a comment on *Civil Disobedience*—Amelia could feel her face visibly registering frustration and annoyance. And even while she felt ashamed, she hoped he would notice and give up his insights so they all could leave.

Caroline will never be like that. She is already so even-tempered. Caroline will take a bottle, she'll wait to be picked up, she'll do whatever is required of her without difficulty. She will sit across from a stuttering boy, beyond the end of class, nodding and smiling her encouragement.

Outside, a car rattles down the street and the room floods obliquely with its headlights. Amelia removes her hands from Bast's neck. Caroline is a kinder person, already, than she.

Caroline smiles for the first time at Chris, while he gives her a sponge bath in a wide rubber basin in the kitchen sink, one hand supporting her head, the other spanning her entire torso. Amelia flies into the room when he calls her, prepared to face disaster. And sees instead Caroline, balanced between her father's hands, a funny kind of grin across her face as she looks up at him. Who could blame her, Amelia thinks, watching the two of them. It's a wonder stones haven't smiled back at him.

"Look at that," Amelia says.

"We have to start writing these things down," Chris says.

"My mother would tell us it's just gas." Amelia sits down at the kitchen table.

"Your mother thinks Bast has devil's hair in her tail," Chris says. "She can't convince me Caroline's not smiling."

Chris lifts Caroline out of the basin and dries her off with a towel, looking proud and besotted. It's not, Amelia thinks, that Chris loves Caroline more than she does. It's that he enjoys

the love more. Amelia's feelings for Chris have always been intense and liberating, signaling the beginning of safe, happy
adulthood. But she dislikes the weight and imperative of what
she feels for Caroline. It makes her feel trapped and out of control, the world once again a dangerous, unnavigable place.

Amelia drops her head into her hands and presses her
thumbs into her temples. Was she always like this? She could
swear she wasn't, that she used to be capable of sitting for a
moment, observing a simple scene—a happy scene—without
roiling through the intricacies of life. She wishes again that she
could be more like the people from the want ads, the owners of
Patches, sweeping away difficulty without thought, guilt, or
concern.

"Are you okay?" Chris asks.

"I'm fine," she says, careful to speak in a kindly tone. "Just
tired." But in her mind, she composes an advertisement:

> *Treasured infant needs new home. Caroline is five weeks old,*
> *healthy and beautiful, only cries when she's hungry. Has*
> *been breast-fed but will take a bottle without complaint. We*
> *must give Caroline up, because her mother is overwhelmed by*
> *the scope and enormity of parenthood.*

Amelia almost laughs out loud, but prevents herself, not wanting to explain to Chris. And then she thinks, with a hideous
sinking, that this is the first facet of herself she'd be frightened
to expose to him. All other flaws and foibles he's forgiven her,
even loved her more because of them. But this, she feels certain,
he would find repugnant. How terribly sad, Amelia thinks, as
she envisions this gap open between them.

"We should find a baby-sitter," Chris says the next morning.
Amelia has just laid Caroline in the crib after feeding her. Still

awake, Caroline blinks contentedly, her tiny fists opening and closing.

"You could get a break," Chris says, as Amelia sits down on the bed. "Work on your books. Go for walks."

The idea cheers and at the same time terrifies her. Amelia barely trusts herself with Caroline. How could she hand her over to some stranger? She imagines a teenager, watching TV while Caroline is left to cry herself to sleep. The same languid girl cracking gum and talking on the telephone, while Caroline dies a crib death, or of a broken heart.

Amelia kisses Chris good-bye at the door (like a wife from a fifties sitcom, she thinks grimly), then goes back upstairs. Caroline is asleep, as usual doing just what's expected of her, just what makes life easiest. Amelia considers scooping her up, taking her to the car—driving to Chautauqua and attempting another hike.

But the thing is: Amelia doesn't want to hike with Caroline. She wants to hike alone. She wants to hike in her old body, which marched easily uphill, never feeling responsible for anyone's well-being aside from her own.

Outside Caroline's window, Indian summer beckons with its too-strong sunlight. Amelia thinks of the day she and Chris decided to marry, camping in Arizona. They'd set up their tent cross-river from the ruins of a remote health spa that had enjoyed a few years of operation before burning to the ground. Only the cement foundation and the outline of walls remained—in addition to man-made hot springs, still partitioned by cedar rails.

Amelia remembers walking down a red dirt path, sunlight boring into her bare shoulders. She remembers that the sign pointing toward the hot springs looked like a mistake; she would have pictured a lull in the river, a calm, shallow spot, easy to wade across. Instead the water rushed as deep and fast as ever, two hurried sections of it with a tiny islet in between.

They could see, just barely through the trees on the other side, rising, blackened pillars—the ghost-town spa.

"Are we sure this is right?" Amelia said.

"It must be," Chris said. "The sign. And isn't that the building?"

"Maybe it's shallower than it looks."

Chris stood downriver from Amelia as they faced the water. I can do this, Amelia thought. She followed Chris's steps into the water, her body resisting her brain's order of movement, but obeying nonetheless.

And being betrayed. The water was even deeper than she'd imagined, enveloping her up to the waist. The current, so fast. Amelia's sandaled feet barely touched the rocky riverbed before being swept up, violently. The water lifted her without thought or effort. Almost as soon as she entered, she found herself running with the current, downstream.

Until the day she dies, she will remember the relief of Chris's arm—shooting out like an old vaudeville hook, encircling her waist. How could he stand so still and evenly in the midst of that current? He pulled her body back upstream, beside him, holding her upright.

While she shivered against him in animal panic. "It's okay," Chris said. "I've got you. We're going to count the steps across. It's not far."

"I can't," Amelia croaked.

"One," Chris said, holding her straight, blocking the treacherous path downstream with his unfathomable ability to stand steady. "Two. You can do it. I've got you. Three."

Amelia remembers reaching the islet, feeling like a shipwreck victim come to shore. Feeling the out-of-time, adrenaline-filled giddiness brought on by a near-deadly mishap. The incongruity of her skin, soaked with the cold water and the hot sun. And she remembers her two choices: continue across, toward the spa, beckoning from behind the trees. Or continue across, back to the original shore. She remembers deeply wishing she could just stay there on the islet, rejoicing in her safety, never touching water again, till whenever the river ran dry. She would have given anything not to cross again, but stay, leaning against Chris—her rescuer. An intense mixture of feelings: to be delivered—only to immediately face your fears again.

While Caroline sleeps upstairs, Amelia steps out onto the front porch. She looks up at the Rocky Mountains, fearless and permanent against the autumn sky.

She walks down the flagstone path to the sidewalk, one ear cocked toward Caroline's window. No sound from up above. She takes a few steps along the sidewalk, until she's standing in front of the next-door neighbor's house.

She remembers that night on their camping trip, when Chris—buoyed by his heroism—proposed. She had said yes immediately, not one moment needed for consideration. Thinking about it now, Amelia is amazed she didn't feel a sense of inadequacy at not being able to cross the river. But she only remembers feeling delivered—and wholly thrilled that they would be married. That the afternoon's deliverance would last, would sustain her the rest of her life.

Amelia longs to continue down the sidewalk. Only around the block. What would it matter, with Caroline sleeping? Amelia guesses this is what bothers her most: there can be no more flights of responsibility. Never again can her personal failures be forgiven. She can never be the person carried across the river, but now is beholden to do the carrying. And she feels frightened, worried she's not up to the task. But also, and more poignant, a sense of no return. The same sad, vaguely bitter feeling she'd experienced as a teenager when she'd lost her virginity. That something which had defined her would now

be permanently out of reach, a word only used to describe someone else.

From next door—from her own open window—Amelia
hears a thin, mewling sound. Not Caroline, but Bast. She realizes, with panic: not only has she left Caroline alone in the
house. She has left her alone with the cat.

For the first time since midpregnancy, Amelia runs. With
their old elasticity, her legs swiftly retrace their steps back upstairs, to the bedroom. Where Caroline sleeps—safe and unharmed, Bast perched on the windowsill, staring outside, not in
the least bit sinister. As if she had merely been calling Amelia
back to motherhood.

Amelia lifts Caroline out of her crib and carries her to the
bed. The baby doesn't wake, but simply breathes, the barest
draft crossing Amelia's cheek.

Caroline's breath will make its way through the window and
the thin mountain air. It will battle through poisonous smog, asserting the strength of its own chemical compound. Trees and
plants will breathe this bit of Caroline, her diaphanous exhalation translating into a film of blue-green chlorophyll, pumping
through stalks and leaves. The world around will flourish just a
little more from the contribution of this embryonic gust, given
with such innocence and willingness.

Amelia thinks again of the Wordsworth poem, and leans
forward to inhale the deep infant scent of Caroline's crown.
She imagines a book she might make for Caroline: with etchings of baying wind and sea, of lulling meadows. She will bind
it in leather, a single edition, and engrave it for Caroline to
keep. "The world is too much with us; late and soon, / Getting
and spending, we lay waste our powers; / Little we see in Nature that is ours; / We have given our hearts away, a sordid
boon!"

The bedroom seems infused with a supply of light and
warmth as endless as the porch of their old Left Hand Canyon

house. Caroline lies on her back, sleeping soundly, safely nested on the soft down quilt.

Bast alights beside them and circles the baby. For a moment Amelia wants to push her aside—frightened by the cat's proximity. But not Caroline. Innately brave and unworried, she simply breathes and sleeps. Confident in her own continuance, her own supply of oxygen—which must be enough to go around, to share; to declare her belonging to the world at large, and carry her mother through its eddy and peril.

Caroline wakes quietly and yawns—a gaping, animal gesture. Seeing Amelia's face, the baby smiles: an expression that looks not only happy, but frankly loving. Delighted. At the sight of her *mother*—the word singing, speaking in Amelia's mind, referring to herself for what seems the very first time. Amelia feels a swell, joyfully unambivalent. So compelled to kiss her daughter, a thousand men could not restrain her.

The baby's lips are pliant, tender, and fine. Amelia presses her own mouth against their most natural smile. And she finds herself not merely kissing, but sipping—the way she would suck blood from a wound of her own. Tending something that belongs to her irrevocably, while exuding the salty, primal taste of sustenance.

lieutenant island

After her second husband died, unexpectedly but not young, Tara made two purchases everyone advised her against: the telescope, a Bushnell Spacemaster from the Bird Watcher's General Store, and the house on Lieutenant Island.

The former, she knew, was available at half the price, including its tripod, over the Internet. The latter she bought with money from selling Martin's house in Piedmont, to which the new house could not be compared. Martin's had been a suburban Tudor, very traditional and expensively furnished, with convenient access to both Berkeley and San Francisco.

The house on Lieutenant Island was a rambling, weathered, and overbuilt shack, pieced together from various schools of architecture: a round turret awkwardly attached to the original saltbox frame, a widow's walk with questionable rails, a dining room with exposed posts and beams, a cavernous kitchen with Spanish tiles better suited to an adobe villa, five bedrooms that Tara could never begin to fill. The house came with ancient beach furniture, ripe from years of absorbing salt air. The walls and floorboards were permeated with a dank, musty odor that Tara didn't mind at all. To her it smelled like summer. When she opened the front door and inhaled the moldy oxygen, she felt she'd arrived less at a place than at a season.

Lieutenant Island was a small and swaying piece of land, shaped like an angelfish: Tara's house sat toward its lower fin. By Cape standards, the area was sparsely developed, with wide stretches of untouched beach between clusters of summer homes. During World War Two the island had been a hub for black market trade, its remote accessibility ideal for covert shipments.

Never mind, thought Tara, that her spit of shore provided access to nothing but the Wellfleet Bay Wildlife Sanctuary. Never mind that this had been the island's only house for sale. Never mind its poor, almost nonexistent insulation and its lack of year-round neighbors. Never mind that the narrow one-lane road was washed over for hours each day, leaving the bridge to the mainland uncrossable, trapping Tara on or off the island, making her life—her trips to town or days at home—ruled, absolutely, by the tide.

Never mind all that. Tara wanted the house, and Lieutenant Island. Six months after Martin's embolism, she sold his place to the first bidder, sold it fully furnished, spending an imprudent portion of the profits on her relocation. She packed up her clothes and Pagan, her fourteen-year-old Maine coon cat, and very little else. She arrived on Cape Cod toward the end of March, bought a tide clock and the telescope, feeling a vague sense of calm throughout, and a finite sense of purpose. She recognized that if her advisors were correct—if she ran out of money and lost the security Martin had tried to leave her—the risk was comparable to the one she'd taken marrying Martin (so much older) in the first place. She hoped that the serenity of her second marriage, despite its brevity, would spill into the rest of her life, forming and guiding it.

At least I'll have had this time here, Tara thought, this year or two or three. Lieutenant Island had existed in her mind, romantic and ephemeral, for so long. She didn't need it forever. She only needed it for this while.

Five years before, during her troubled but passionate first marriage (before she left Greg and lost track of him, before he married her old friend Libby), the tide on Lieutenant Island had stranded Tara with her then-husband. Ever since, there had been something about it: a surreal blending of time, place, and emotion. She had spent exactly one day there with Greg. But for her that day ran the entire course of their marriage as it might have occurred in a parallel universe: ending on a happy note; or rather, not ending at all. In Tara's mind, her connection to Greg had never been entirely severed, so that now, since she'd moved alone to Lieutenant Island, after Martin's death: that first day with Greg might as well have taken place the day before. Something as simple and flawless as a group of sanderlings flying over the shoreline would suggest not the things that had toppled their marriage, but what made it for Tara a union that, despite divorce and subsequent marriages, had somehow lasted.

Tara had been married to Martin for nearly three years. She had loved him fondly, respecting and admiring him with no sense of hunger or imperative. And she was grateful to him, for the tone and substance of the life he gave her—and continued to give her, through memory and bequeath, even after his death. Back when she was with Greg, Tara would have considered such a marriage mercenary. She would not have understood Martin's need (after his own good marriage, ending in his first wife's death from cancer) for someone to take care of. But Tara's older self realized: the things she had offered Martin— her youth and noncombative companionship—were in ways more valuable than the consuming and uncontrollable love she had always felt for Greg.

Tara missed Martin. Evening on Lieutenant Island fell with the early dusk of winter. When the beams of her old house swelled with silence, in the still gray between sundown and electric lights, she longed for his opinion and conversation, his steadying and fatherly counsel. Still. While she often felt his absence with sharp regret, Tara realized without surprise that, unmarried again, she mourned not so much the loss of Martin: but the loss of Greg.

Now, living alone on Lieutenant Island, Tara would recall the original day there—her reaction to discovering herself stranded. And her stomach would knot with embarrassment: the way she'd panicked when they started down the road to find it washed away, the mid-arc of the bridge curving inaccessibly in the water, like something out of a ghost town. No way to drive through without inundating their already fragile car with salt-water. In her agitated state, Tara had blamed Greg for the stranding. Five years later, she wished she could return to that moment the same way she'd returned to the place, this time to do things differently.

But of course there was no changing the past. That morning with Greg she had been expected in Wellfleet, clerking at a store that sold cat paraphernalia and souvenirs. Although Tara hated the job, found it dull and stultifying, the thought of missing her shift without warning or explanation flooded her with the helplessness of a shipwreck—stuck indefinitely on a remote and unfamiliar piece of land. In those days, in that marriage, Tara indulged her temper with a child's immediacy. Stranded on

Lieutenant Island, she had raised her voice to a furious and irrational pitch, pummeling Greg with her left fist when he tried to hold her in place and calm her down. She had allowed herself an unrestrained show of unjustifiable emotion, because that's what she used to be able to do—explode—with minimal provocation, her love for Greg confused with a tumble of fury that Tara still did not quite understand. Remembering it now, she could visibly cringe with shame, the anger that had once been so habitual now seeming as unavailable as that road, buried under high tide.

No cell phones, no pay phones. No way to tell her employer she would simply not appear. Replaying the day in her mind, Tara sometimes would imagine walking up to the house that now belonged to her. Making the calls she needed instead of lashing out at Greg, who had promised he could time their visit to avoid this very circumstance. Who had promised they would not be marooned.

She remembered a resident bird-watcher, wearing hip waders and carrying binoculars, who turned a startled glance at Tara's shrill, rising voice, then quickly looked away. Humiliated, she ran down the beach. The sky stood absolutely clear above her. The ocean spilled across her sneakers, then retreated out to the ends of the world. Amazing, that she could feel so claustrophobic amidst this most far-reaching of scenery. She stopped running, and let her chest rise and fall with calmer breaths. Greg approached cautiously. When he put his arm around her shoulders, she let it stay there.

And then the sanderlings appeared. What seemed like hundreds of them, breaking into flight like pairs of slow-motion swing dancers. "Look," Greg said. "They're jitterbugging."

Tara felt a rise of emotion, watching the birds fly and flutter in butterfly formation. Their synchronized parallels: outward and in, upward and down, in a display of grace so mystical, Tara thought they might disappear if she so much as blinked. Aurora borealis, the bird ballet. She was not, and would never be, a religious woman. But she felt that day, and every day since—whenever she saw the sanderlings at work—that they'd been sent directly from God. A sign that everything was, and would remain, exactly as it should be. Her job shrank in her mind to precisely its actual size: one tiny room in a tiny town, one shift of thousands lost. She herself became one small creature among billions, standing on what amounted to the smallest fraction of the merest third of a vast and far-reaching planet. There was no reason on earth not to leave anger and worry behind, and simply enjoy the day.

They walked back toward the sunken bridge, stopping to watch a pair of osprey feed their reptilian newborns—the male swooping into the nest with a fish in its talons. The female doling out morsels (not regurgitated, Greg explained, but carefully, precisely small) into the gaping mouths of their black, gangly, groping offspring. They walked past an area squared off by string, supposedly a piping plover nest, but littered with a candy wrapper and an ocean-faded beer can, empty of any bird life. Later they discovered an actual nest in the dunes (hidden amidst the beach grass) and they backed away carefully so as not to disturb it.

They swam together in the deep, high tide, Tara wrapping herself around Greg with the ridiculous notion that his body would provide warmth in the middle of the freezing ocean. They found a belted kingfishers' tunnel, fifteen feet long: its entrance reeking of rotted fish, and marked by two slight grooves—the birds' narrow footprints. They heard the kingfishers' cries of protest, like monkeys chattering, at seeing people so close.

At the end of the day—waiting for the road to clear, sleepy from walking the length of the island several times over in the hot sun—Tara and Greg watched three British children play in the water, their crisp young voices ringing out from the surf, perfectly formed sentences chiming as they splashed through the waves.

When Tara remembered that late afternoon—the sun finally low in the sky, her exhausted head resting on Greg's leg—she felt an odd sense of peace. Some primal, happy pounding, an affectionate squeeze of her cerebral cortex. "I was so angry when the tide came in," Tara told Greg. "Now I never want it to go out."

The memory of that moment always created in Tara a profound swallow, the most tender warmth. No matter where she was, in her life or in her day: behind the wheel in standstill traffic on the Bay Bridge, pressing a melon at the Star Market in Orleans, even in bed with Martin.

She could remember being stuck with Greg on Lieutenant Island. And in the small round circle beneath her ribs, that core orb she called emotion (that core orb she called herself), it would be just the same as being there.

Tara and Greg first met riding up a chairlift in Colorado. She'd been out of college one year, living in Telluride, selling lift tickets for the mountain resort, not thinking about much beyond snow conditions and ski equipment. Until the day she found Greg beside her, felt that strange instant intimacy of being scrunched and strapped together in a tiny, rattling space. Greg's left-handed gestures repeatedly bumped into Tara's right. They chatted, Greg's idea of small talk—him identifying every plant, shrub, and habitat below as they teetered through the trees. He talked about veterinary school, which he attended in Fort Collins, and Tara remembered feeling obliquely criticized: for lacking a life of the mind, for never thinking about the world below, but just swinging the dead weight of her ski boots and waiting to be delivered on the slope.

She remembered sandy, longish hair falling across Greg's brow and into green-flecked eyes, making her right arm itch with the urge to reach over and stroke it back into place. She remembered an involuntary tug at the base of her abdomen, impelling her footsteps toward him when they loaded off the lift. It was Tara who asked Greg to ski with her, and then Tara who proved the better athlete—faster and more graceful, beating him easily and prettily on every run.

In her early twenties, Tara had lived exclusively in her body. She cared about skiing, running: the adroitness of her movements, the fitness of her muscles. But while Tara had some degree of physical talent, she never had *enough*. In the local slalom, she always placed a respectable but unimpressive fifth or sixth. She had not been accepted onto the Ski Patrol. In the world of mountain towns, she was one moderately gifted athlete among thousands. Eventually she would have to think of something else to do.

Tara had been instantly fascinated by Greg's broad purpose and passion—for veterinary school, for science. She saw him watching birds and coveted that focused gaze herself, for something, anything.

She confided this to Greg, at the end of the day, as they sipped Sam Adams and watched each other from across the small square table at the Mountain Village Bar.

"It's a matter of deciding what you care about," Greg said. Tara noticed, with oblique panic, his eyes harmlessly flit as a pretty woman walked past. She thought inexplicably: I care about you.

They ate dinner in the bar, ordering identical drinks and meals. After dark they played ice hockey in the town park's deserted rink. While Tara glided around him in rapid circles, Greg tripped in his skates, confident enough to laugh at his own awkwardness. The first time he reached out to grab her elbow, his grip pulsed through her layers of wool, polypropylene, and Gore-Tex. Tara felt the most heady elation as Greg slid her toward him over the crackling surface. She kissed not so much his lips as his broad, delighted smile.

The four days Greg stayed with her, after that night, Tara felt a fantastic kind of completeness. They hiked up the Judd Wiebe trail through heavy snow. When Greg pointed out a red-shafted flicker, when he stopped her so they could watch a golden eagle circle overhead, Tara's physical form and prowess became suddenly enough to sustain her: complemented by Greg, and everything he knew about the world.

Telluride had an infamous man-to-woman ratio of eight to one: Tara could enter any bar and be surrounded. After Greg returned to Fort Collins, she would listen dully to endless boasts about moguls and powder, the same conversation night after night. After too many complimentary drinks, she would go home to her small apartment over the Roma (music from downstairs loud in her living room) and phone Greg. "Come," she would beg him drunkenly. "Come this weekend, to visit me."

Ages and ages before, when Tara learned to ski, there had been a distinct moment in the process, between control and loss at an increased velocity. And later another, when she realized her abilities didn't change, no matter the turbulence or speed. She could release her inhibitions and let her body do what it knew. She could make the same turns. She could perform as she needed.

Loving Greg was like learning to ski on a black diamond run. Caught in the rapidity of emotion, Tara had no tools to conceal the anguish of doubt, the fear that he'd find someone smarter, more focused than her. Back then, when Greg (for any reason) refused her, Tara would explode into sorrow and rage. Sometimes, goading Greg into shouting back at her, Tara would hear the anger in his formerly calm voice as victory:

evidence of the level of feeling she was capable of wresting from him.

But then she would awake the following morning, with her cat Pagan curled up in the covers, and find herself awash with turmoil and self-loathing; remembering Greg's voice over the phone, "I only want to make you happy."

"Deep breaths," Libby would say, when Tara called her in Boston. "Keep what's inside inside. And drinking doesn't help," she'd add—hearing the rattled hangover in Tara's throat. In college, Libby had not been Tara's closest friend. But she had always been practical, cerebral, and controlled. Tara naturally gravitated to her when faced with her own sloppy upheaval.

That April, when the mountain closed, Tara moved to Fort Collins to be with Greg—marrying him when he asked her the next year as a matter of course, thinking the promise of permanence might assuage her insecurities. But between stretches of laughter and lovemaking, they fought. They fought about Tara's cat, who left magpies and mourning doves slaughtered on their lawn; about veterinary school, which Greg quit against Tara's wishes; and about money. They fought about doing dishes and cleaning the bathroom. Tara was afraid to stay alone in the old Victorian house Greg rented, so they fought when he traveled. When Greg started working on his biology degree, they fought about female field partners. They fought about everything trivial and mundane, and about everything significant and consequential.

Three years into their marriage, when Greg finished his degree and received a commission from the Audubon Society to spend the summer on Cape Cod and study the nesting habits of ospreys, they fought about the mountains, which Tara couldn't bear to leave even for four months.

·   ·   ·

The ospreys, which had been on the brink of extinction due to DDT, were suddenly on the rise: proliferating in New England, arriving in force to build their enormous ramshackle nests on platforms raised by Com Electric. That first summer, while Tara worked at the shop in Wellfleet, Greg would travel the Cape with his tripod, telescope, and frayed beach chair piled in the back of their thirdhand station wagon. He'd camp out by Quivet Creek, or along the National Seashore, or on Lieutenant Island, and watch the birds through his high-resolve lens, staring with the patience of a monk, observing all their habits from first nesting to final fledgling.

Despite Tara's never feeling at home on Cape Cod, this stretch of their marriage yielded some of its happiest moments. On afternoons or mornings off, Tara would sometimes visit the osprey nests with Greg. At Quivet Creek they'd walk through the cemetery, Tara committing the odd, old-fashioned names to memory: Moody Sears, Heman Sears, Constant Sears, Nabby Sears—all dead before 1890. Jerusha and Jeremiah Long. Mehitable Snow, Nightingale Judge, Thankful Hall, and Zebina Doane—all born before 1790. The best headstones were unreadable, time having worn down and rendered the carved words indecipherable, almost level with the original slate—and covered with orange lichen so thick and native, it would have felt criminal to scratch any of it away.

Toward the path that led to the marsh, the headstones became more ordinary, bearing modern names and laments, settling into the perfectly trimmed Kentucky bluegrass. Tara and Greg would leave well-groomed civilization, past and present. They'd go into the brush between red and black oaks—Greg with his baseball cap, Tara wearing long sleeves and pants to guard against deer ticks and poison ivy. They'd hike through the greenbrier, bayberries, and tall reeds that rustled overhead—Phragmites, their dust-mop tops bowing and nodding with a sibilant whoosh. The path opened into that greenest wetland green, meandering through bluest summer-sky blue. Greg would set up his telescope and beach chair at the edge of elder bushes and spartina and quiz Tara about the plant life. "What's this?" he'd ask, crushing a juniper berry between his fingers, releasing the faint, thin odor of gin. Or he might point out a red-tailed hawk, chasing the ospreys through the air space around their nest. "Listen," Greg would say. "That's the osprey's warning cry."

Tara would sit in his lap, the two of them perched in the rickety chair, Greg's arm across Tara's waist, holding her against him. When he spoke his breath gusted gently across her cheek and lips. Tara could imagine the two of them as a single entity with a common purpose. In perfect sync as they swatted away greenflies or mayflies, Tara flattening the mosquitoes on Greg's arm with the same bloody squish as her own. He shared the telescope with her, marking Tara's observation of the birds as important as his, so that even when Tara watched the osprey through blurry, far-away binoculars, she felt necessary to Greg, perhaps even to the birds themselves. She felt happy and significant, and precisely where she belonged.

But these moments weren't frequent enough to hold the marriage together. Most of that summer, Tara worried their time here would end and Greg would want to stay east. During Colorado summers, Tara had biked to stay in shape for skiing— but Cape Cod's lack of hills made this seem worthless. So she'd run, and complain about shinsplints. She would stand for hours in the tiny, one-room shop, staring at cartoon cat faces and pining for the mountains, hours on her feet aggravating her painful shins. She repeatedly, against Greg's sharp correction, misidentified birds, calling crows ravens and finches sparrows. And she blamed Greg: for the lack of hills. The lack of money, which necessitated her reluctant life in retail.

At night their angry voices floated through tattered window screens, disappearing into the salty air. In the morning, waking beside Greg, Tara's chest and muscles ached with the complicated exercise of loving him. At times she wished she could discard herself entirely: becoming Greg, slipping into the breadth of his knowledge and competence the way she might pull on one of his old flannel shirts. In four years of marriage, she had lost the use for her spare talents—while never quite mastering what she admired of her husband's.

Perhaps, Tara thought now, it was because she'd felt so out of her element that she gave up. Perhaps she'd simply been too young. Perhaps she relied too much on Greg, and not at all on herself, to arrange a life that would provide fulfillment. Perhaps she'd lacked a sense of the permanence of her actions: believing, foolishly, that Greg would always exist, somewhere, for her to return to.

Looking back, Tara remembered a peculiar shift. An idea forming, that passion caused misery and calm might provide happiness. At the Star Market in Orleans, she stood behind a couple, obviously married but not feeling the need to touch despite being squeezed together in the narrow grocery aisle. She watched the man pay while his wife waited, a healthy stack of bills in his palm, gray hairs curling onto his wrist. Amazing, Tara thought: something concrete and useful, handed over without complicated process.

She started to imagine a serene and quiet life, every bill paid before its due date. Tranquil good-mornings and quiet but companionable breakfasts, after which each partner would move easily away from the other, to attend separate business: wife never worrying about husband, husband never worrying about wife.

. . .

Tara made everything about their divorce civilized in the way their marriage had never been. She simply left—against Greg's protests, his pleas for her to stay—but too quickly for any continuation of their usual acrimony. In their four married years, they hadn't amassed enough possessions to incite property disputes. They didn't have children. Tara made it clear she did not want Greg following her, and he complied with an ease that bordered on hurtful. So uncomplicated, it turned out, after all those battles, to dissolve their union.

"It's not you I'm leaving," she told Greg, before heading back to Colorado. "It's the person I am when I'm with you."

By the time Tara received Libby's letter a year later (the envelope instantly recognizable, even from a distance, addressed in Libby's peculiar geometric handwriting) she couldn't afford to mind. She had already found Martin, who was more than thirty years older, and who made Tara feel tended and guided. He was like an instructor, allowing her to learn on gently graded slopes. Tara discovered how easy it was, to comply and agree when she didn't feel her very life depended on Martin's love. Not precisely returning Martin's feelings, she could accept them without question. Tara abandoned her mountains, and skiing, and moved to California. She typed her reply to Libby. It's all right. Greg and I are divorced. He's free to do what he wants.

Tara and Greg did not keep in touch. Instead Tara studied birds: buying feeders and field guides. Joining Saturday morning groups, walking in Muir Woods or at Point Reyes with gray-haired ladies Martin's age, all of them peering through raised binoculars at a spotted towhee or a turkey vulture.

And now Greg could be anywhere, with Libby as his wife or not. He could be working on his Ph.D. He could be teaching at a university. He could be conducting a study in South America, Canada, anywhere. And he could, still or again, be living on Cape Cod.

During her first month on Lieutenant Island, as the avian population increased with the warming weather, Tara noticed small birds, which—back in Pagan's hunting days—would have been placed in peril. When Pagan was young, and Tara and Greg lived in Colorado, they used to outfit the cat with bells. Greg believed cats belonged indoors. "Think of the damage to the ecostructure," he'd scold Tara, whenever Pagan deposited a slain bird or rodent by their doorstep. Greg complained that he couldn't, in good conscience, hang his bird feeders. "It's like setting a trap for them," he said.

"Put bells on her," a letter from Libby advised, in her strange handwriting. Libby loved meting out advice in any and every field. She annoyed Tara, but at the same time compelled her to obey. Tara bought bells: small round jingle bells, and miniature brass cowbells, and combinations of the two that surrounded Pagan with a clamorous tinkle. But the bells ran out as regularly as cat food. Pagan became expert at discarding them, suddenly appearing bare-necked, in startling silence. And she made the most of her time between collars. Sometimes, as if to taunt Greg, she would capture a live robin or Stellar's jay and release it in the house. Cursing both Tara and the cat, Greg would capture and rescue the frantic bird. "Extra field work," Tara would say, when the birds flew upward, delivered, from Greg's hands.

On Lieutenant Island, the younger Pagan would have had a whole new world of prey: prairie warblers and song sparrows; grackles, catbirds, and Eastern bluebirds. Finding the corpses on her doorstep, Tara would have heard Greg's voice in her head, urgent and admonishing, accusing her of rendering the area's sanctuary status null and void.

But at fourteen, Pagan seemed done with hunting. The last time Tara had seen her exhibit predatory behavior was back in Piedmont. Pagan caught a vole and then immediately released it, not bothering to attempt a recapture—as if finally assured of her abilities and therefore not interested in indulging them. After years of ignoring toys, she finally played with catnip-filled mice and crumpled wads of newspaper.

The summers had become difficult for Pagan. She hated the heat, and by August her long gray coat would be snarled and unwieldy. In California, Tara began having her shaved in the spring. Without her abundant gray coat, the cat became an unidentifiable Dr. Seuss creature, a mane-like fringe around her face, and velvety stubble—a feline crew cut—all she had in the way of fur. The black stripes beneath her coat stood out like the pattern on an old-fashioned football uniform. Pagan's stomach, usually camouflaged by fluff, would hang, swinging, vulnerable and exposed. "She looks like she's wearing a cat suit," Martin used to say.

Pagan appeared to enjoy the spring cat suit, the release from heat and the reprieve from grooming. She pranced and minced as if she'd just won a beauty pageant. In the mist or sun of Lieutenant Island, Tara would find her lolling on the concrete patio or on the front stoop, not hunting the birds on the beach, but staring at them. The cat would stretch indolently and watch a flock of sanderlings perform their airborne magic. Pagan never made any pretense of stalking; but every once in a while, as she watched, she'd emit an odd, nearly silent chattering—high-pitched and filled with longing.

When Tara left Lieutenant Island to run errands, she would plan enough to keep her occupied for long stretches—till the tide went back out. She would save up time, writing out lists of what she needed. She'd shop in the morning for things that would last in the car—dry cat food, toiletries from the pharmacy, anything for the house. She'd postpone groceries until the end, giving herself just enough time to drive back over the bridge as the water began to rise again. On the day she found Libby, Tara made a trip to the Bird Watcher's General Store. Though not yet officially summer, the season seemed suddenly under way. Tara fought through traffic—the thick stream of drivers with their endless, clueless signal lights—on Route 28 and 6A.

The Bird Watcher's General Store fit into the collection of tacky summer T-shirt shops and lobster restaurants that made parts of Cape Cod look like a third world tourist economy. Birdbaths crowded its wide front porch, and lobster buoys decorated with paintings of chickadees hung from the eaves. Inside, the store smelled like sawdust and new wood. Bird-watching paraphernalia (binoculars, field guides, lens cleaning kits) were outnumbered by kitschy souvenirs: T-shirts, shower curtains, boxer shorts, singing clocks—anything that could be adorned with the imprint of a bird. Tara strode past all the costly, colorful whatnot and headed downstairs, into the serious stacks of bird seed. A chipmunk darted out through the open basement door as she thumped a sack of thistle to the floor.

Tara couldn't think of a reason not to buy bird feeders. Pagan didn't hunt anymore. And just in case, Tara could buy a collar with a bell, from the pet-food aisle of the Star Market.

In the back room Tara picked up a plastic bird-seed scoop and read a few handwritten descriptions. The employees here had a sense of humor. "Aviarium," one sign read. "$79.85. This is the feeder with the one-way mirrored coating that lets you watch the birds from inches away no matter how ugly you are."

It was the sign on a baffler, though, that caught Tara's attention. Something square about the numbers, even the zeros.

And the dollar sign like a narrow rectangle, the curves oddly sharp and straight—like an unbent paper clip. No nonsense in this description. "Guaranteed to keep squirrels away when hung properly," it read, in letters that looked more like assorted shapes. Not to be confused with plastic imitations. $24.95."

Nobody else wrote like that. Tara turned to read the sign on an adjacent finch feeder. "Seed: Thistle," the sign advised. "Pro: Attractive cedar. Con: Squirrels can chew it up." Tara might as well have been staring at photographs, eight-by-ten glossies, hung about the room. Hard to decide whether the opening in her stomach indicated excitement or dread.

She replaced the scoop. This project could wait for another day. On her way out, she interrupted a clerk unwrapping a box of Christmas ornaments shaped like cardinals.

"Excuse me," Tara said, one foot already on the porch. "Is Libby working today?"

"No," he said. "She comes in Tuesdays and Fridays."

Outside, traffic whooshed by at a decidedly unvacationish speed. Slipping into the leather interior of Martin's Volvo, Tara ran her fingers fondly over the display panel: an odd thing to do, absently admiring its technology, the nicest car Tara had ever driven. She remembered a conversation with Libby, years earlier, when Tara and Greg were still together. Tara had asked about one of Libby's old boyfriends, whether he'd ever married. "Are you kidding?' Libby had replied. "He is hopelessly, hysterically in debt. Who could possibly marry him?"

When Tara had been married to Greg, she'd work her retail job five days, a forty-hour week. He'd had enormous student loans from the veterinary school he'd never finished. He must be doing better, Tara thought, if Libby has stayed with him. If she's only working two days a week.

.　　.　　.

At home the water had receded, leaving the road damp but clear. Carrying her first load of groceries, Tara felt a swell of happiness and relief at the sight of her house, rising up behind the dunes, languid and imperial in its eccentricity. Pagan, mirroring the house in mood and peculiarity, stretched out on the deck, elongating her shorn, misshapen body with a faint chirp— the barest feline expression of pleasure at Tara's return. Tara dropped her purse and shopping bags and sat down next to Pagan, jiggling her fingernails over the cat's belly.

Toward the shore, the tide pools emptied themselves back into the ocean, clearing the sand. Amidst the complicated spilloffs and trills, a great blue heron sat perfectly still. Tara always had to blink when she saw these birds, so narrow and prehistoric. "I think herons are related to grasshoppers," she once told Greg, and he'd laughed. But that's what the bird looked like to Tara: a majestic, overgrown grasshopper—balancing on one impossibly thin violin bow of a leg.

Tara stroked Pagan and tried to remember if Libby had ever been interested in birds. The Libby Tara knew liked arty movies. "Films" she'd always called them, drawing the word out into multisyllables. Libby grew up in Manhattan, a pavement child, referring to New York as "The City" regardless of where she was geographically, drawing perplexed glances when she visited Tara in Colorado or on Cape Cod. She liked long afternoons in coffee shops, smoking and writing notes in her journal. She liked dark, impeccably ironed clothing and always insisted on the correct glass for any beverage—making distinctions between red wine, white wine, and water goblets which Greg, who liked to drink from mason jars run once through the dishwasher, would undoubtedly consider absurd. Libby cared about maturity and self-improvement. Manners and good behavior. Other than suggesting putting bells on Pagan, Tara wasn't sure she'd ever heard Libby refer to birds

at all. Libby had not been interested in much that pertained
to the outdoors: not hiking or camping—not even walks on the
beach.

Pagan struggled to her feet and rubbed impatiently against
Tara, wanting to go inside. Clearly, Tara thought, Libby had
chosen to work with birding paraphernalia in order to ingratiate herself to Greg. Ingratiate? Not the right word at all—she
was married to the man. Still. The idea brought an unpleasant
taste to Tara's mouth. A depressing, sinking kind of dismay. If
Martin were alive, and she'd been sitting on the front stoop
this long, now would be the time he'd come to join her. He'd
bring her a cup of tea or a glass of wine, and sit down behind
her. Hand her the drink and rub her shoulders as she took the
first comforting sip.

In Martin's absence, Tara felt angry. She gathered her pack-
ages and stood. As she pushed the unlocked door open with a
shove of her hip, Pagan darted inside. Tara's anger rankled in
her chest, uncomfortably familiar, as if a problem she'd considered solved had unexpectedly reappeared. The same way she'd
feel if she found a bird—a swallow, a sparrow, a goldfinch—
dead on her doorstep.

The morning after she discovered Libby, Tara woke to a window filled with ocean and found herself returned to the new
incarnation: calm, forgiving, implacable.

She carried her telescope out to the beach. Low tide, and a
ruddy turnstone—colored like a calico cat—hopped beside a
tidal pool, flipping over pebbles and shells. Toward the south
side of the island, Tara saw a whimbrel hunting fiddler crabs—
investigating the thousands of tiny holes bored into the sand
with precision by swaggering, lopsided little beasts. All along
the shore, cormorants posed in troops atop waterlogged rocks,

lifting and spreading their bat-like wings to dry in the sun. A gull flew overhead with a sinister cackle, and Tara found two horseshoe crabs marooned on the flats. With no chance of dragging themselves back to the water before the tide came in, it looked as if their hundred years were up. So she lifted them one at a time by their thorny shells and carried them back to the surf. For Tara the ocean was a constant frame of reference, both daunting and comforting in its permanence. Industry might kill all its creatures and empty it of life, but still: there all that water would be.

The best view of the osprey nest was just yards from Tara's house. When she took her eye away from the viewfinder, she could see Pagan—taking mincing steps through the sand, watching various tiny life forms scuttle through the dunes. An incongruous sight, a cat on the beach. Particularly Pagan, in her shorn state, with her vaguely arthritic movement. The occasional passerby would do a double take in the midst of their nature watching: "What sort of creature is *that?*"

Years ago, when Greg began his study, Tara learned what the DDT had done to the osprey: destroyed their eggs, softened their shells. The poison had passed through the water to the fish and on to the fish hawks. Who would go about the nesting process, the building, the waiting, and finally the migration—after unfruitful attempts, shattered shells, and ruined embryos.

Now, too early in the season for fledglings, the osprey busied themselves with preparation. The female sat patiently atop her hard-shelled eggs for endless hours while the male fished. Very occasionally, she'd leave the nest to bathe. The two birds seemed to Tara the model of cooperation—the male returning with fish in its talons, the two of them feeding together. Greg had told Tara that although ospreys were mostly monogamous, their strongest connection was to the nest itself. Regardless of what happened to the mate, they would always return to the same spot. So this would very likely be the same pair—the original pair—of birds she and Greg had watched, more than five years ago, the day they'd been stranded.

Later that afternoon, Tara sat at her long dining room table (a family's table, not meant for one person) writing out checks, paying bills. The tiresome business to which Martin had tended. Now Tara resigned herself, trying to fill in amounts and sign her name the way Martin used to, without anxiety or resentment.

Affixing a commemorative bald eagle stamp to Atlantic Bell's envelope, she remembered a day with Greg: the time she'd correctly identified a marsh hawk on Sesuit Neck. They had been returning from an osprey nest at Chapin Beach: late in the summer, the two fledglings had grown to almost the size of their parents. Tara and Greg watched the birds practice flight, peering over the edge of the nest as if gauging the distance to the ground. They would balance awkwardly, their bird legs trembling, and flap their wings in a tentative testing motion without actually leaving the nest.

Tara had forgotten to wear sunscreen. As they drove back, the skin over her cheeks felt warm and tight. Crossing Old Town Lane, Greg slowed the car down and pointed at a large bird sitting in a field of overgrown grass. Tara rolled down her window and examined it—its owlish face, its narrow, oblong skull, its white rump. "It's a marsh hawk," she told Greg.

"That's exactly right," Greg said. Tara felt her sunburn flush further at the pleasure in his voice. She pressed her ponytail against the overheated headrest, listening to Greg explain why the hawk was a juvenile—the color and density of its feathers, its reluctance to fly away despite their car's proximity. "I almost thought it was an owl," Tara admitted.

"Yes," Greg said. He banged the flat of his palm against the steering wheel. "Yes, Tara." He told her that marsh hawks had well-developed facial disks, like owls: "It helps them find mice in the tall grass," Greg said.

Tara had to laugh at herself for feeling so profoundly accomplished, for her overinflated delight. Greg reached across the bench seat and grasped her hand. Tara tangled her fingers into his and shrugged with a buzzing kind of contentment. The ripe ocean air, the crackling dryness of her skin, and Greg's approving grip: all this conspired to make her feel happily childlike, happily complete.

On Tuesday Libby was in the middle of ringing up a customer when she saw Tara—who felt sorry for this ambush, having had ample time to assemble and conceal the most relevant emotions, while Libby had to react, adjust, and compose in an instant. At the same time, it seemed a fair assignment of handicaps, Libby having always been better contained.

When Libby recognized Tara, there was an instant of unreadable paralysis—her fingers over the cash register freezing, her face suddenly blank. But then she smiled with welcomed surprise: the oh-my-God expansiveness of an unexpected meeting with an old friend.

She extricated herself gracefully from her business and walked around the counter to embrace her predecessor: as if, Tara thought, she meant to make a point—to illustrate that Tara posed no threat. Libby had changed very little. She still wore her black hair clipped boyishly short, its lines updated but essentially the same. Her clothes looked citified to Tara, casual but chic—khaki and navy replacing her old black, a New

Yorker's idea of what a person should wear, living on Cape Cod, working in a birding store.

"Tara," Libby said, on the other side of her hug, her hands still on Tara's shoulders. "What are you doing here?"

Tara offered a brief explanation, of Martin's death, of the house on Lieutenant Island. "I've been watching birds," Tara told her carefully, "and getting myself back together."

Libby nodded with appropriate sympathy. "I wish we'd known," she said. "We would have gotten in touch."

"So you're still with Greg?" Tara blurted, conscious of her lack of subtlety, at the same time feeling entitled—Libby after all, having married Tara's husband.

"Sure." Libby laughed in an uncharacteristic, nervous way. "Till death do us part and all that," she said.

Libby's hand flew up to cover her mouth. "God, Tara," she said. "I'm so sorry. How stupid. It just popped out."

Regretful, Libby's unlined face looked somehow older. Tara decided that Libby, despite flawless skin and perfectly arched eyebrows, managed not to be at all beautiful. She supposed she used to consider Libby pretty, when they were friends.

"It's all right," Tara said. "It's a hard thing to get used to. Me, a widow. On top of everything else, it's just weird."

"It is weird," Libby agreed. "You're so young." And then added, "Everything about this is weird. You and me. You and Greg. The last time I saw you, you and Greg were married."

They spoke for a minute more. Libby told Tara about Greg's good job at the bird sanctuary in Wellfleet, and about herself teaching a poetry class at the community college. They each mentioned mutual friends they'd heard from recently. They exchanged phone numbers, and said good-bye.

"I am so sorry about your husband," Libby said as they parted. "Please do call us."

"I will," Tara said, patting the scrap of paper in her pocket. "I promise."

• • •

Back home, Tara couldn't resist climbing up to her widow's walk. When she'd left the Bird Watcher's General Store, the day had been temperate but overcast. Now heavy winds circled, blowing in from the north and winding up to gather speed. A dense ceiling of darkening clouds rested low over the ocean. Tara felt like a ghost story, hanging on to the rail while her hair and skirt battered backward. Pagan appeared up the old stairway, her new cat bell jingling, and twined herself through Tara's legs. Tara picked her up, curling the cat like a baby into the crook of her elbow. Not so long ago, Pagan would have disentangled herself with an indignant yowl; now she just rested with a vague purr, too content, or too lazy, to pull away.

"We've changed," Tara said, squeezing Pagan until she let out a disgruntled chirp. Tara dropped her to the wooden planks with a thud. Pagan bristled hairlessly, then perched to wash herself beside the rails, licking her paw and wiping it across her face, now and then glancing up from her work to watch the ocean roll in, and the birds down on the sand.

There were birds on the decline nationally that Tara saw in abundance on Lieutenant Island. Like the American black duck. Elsewhere in the country, ornithologists searched in vain for the species: Tara, from the roof of her house, could see several, floating together on the crests of wind-rocked waves, occasionally turning upside down to troll for snails, yellow bills submerged and tails in the air like something out of a children's book. In the shallower water, Tara saw two sandpipers, greater yellowlegs, rushing around clumsily as they fed. A cedar waxwing flew past her, downward, alighting on a lower porch rail. Tara felt the first lashing mist of rain and tilted her face toward it. "Your face looks prettiest when it's tilted up," Greg used to tell her. "I don't know why."

"Cedar waxwings," Tara said out loud, to Pagan, or the sea ghosts, or just to the mist itself, "eat mostly berries. They breed in midsummer, so the crop will be ripe when their young hatch. It's very unusual for birds to eat mostly berries."

Tara ran her fingers across the damp rail, its wet splinters harmless and smelling of wood rot. She turned and looked out toward the bridge. High tide covered the road, and no one would come or go for hours. She inhaled the sense of safety this lent her, and the unreasonable sense of permanence. She tapped the piece of paper in her pocket, Greg's phone number, seven digits that would beep and then reach him—his voice, after all this time. Of course she would call. She would have him here to dinner, with Libby, the three of them together.

The rainfall accelerated in a single instant, as if someone had opened a water hatch. Sudden torrents, pouring down to drench their roost. Pagan made a swift dash downstairs. But Tara just grasped the rails and tilted her face upward, letting the cold water soak through her skin, hair, and clothes. Feeling strangely and excitedly like herself—for the first time in a long, contented while.

Over the wire, the numbers did not yield Greg but Libby—through several phone calls, several unworkable dates. Until finally Tara, consulting her tide chart, was able to find a time and date that worked for them—a Friday night, nearly two weeks after Tara and Libby's meeting.

"I'm easy," Tara said. "When the tide's in, I'm here. When it's out, I try to get things done."

"Sounds nice," Libby said.

"You may have to stay," Tara warned her, "if we take too long, and the tide comes in. But don't worry—I've got plenty of room."

Tara didn't want to overthink details. She would appear as

her best self, the way Greg remembered her—not flustered or dressy, not asking if she looked all right. Hair down, once brushed, and curling from the peninsula's notorious humidity. Jeans and a T-shirt. The faintest bit of bird-searching sun across her face. So that if he happened to tell her she looked well, she could respond with incredulity ("I *do?*"), a happy flush of surprise.

She planned simple food: swordfish, marinating in ginger and teriyaki, waiting for Greg to grill. Rice pilaf and a salad. Raspberry sorbet. Everything store-bought, nothing hand-made, nothing overdone. Two magnums of merlot, the first alcohol Tara had bought since moving east. Moderate Libby would sip, perhaps a glass or two; but Greg and Tara would drink deeply—Greg having already consumed two or three beers, from the six-pack of Harpoon IPA Tara bought for him.

If it were Martin coming to dinner, Tara would have to guess what to do for him, remembering what he'd appreciated in the past, asking the butcher and wine merchant for advice. Martin would respond with flattery and thanks, out of politeness and because he loved her. But she wouldn't really *know,* the way she did with Greg.

On Friday evening she considered the various ways to watch for their approach. From up top the widow's walk was a temptation. Greg's car—perhaps even his old station wagon—would be mud-splattered and overused, rambling across the bridge. Tara could watch them park and make their way over the dunes, carrying whatever offerings Libby would have chosen. But there Tara would be, perched on the roof like a weather vane, her anticipation too visible, too indicative. And she would miss Greg's face, up close, taking in the house, which he would so love. Taking in the island, and what he remembered about it. Which—Tara felt sure, despite the many times he must have returned, to count birds (the ones on the decline, the ones on the return, the ospreys themselves)—would be her, the day they had spent here together. Which was simply too large to exist, the way it did in Tara's mind, alone.

Libby and Greg arrived just as the tide went out. Not surprising: Greg always heeded the numbers on a clock with a scientist's precision. From the kitchen Tara heard his car, sounding the way she knew it would. Sand-damaged, full of rattles and creaks.

Nothing about Greg could surprise Tara. There were no possible changes that she would not be able, in some way, to account for. Tara felt this in the sound of his car door closing. She felt it in the sound of his voice, talking to Libby, his approaching footsteps, the sway of his silhouette behind the ruffling curtains. Everything about his impending nearness seemed as eerily familiar as a childhood memory.

Libby entered first. Carefully dressed, in a long beige skirt and white button-down blouse, a precisely oversized Tencel jacket. She looked tamed and meticulous. Ironed and combed and made-up. Tara felt a moment of uncertainty, one hand fluttering to her hair, feeling unkempt and childlike. Then Greg, in his old costume, shorts and T-shirt and long-sleeved flannel shirt. The room flipped, the perspective shifted; time and place becoming something altogether different from what they'd been just seconds before.

His face looked dimly older—like Tara, with his twenties just far enough behind him to have lost some remnants of youth, while retaining its general form. Faint lines had begun a map of his habitual expressions: Tara could have drawn a picture, before seeing him—across his brow, around his mouth. Between his eyes, the vertical crease that had always appeared while he was studying birds, or in the midst of an argument, now permanent.

Libby and Greg, standing more or less together on the other side of the kitchen table, were approximately the same size—two or three inches apart in height, Libby faintly broad for a woman, Greg slight for a man. They can probably share clothes, Tara thought. Tara used to pull Greg's jeans on as a joke—the way they swam around her waist. But while Tara stood a good head shorter than Greg, the instant he walked into the kitchen she and he seemed exactly eye to eye. She smiled—the most genuine expression to cross her face in ages. And Greg's return smile (his only greeting—Libby said hello, not Greg) felt like looking into a mirror. What Tara had feared would be weirdness was nothing of the kind: the most normal thing in the world, for them to be in a room together.

"This place is great," Greg said. "What a house." He circled the table in an expansive way, broad steps, peering around doors, taking inventory. Libby kissed Tara's cheek, but Greg did not touch her. Instead he set about touching her things—opening cabinets, pulling aside curtains. As if assessing the place, deciding where he'd put belongings of his own. He ran his fingers (without a wedding ring, Tara noted) around the edge of a photograph on the refrigerator door: Martin, in a coat and tie, standing in front of his house in Piedmont, looking like he could be Greg's, Libby's, or Tara's father.

"Is this Martin?" he asked.

"Yes. That's Martin."

"I'm really sorry to hear about him," Greg said.

"Yes," Libby agreed. "We both are. So sorry."

"Thank you," Tara said.

Pagan marched into the room, more quickly and confidently than she normally would for company, her tail bristling with pleasure. Until the cat made a beeline for Greg, Tara had been so absorbed in the details of his face, she'd missed the absence of hair: not lost but cut, buzzed short like the cat's. When Greg gestured—pushing his hand against his forehead—there was nothing beneath his palm but skin and stubble.

"Who's this?" Greg said, as Pagan purred and pressed herself against his legs, the bell on her collar jingling.

"Greg," Tara said, startled. "That's Pagan."

"Pagan," Greg said. "What happened to her fur?"

He knelt and picked her up, cradling her the way Tara usually did. The room drowned in Pagan's loud purring. Tara felt uncomfortable, as if Pagan were revealing her own happiness.

"Shaved," Tara said, with vague rebuke, "because of the heat. She recognizes you, without your hair."

"She does seem to recognize you," Libby said, including herself in their past. "Pretty amazing."

"Pagan's a murderer," Greg said to Libby, scratching the cat under her chin. "But she's very deep."

"She doesn't kill birds anymore," Tara said, reaching into the refrigerator for a beer. "Too old."

Greg knelt and carefully returned Pagan to the floor. Tara opened the bottle and handed it to him—their first touch, the tips of his fingers against cold condensation as he took it from her hand.

"Libby," Tara said. "Would you like a drink?"

"I'm okay for now," Libby said, as Tara poured herself a glass of wine. The initial sip, after so much time abstaining, clouded her vision with an instant delicious fog.

"I'll give you two the grand tour," Tara said. "Okay?"

She led them through the house, opening doors with a wave of her hand and a swift explanation: dining room, study, guest rooms, my room. She loved watching Greg's wistful admiration, his hand finding something of hers to touch in every room. Tara marveled at Libby, whose demeanor remained absolutely calm, refusing to bristle or jockey for Greg's focus.

Whereas Tara could already feel her own need: to be between Greg and Libby, to call things to his attention. At the same time, she derived a certain sense of pride—at her ability to be here, with Greg and another woman (another wife), and behave calmly, civilly, at all. She led them downstairs, through the back door, and out onto the sand.

"Look at this place," Greg said. "It's perfect." He let his arms fall wide, as if embracing the location—the beach, the water.

"I've never been out here," Libby said. "It's beautiful."

Tara smiled at Greg. Jubilant.

"I can't believe," Greg told Tara, "that you stay here by yourself." He turned to Libby. "Tara used to hate that," he said. "She had a phobia of being alone in a house."

"I remember," Libby said, reminding them.

"Half the time, you're probably all alone on this island. This time of year," Greg said.

"Sure," Tara said. "I guess I've changed."

Libby turned away and walked a tactful distance down the beach, scattering terns from their shore-side roosts. The birds inundated the overhead sky.

"Look," Greg said, pointing toward the surf, the stretch of beach abutting the parking area. Without his hair, Tara had no incentive to touch him: a sad, fantastic relief. "That's where those British children were playing that day," he said. "Do you remember?"

"Of course I do."

Beneath her smile, Tara felt something larger—a quaking, a renaissance. *He remembers that day as clearly as I do.* Behind the place where she and Greg stood, the tide gaped, allowing the road its exit toward the bridge. Soon enough the water would reclaim the sand, its passageways and escapes. What mattered was Tara and Greg: standing, at last, on this very spot.

.   .   .

"Jealousy," Libby had once admonished Tara, paraphrasing Margaret Mead, "doesn't show how much you love someone. It shows how insecure you are."

As evening slid to shore—the island allowing a westward view of sunset—Tara stood out on the deck, talking to Greg while he grilled the swordfish. Libby setting the table in the dining room, leaving them alone together. If it were me, Tara thought, I would not be keeping a polite distance. I would be out here, touching him. I would be sending intermittent warning glances, a continuous reassessment of the situation.

If it were me, Tara thought, adjusting with new honesty. If Greg and I were his second marriage, and Libby his first: we wouldn't be here at all.

The last time Greg and Tara had been together, she was leaving him. She remembered the day, in late September: standing upstairs, scanning their bedroom for something she'd forgotten—the way she would leaving a hotel. Pagan had already been captured; she crouched in her cat carrier, letting out intermittent yowls of outrage. Tara had decided she'd left nothing important behind when just outside came a sudden blizzard of birds: tree swallows—staging, preparing for their migration south.

It seemed like pure hundreds: a great, swirling constellation of birds. Tara couldn't resist walking to the window. The swallows would alight en force—a blanket mass of them, perching in the bushes out back, or lining up on the telephone wires like an organized battalion. Then they would rise together, flashing white bellies, crisscrossing each other with dive-bombs and fleet upward lifts. A chaos, but jaggedly choreographed, with absolute direction—like a whirlpool, or a windstorm.

Greg walked into the bedroom and stood beside her, resting his hands on the windowsill next to hers. "There's so many of them," Tara said, the first words they'd exchanged in weeks that didn't pertain to their impending separation. "It seems like hundreds and hundreds. A thousand swallows."

"In the old days," Greg told her, "before the bird populations were decimated. Daylight would be lost, during staging and migration. Because of all the birds."

And Tara could see it, exactly: fill still more birds into the spaces between the ones before her, and the sky would indeed go black.

Now, standing next to Greg on Lieutenant Island, years later, another season, the birds on the opposite end of their migration—having just arrived north. Tara remembered how very much *with* Greg she had felt that day, how connected to each other they'd both still been, despite her being moments away from gone. How very wide a gap, between leaving and left.

"See the nest," Tara said, pointing to the platform. "The ospreys are back."

Greg nodded. "They're all over the Cape now," he said. "Remember the nest on Chapin Beach? Last year they had four fledglings. All of them survived for the migration."

Tara looked out toward the water: a new moon, and the sand sprawled back twelve or thirteen feet. Wellfleet Bay had the lowest tide on Cape Cod. Tara found herself strangely wistful—worried that the tide would stay out too long, that the bridge would stay passable, that Greg would be gone this evening.

"Look," she said. "Out by the shore. A big turtle."

Greg flipped the swordfish and put the spatula down. "That's a diamondback terrapin," he said, in his old correcting voice. "Let's go look."

Libby was still inside fussing with the table as Greg and

Tara walked toward the surf. A few feet before the terrapin, he held his arm out—a straight barricade, halting Tara, his flannel-shirted forearm knocking against her stomach. He knelt in the sand, and Tara knelt with him—a studious, obedient mirror.

Greg pointed, his fingers tracing the shell's patterns into the air. "They're called diamondbacks because of the shapes on their top shell."

"It's so huge," Tara said.

"It's a female," Greg explained. "The females are bigger. And the males don't really leave the water. She's here to dig her nest."

Greg stood up and brushed sand from his knees. "We're only finding older ones," he told Tara. "Which means something's happening to the hatchlings. People trolling for shell-fish, with nets. And cars, four-by-fours, driving on the beach."

"That shouldn't be allowed," Tara said. "In a wildlife sanc-tuary."

"Some people might say a cat shouldn't be allowed," Greg said, maybe baiting her. "In a bird sanctuary."

"I'm telling you," Tara said, not allowing herself to ruffle. "Pagan's harmless now. She's mellowed."

"What about you?" Greg asked. He didn't look at her, but out at the water—squinting, as if pretending the question didn't matter. "Have you mellowed?"

Tara nodded. "I have. I think I have."

"Was it worth it?" Greg said. "Is mellow everything you hoped it would be?"

"Hey!" Libby's voice echoed smoothly from Tara's back deck, her timing as precise as if she'd been listening. Greg and Tara turned to see her scooping the smoking swordfish off the grill. Greg jogged up the sand—back to his cooking, and his wife.

Tara twisted her hair into a knot at the back of her neck, then let it fall. She followed Greg, her sneakers sinking dully into the sand. It had been amazing, really, what Pagan used to be capable of: catching birds, airborne creatures. Plucking them out of the sky. And Tara thought: how stupid I was, how callow and lacking foresight. Longing for calm—in the face of all that passion.

Sitting down to dinner, Tara filled three new wineglasses. Her first taste, after the brief hiatus—the head-clearing biology lesson—plunged her immediately into the first stage of drunkenness. She pushed the glass aside. The narrow scope of her dining room, the original frame of the house, its posts and beams, its old-fashioned light, made her slightly dizzy. The scent of low tide, never kept out by windows and walls, began to fade as water crept back up the sand.

Tara sat at the head of the table; not between Greg and Libby but with both of them on one side—Greg next to her, Libby a seat away. Greg close enough so that his left-handed elbow bumped Tara's right.

"Tara," Libby said, after complimenting Greg on the fish. "I find it so interesting that you ended up back east. What do you do now in place of skiing?"

"I wasn't skiing in California," Tara said. "Sometimes we'd go up to Tahoe. Last winter we had a vacation in Crested Butte. But really it hasn't been a part of my life for a while."

"So what do you do instead?"

"Mmm," Tara said. "Quieter things. I used to think I needed all that. Speed. Constant speed and movement."

"You were so good at it," said Libby, who'd never seen Tara ski. Tara looked at Greg, who, it seemed, was trying to control a glare, spearing pieces of swordfish with abrupt jabs.

"Thanks," Tara said. "But I'm into walking now. You see more."

"It's funny, isn't it," Greg said. He reached across the table for the wine bottle and topped off his glass. "She used to hate it here," Greg told Libby. "All she ever talked about was Colorado.

The mountains. High drama, because she couldn't stand to live away from the mountains."

"I know," Libby said, her calm, mascaraed lashes blinking at her plate. She curved the fork into her fish, placing a small piece between her teeth noiselessly.

"And now, five years later, here she is." Tara detected something more than irritation in his tone.

"Here I am," Tara said.

"Why'd you come here, anyway?"

"I guess I decided I liked it," Tara said. She retrieved her wineglass and drank. Matching Greg, falling in step.

"Your timing is peculiar," Greg said.

"Well," Libby said, with philosophical brightness. "Different people come to places at different times in their lives. Tara suffered a loss. It makes sense that she'd want to come back to a familiar place."

"A familiar place she hated," Greg said—but more tempered than before, reminded of Martin. His death.

"I never hated this place," Tara said. "I never hated Lieutenant Island."

Greg caught her then, looking up from his food. For one second, Libby dissipated almost entirely. Tara existed squarely in the spotlight of Greg's glance. For that moment the table became a séance—a ghostly sort of recall, an eerie resurrection.

Then Greg looked away. And there was Libby, unfazed by Tara, picking at her rice pilaf—too daintily ladylike to finish her dinner.

"So," Tara said. "I never got the full story. How did you two meet?"

Libby cocked her head.

"I mean obviously I know how you *met*," Tara said, "but how did you end up getting together?"

"I had to make some trips to Boston," Greg said. "Libby was the only person I knew there."

"So you stayed with her."

"Yeah."

"Speaking of funny," Tara said.

Greg finished his wine. Tara poured him, and herself, another glass. She saw him move his finger, almost imperceptibly, toward her hand, which hovered inches above his.

"I wonder what the tide's doing," Libby said. "Do you think we'll make it home tonight?"

Tara leaned to her right, checking the tide clock in the kitchen. "Oh," she said. "Doesn't look good."

They got up from the table, the three of them, and walked outside. A good, clear, full-mooned night. Tara leading, Greg just behind her. Out by Greg's car, Tara raised her hand to her eyes.

"Sorry," she said. "The road's washed away. You could stay up and wait for the tide to go out, but it'll be hours. Probably easier to just sleep here."

"No problem," Libby said. "We expected as much. It'll be fun, waking up in this house."

Libby and Greg collected matching overnight bags from the car. Tara frowned. Libby could be as calm and well-behaved as she liked. Tara owed her nothing.

Libby and Greg cleared the table while Tara put new sheets on a bed in one of the upstairs guest rooms. She moved in sort of a cloud, operating from memory, vaguely worried about her sense of imbalance. Pagan padded into the room and stretched out on the round, woven rug. Tara tucked in the last blanket, smoothed the coverlet, and sank down onto the floor, her head resting against the bed. One minute, she thought. I'll sit here one minute, and then I'll go back.

Downstairs, the sound of water and rattling glass began, accompanied by footsteps, intensely familiar, coming up the stairs. In a moment, Tara smiled—at the shape of Greg, standing in the doorway.

"Hey," he said.

"Hey."

He walked in and sat on the other side of Pagan—who didn't start or move as she would with a stranger, but turned over, exposing her stomach. Greg rubbed her shorn belly, making it ripple like a bowl of gelatin. Pagan grinned and purred.

"Funny," Tara said. "You, me, and Pagan. Together again."

"Sure," Greg said. "Everything's funny. Hilarious."

"A riot," Tara agreed.

Below them, the sound of Libby clanking gently in the kitchen.

"Listen to her," Greg said. "Can you imagine if it were you I'd left down there, when we were married? You'd be slamming dishes into the sink. You'd be making a racket."

"I wouldn't be left down there, doing dishes."

They lowered their heads, synchronized. Both pretending to concentrate on the cat—whose breadth provided little enough distance for Tara to smell Greg's breath, like liquor, like red wine, like her own.

"Libby and I are very different," Tara said, testing the obviousness of her words.

"True," he said simply. "Libby's very reasonable."

Tara laughed, a short and sudden burst. She punched Greg on the shoulder, gently, her fist pressing against the worn cotton that draped his clavicle: reminding her of that first kiss, sliding together on ice skates.

"Tell me something about your husband," Greg said, after a minute, his voice hoarse and careful.

Tara blinked at him. In her wine-soaked mind, she saw a strand of hair flop across his forehead. She lowered her eyes to Greg's bare hands on Pagan's belly, and remembered the broad gold ring he wore when he was married to her.

"Like what?"

"I don't know," Greg said. "Anything."

"All right," Tara said. She stroked the underside of Pagan's chin, and the cat stretched her legs with a human sigh.

"When I first started spending time with him," Tara told Greg, "I didn't want to hear about love. I didn't trust it, not the concept or the word. I wanted it so much that I didn't want to think about it. He and I had dinner a lot. He stayed at my house for some weekends. We were dating, you know. But I was afraid—that he'd say it, that he loved me, and not really mean it." She looked away from Pagan, back to Greg, who kept his eyes on the cat. Their hands moved in identical circles, on different parts of her stomach, their fingers struggling to avoid connection.

"Anyway," Tara said, "I could tell he was getting ready to tell me he loved me. And I wanted him to, badly. But at the same time I couldn't stand the idea. The degree of risk. You know? So I just came out and told him not to. I told him I didn't want to bring things to that level, I wasn't ready. I wouldn't believe him. So he started telling me anyway, but very quietly. In the middle of a hug, or a walk, he'd mutter something, and I'd pull away and look at him. I'd say, 'What did you just say?' And he would pretend: 'I said, it looks like rain,' or 'I said, let's have fish for dinner.' But I would know what he really said, that he loved me, and we'd both laugh."

Greg had stopped petting Pagan. He placed his hands on his legs, stretched out bare in front of him. The clanking downstairs halted, and it felt like the pause of important mood music—a wedding band's break, or the abrupt end of a record.

"That was me," Greg said. "Not Martin. I was the one who did that."

Tara paused, her eyes fixed on Pagan. And then she agreed. "That's right," she said, "you were. It's weird. I guess in a way I feel like I've only had one husband."

"I know," Greg said, separating his words precisely. "I know exactly what you mean."

Pagan got to her feet, arching her spine. Through an odd quiver of follicles, Tara could see the movement required—when the cat had her full coat—to raise hackles, to increase volume. As Pagan marched out of the room, Libby appeared in the doorway. Tara recognized an emotion (a falling, a sinking) on her face. And then an attempt at rearranging, into a smile: a visible rewriting of the scene before her, from Oh, no into Oh, there you are.

"Oh, there you are," Libby said, and smiled.

Greg turned his head toward the sound of his wife, and Tara saw in the incline of his jaw an unwillingness to turn away from her. In her wine-warmed mind, she felt a rippled tide, whitecapped waves of excitement.

From outside the open window came an odd staccato coo, sharp bird yelps, each one picking up speed. Shrill and muted at the beginning, like a child's mouth harp; a few seconds later, urgent and continuous like a whistling teakettle. Tara reached out, across where Pagan had lain, and grabbed Greg's hand.

"Listen," she said. "It's the osprey. The warning cry."

Libby's smile stiffened. But Greg's fingers closed around Tara's. "You're right," he said. "You're exactly right." Greg's hand around her own felt to Tara so private, she almost thought Libby wouldn't be able to see—Tara's palm against her husband's, her knee resting against his calf.

"You're exactly right," Greg said again.

Libby disappeared from the doorway, and the bird sounds quieted. The room felt light, mobile, a swirl of salty air. Tara felt a swell behind her eyes. A happy sort of stinging. She heard the front door open, then close. Greg didn't move.

"Don't worry," Tara said. "There's nowhere for her to go. We're still stranded here, till the tide goes out."

And that was exactly the thing of it. Tara imagined Libby moving across the dunes, the pressed hem of her skirt dragging through eelgrass. She saw her fists closed and swinging as she strode past Greg's car in the otherwise empty bird sanctuary parking lot; walking to the edge of the road—at this time of day not a road at all, but a tide pool. No access. No leaving.

Upstairs, Greg stood and walked to the window. Tara recognized in the tilt of his hip, the angle of his head, a certain level of confusion, frustration: just shy of anger. Pagan reappeared and in a quick leap alighted on the bed with a nostalgic jingle. She perched at the end, washing her paws and face—waiting for Tara and Greg to join her. As if no time had ever passed.

Tara moved from the floor to the edge of the bed, and watched Greg's face, turning back toward her. And it didn't matter: the vertical crease between his eyes, or the new lines— like sadness—around his mouth.

"Do you see what I mean?" Tara asked Greg, with a drunken, slightly velvet lisp.

"You didn't say anything," Greg said. His voice sounded hard but very close. Tara inhaled a stream of air through pursed lips, like smoke from a pipe, and waited for the happiness to take. Behind her, she heard the noise of Pagan settling—the rustle of the sheets, the well-oiled, throaty purr. From across the room, the sound of Greg's light breathing mingled intimately with Tara's; and the summer crickets, and the gulls, and the ospreys. And the cat behind her—the definition of contentment.

Greg moved away from the window, coming back toward Tara. How exhilarating, his approach for her: like going downhill, faster than she ever thought she'd allow herself, the moment she let her knees collapse, and the speed itself owned her, and she owned the very world. Tara recognized this. She knew it. She could handle it, easily, when Greg knelt in front of her, and rested his forehead on her knee, not entirely, but with a reserved pressure that required the restraint of his entire upper body. He put his arms around Tara, his hands gathering up the material of her T-shirt at her back.

They would kiss in that next instant. Not, Tara realized, because either of them had changed. But because, alone in a room together, there was nothing else for them to do.

Tara wished the tide into her own upstairs hallway. Never mind if it washed away the house's foundation, the musty old furniture, the secure, serene present. Never mind Libby, or even the birds: sacrificed to the undertow.

Lieutenant Island could be just this room. With Tara and Greg, left alone: to battle it out till the sun came up. While all the time in between, its people and its evolutions, floated away on the wide, unchangeable sea.

acknowledgments

I owe a thousand thanks to Peter Steinberg, my agent, for his hard work, intelligence, and good humor. And to Carla Riccio, my editor, who shines so brightly with talent, insight, and warmth.

Thanks to my parents, Carol and Georges de Gramont, for their bottomless well of love and support. Thanks to Barbara Gessner for taking me into her family and home. Thank you Pres and Eileen Bagley for loaning that beautiful house by the sea. Thanks to Brad Watson, the world's most generous writer; and thanks to Danae Woodward, my original source of encouragement and friendship. Special thanks to my grandmother, Cyrilla Carmel.

Kathy Tuxbury introduced me to Lieutenant Island and gave me loving, comprehensive detail about its bird life— and she is in no way to blame for the liberties I took with its tides.

For years of camaraderie, support, and/or inspiration, I thank Abby Jones, Leslie Rechner, Dan Pierce, Mark Honerkamp, Melinda Murphy, Russell Woodward, Karen Auvinen, Heidi Pomfret, Allison Boyd, Hilary Horan, Matt Hall, David and Tomi Sears, Beth Hackett Pride (wherever you may be), Jennifer Whitten, E. J. Bernacki, Ben Jones, Randy Ricks, Alice Fiori, Joe Reorda, Luis Urrea, Reg Saner, and Mark Spitzer. And

Melinda MacInnis, who always made sure there was a room in her house for me.

Thanks to Alex and Jacqueline de Gramont. Thanks to Heidi, Jennifer, and Scott Gessner.

Many thanks to teachers Crawford Blagden, James Yaffee, Adrienne McDonnell, Ron Sukenick, and Suzanne Juhasz.

Thank you Pat Bellanca at the Harvard Extension School. Thank you Bess and Jack Moye at Cabbages and Kings Bookstore in Chatham, Mass. Thanks to the Seaside Institute, for an uninterrupted month just when I needed it.

Thank you Dolores Dwyer for careful copyediting. Thank you everyone at The Dial Press, especially Susan Kamil. And thanks to everyone at Donadio and Olson.

To David Gessner, I owe a million thanks plus all my love till the last tide goes out. And then some.

about the author

Nina de Gramont teaches fiction at the Harvard Extension School. She lives on Cape Cod, Massachusetts, with her husband, David Gessner.